Second

Destiny

GLORIA SILK

Cover Designed by Linda le Breten of LLB Studio
Interior Design by Woven Red Formatting Services, www.wovenred.ca

Second Destiny/Gloria Silk—1st edition
ISBN: 978-0-9936952-1-6

To Austin and Natalia, my two constant loves.
Thank you for your support in so many ways

Acknowledgments

This story is the culmination of my long awaited dream of seeing my fiction come to life, and hopefully, to be shared with readers all over the world.

Huge thanks to *all* the effervescent members of the Quince Apple Group, and especially to Storm Grant, Joan Leacott and Bonnie Staring, and with heart-felt gratitude to my long-time mentor and friend, Kate Freiman. Thanks for all your graceful patience, your sense of fun, and insightful critiques and discussions.

Also thanks to my reading and writing team of friends: Yvonne Finn, Bethea Reznik, Anya Richards, Mike Spiers, Alan Stuart, Stella Yosefi. Of course, thank you to the others who also helped make my work so much better over the years.

Finally, my love and appreciation to my own personal hero—and patron of my arts—Austin, without whose unfailing support my dreams would not come true.

Glossary

Bhaiya	Brother (Hindi)
Brahmacharini	An unmarried woman pursuing virtuous spirituality through committing her life to helping children and the needy. (Hindi)
Challa (ha-lla)	Braided egg bread (Hebrew)
Chalo (cha-lo)	Let's go (Hindi)
Chuppa (hu-pa)	Wedding Canopy (Hebrew)
Holi	Hindu festival
Hora	A type of circle dance (Hebrew)
Jaan/Jaanu	My heart (Hindi endearment)
Klezmer	Traditional Eastern European Jewish music
Mandap	Wedding canopy (Hindi)
Mazal Tov	Congratulations (Hebrew)
Mensch	Decent human being (Yiddish)
Mera beta	My son (Hindi)
Pakoras	Fried snack, fritter (Indian cooking)

Pandit ji	Priest (Hindi)
Parsha	A portion of Torah (Hebrew)
Rabbi	Preacher/Reverend (Jewish)
Samosas	Triangular vegetable of meat fried snack
Schmooze	Talk intimately and gossip, charm
Sherwani	Knee-length coat worn by South Asian men
Shul	Synagogue (Yiddish)

Prologue

North London, June 1995

LIA COULDN'T DO it. She knew she couldn't go through with this crazy idea when she heard the second urgent blare of the ambulance that had just flown by them. A few minutes ago, she was on top of the world, running into the arms of the love of her life. She had bolted out of the synagogue and abandoned her family and bridegroom, intending to elope with Devraj, her gorgeous Hindu prince who seemed to have sprung straight from the Bollywood movie set.

Now, here she sat next to him in his cramped sports car, in a soaked wedding dress.

"What are you thinking, Lia?" Devraj scanned her face, frowning.

"Devraj." Hardly breathing, the pain in her chest grew triple-fold as the ambulance ominously went silent a few yards behind them. She didn't dare look back, but knew it had stopped outside the synagogue.

Her strong instincts warred against everything else, screaming at her what she already knew. What she had done.

Her grandfather's heart must have given way under the shock she'd just inflicted.

"Here we go again." Devraj said through gritted teeth. Sighing, he brushed his fingers through his still damp hair, from the rain in which they'd hugged and kissed only minutes ago. "Don't say it. Don't fall for this. What if it's a coincidence? What if your grandfather is fine and it's a ploy to get you to do what they've always expected from you?" The agony bordering on anger shone clear in his beautiful hazel eyes, his tension reverberating within the car.

Lia bit her trembling lower lip, staring at her clasped, cold hands on her lap. The damp, limp dress full of ridiculous lace and satin made her feel like a foolish child playing dress-up. "We both know this can't happen. I know what we both want more than life itself, but I also know what I have to do."

"No, Lia, be strong for us. I beg you. We love each other and we'll be fine without any of them, your family, my family, Jewish, Hindu, none of it matters. Only us." He grabbed her arms and the seat belt stopped her from being pulled into him, enveloped in his arms.

"I'm so sorry, Devraj." Tears blinded her vision of his face, but she couldn't bear to see the suffering she was inflicting on him yet again.

With all her remaining resolution she unbuckled her seat belt with numb fingers and reached for the door handle. "Please help me, Devraj, by letting me go once and for all. I'm not going to marry Howard only for my grandparents' sake but for—"

"No, I won't let you go, I can't." He nearly shouted, grasping her arm. When she looked at his fingers and then at him, he let her go. "Don't marry him, at least wait until your family no longer have such a hold on you. Then we can marry. I'll wait for you forever if I have to. Please, Lia."

She shook her head, closing her eyes. What was the use? They could go round and round like this forever. And remembering Mr. Amit Shah's warning only weeks ago, she now finally admitted that neither she nor Devraj could ever have what they craved.

Opening her eyes, she wouldn't look back at her first love. Grabbing the door handle, she pushed the door open with too much force. She had to go back.

Chapter One

North London suburbs, April 2014

SOMETHING WAS WRONG but Lia couldn't put a finger on it, as she glanced around the long dining table at her in-laws. Her ever-silent father-in-law, Jonathan was nursing his third brandy since their arrival. Nothing new there.

The residual smells of Grace's famous matzo ball soup, with its swirling rainbow of grease reflecting the chandelier lights, intermingled with the fresh yeasty *challa* rolls her mother-in-law had baked, as she did every Friday night for Sabbath.

What I wouldn't give for a bowl of curry, at this moment. She thought. Maybe tomorrow she'd order it with her girlfriends at their bi-weekly lunch date. But tonight routine and tradition ruled this ritual Friday night dinner in London's suburban Oakwood.

Looking around at her two silent children Lia concentrated on being in the moment. The only sounds in the slightly oppressive, antique furnished dining room were the delicate clatter of cutlery against the plates and her husband's response to his mother's probing questions about his latest problems with his business partner. As usual, mother and son were the two centre stage entertainers, while the rest of them were their audience.

Lia observed Howard. Tonight he seemed even more distracted, obsessed, as always searching for bigger ways to promote his cosmetic-surgery practice, and still waiting to be recognized for his genius.

Nothing new here, either.

Looking down at his roast chicken breast through his designer glasses, Howard said, "Of course I want him out, mother. My solicitors agree that Tom's got too unrealistic expectations of me, but I have a busy clinic to run."

Grace expelled one of her loaded sighs. More questions and reluctant answers ping-ponged between them.

Lia was tired of these conversations, but at least no one expected her to contribute to them. Most of the time she felt invisible, but that freed her to observe everyone.

She had a busy, uncomplicated life, with a beautiful home and great friends. Her parents-in-law tolerated her well enough. Her children were healthy and for the most part happy.

If she hadn't pursued her art, it was her own choice, and she'd made peace with it.

She swallowed the sudden lump in her throat and reminded herself to be more grateful.

Her husband of nineteen years may not be the perfect mate,

but he was a good provider and, mostly, an indulgent father to their children.

Swaying her attention back to their children Lia glanced at her ever silent thirteen-year-old son, Gabe, slouching beside her, and then at Danielle sitting across from her.

Lia's spine went rigid.

This was where something was definitely wrong.

Her eighteen-year-old had hardly been eating in the past few weeks, and tonight Danielle seemed extra moody and withdrawn. What was going through the med student's mind, sitting with her head downcast, yet again wearing those dark, tight fitting clothes Howard disliked?

Medicine seemed to be her passion, but she wasn't the talkative type if she did have any issues with her studies.

At least Danielle hadn't gone through with the tattoo or belly-piercing rebellion, Lia thanked God. Where was her funny, vivacious little girl who couldn't wait to spill her every adventure the moment she burst through the doors after school?

And would she ever resurface?

How could she help her sombre demeanor, while the teen looked like a caged animal?

Realizing Lia was again twisting her tight engagement and wedding rings around her finger as if they were a double noose she picked up her fork.

Guilt seeped through her. Were her children noticing her growing discontentment? The English spring weather always brought it on, along with the memories of a lost love.

Danielle broke the momentary silence between her grandmother and father. "Daddy, I have something to tell you." Those wide blue eyes, a warmer shade of her father's shone. Electricity seemed to crackle in the air around Danielle.

"What, sugar-plum?" Howard asked just as Gabe reached across the table for another roll.

"Where are your manners, Gabe?" Howard didn't raise his voice, but just glared through Arctic-blue eyes. "Ask if you want something."

"S-s-sorry, D-dad."

Lia's heart squeezed hard. Gabe's stutter never bothered him when mother and son were alone. These days he spent almost all his hours in his room with his books and computer.

Picking up the basket, she held it out to him.

He shook his head, and putting down the basket, she discreetly patted his knee.

He didn't pull away, but his expression made her question why she never stood up for him, or took his father to task. Oh, she had, after both children had gone to bed—or in the privacy of their bedroom when they'd still shared one—arguing, reasoning with Howard, until she was emotionally exhausted talking to a human equivalent of a brick wall.

"Daddy, will you please listen?" Danielle's voice broke through her thoughts.

Ever patient with his daughter, Howard glanced at her shortly, resuming cutting his chicken with the precision of a perfectionist surgeon.

"I've met my Mr. Right. I've been seeing him for a year and

I love him. I'd like you to meet him." Danielle's honey-gold bob framed her pale face. She sat reed-straight as if expecting an explosion or at least a rare shouting match. "Sanjay is of a different culture—"

At the mention of this familiar name, Lia's airways seemed stuffed with hardening cement, choking the breath out of her.

Someone's cutlery clanged loudly against a plate.

"Sanjay?" Both Grace and Howard pronounced as if smelling something disgusting off the sole of a shoe, at this very table.

A warped sense of *déjà vu* settled over Lia, heat prickling under her arms.

Danielle stared back at her father. "He's of Indian background, but—"

"Danielle, are you out of your mind?" Grace demanded in her haughty over-British voice.

"Let me handle this, mother." Howard continued glaring at their daughter. Wiping his mouth on his damask napkin, he stood up to his full height of five feet seven inches.

Lia couldn't move.

"You've been seeing him for a whole year." His eyes narrowed slightly. "Why now? I thought we talked about everything." Lia heard the tinge of betrayal.

"We do, but at first we were just friends, then it became more important and...I didn't think you'd accept him because he's not Jewish—"

"Glad you know your father so well." He looked at Grace. "That was tasty, mother." He thanked her as he thanked Lia after every meal.

He squinted back at Danielle through his glasses, his thinning oatmeal hair shone on his pinkish scalp under the chandelier lights. "This was in very poor taste, to come out with this nonsense at your grandmother's Friday night table. Now you've ruined everyone's dessert with this rubbish. I won't get angry, but you'll never see this person again. Or mention him. It stops now! End of conversation." Although his voice was firm, he gave Danielle one of the smiles he reserved for his female patients, their best friend and beauty god promising to make them look younger, more beautiful or desirable again.

But as Danielle stared up at him with that brave expression, Lia knew it was far from the end. "No, Daddy. If you won't meet him, we'll elope."

Lia needed water to help her constricting throat, but she couldn't trust her fingers to pick up the crystal water goblet. Hadn't she said almost the same words to her grandfather nearly two decades ago, about a fun loving—Indian—young man?

"If you promise to see Sanjay then I'll continue my studies after—"

"Like your mother did after I married her?" He sneered. "At least that was only art, no loss to the world. But medicine's not to be taken lightly, young lady."

"I don't care about medicine, never have, and I don't want a marriage like *yours.*" Danielle almost shuddered. "I want a real marriage, real love, and I *will* get it."

Fists by his sides, lips even thinner, Howard turned to Lia.

For the first time in years, he glared right at her, not

through her. "Do you know anything about this, considering the background of this...this...?"

"No, but the boy may be—" She started.

"He's nearly twenty-one, Mum. He's hardly a boy." Without looking at her, daughter and father dueled with each other with the same challenging eyes. "Sanjay's smart and kind and such a hard worker, Daddy. He's doing his MBA, and then plans to join his uncle's business—"

Howard's hand shot up in front of him. "Spare me the details."

Watching, Lia's sense of *déjà vu* grew stronger and her chest felt overtaxed from ineffective, too-shallow breathing. Devraj had also been subtly groomed for his family business empire. Her memories were torture enough almost to distract her from the crisis at hand.

"Why have you let this go on, Lia?" Grace asked, blinking profusely while holding her hand against her pearl-clad neck and cream cashmere sweater.

Before she could respond, Danielle said, "Mum doesn't know anything about Sanjay." She scraped her chair against the hardwood floors.

Teetering, it righted itself as if not daring to interrupt the drama.

Her chin jutted out in defiance, like Lia's had so long ago. "I mean it, Daddy. We'll get married with or without your permission. I'm old enough now."

Unlike her mother, Danielle was made of stronger stuff. Her contradictory, secretive behaviour over the past few months made so much sense. Knowing exactly what she wanted, Danielle wore a cloak of confidence of someone who was unconditionally adored. Lia was proud of her daughter, yet feared for her happiness, knowing Howard too well.

This couldn't end well.

"You know the rules." Howard's usually sloped shoulders raised in tension, as he shook a chubby finger at his daughter. "If he's not Jewish you've wasted your time."

"You know that's a load of hypocritical bull." Danielle retorted. "Like *you're* wasting time with some of your 'patients, after going to *shul* on Saturday'?"

It threw Lia off, seeing how Howard's expression changed from a ruddy pink to the puce shade he turned when talking about a defecting patient.

"You've never talked back to me like this and I won't stand for it."

Danielle turned her attention to Lia, anxious eyes sparkling, "Can you talk to him, Mum?"

Lia would meet the young man, but knew she would see a kosher pig fly before Howard would give in or compromise on this issue. That's what she'd thought about her grandparents and she'd been right. Even now with so many years of losing them within ten months of each other, she couldn't let herself think of the loss, not right now.

Was this the full circle through which she could make it right, *if* Sanjay was really Danielle's destined love? Lia was about to speak when Danielle threw her hands up. "What else is new? I should've known. No backbone. Well, I won't turn into you, with no voice, no life. And you're no better than Dad or Grandma. Just like them, you're all about the status quo and appearances." Contempt and defiance made her look older than eighteen.

"Now just wait a minute, young lady—" Grace started, but Lia interrupted her.

"I was going to say that we should at least meet S-Sanjay." Her heart skittered at the exotic name on her lips.

"How dare you, Lia?" Grace accused.

Jonathan cleared his throat and said, "Grace, dear, we shouldn't interfere—" His wife's glare stopped his words and she turned to her son.

"I blame *her* for this disgusting turn of events. What will our friends say if they should ever find out?"

"I'll take care of it, mother. Trust me." Howard glanced at his Rolex. "Later. Right now, I've got to go."

"You can't be serious, Howard." Lia almost whispered in disbelief. "We have to discuss this in private, tonight."

"When have you ever had a say about anything? I'm the head of this family, so don't contradict me." Howard then stared at their daughter. "Understood?"

Danielle continued staring, her bottom lip trembling slightly.

"Don't you want Danielle to be happy?" Lia spoke clearly, to be heard above the egos in the room. "If she believes she's mature enough—"

"I don't *think* so!" He hissed, his fleshy jaw clenched, and then he turned away.

"Dad, please listen to her." Danielle said.

She was once again her daughter's ally.

It felt wonderful. "I mean it, Howard. This could change her whole life. Please let's go home and discuss this, now."

Her alien, iron resolve made Howard's strides falter. He turned to face her. Everyone stared as he pointed at her. "My mother's right. It's all because of you and your family filling her head with those Indian movies, and you dressing her up as an Indian princess for Halloween all those years."

Guilt slid around Lia like a cobra. Although she'd stopped watching Bollywood movies, she knew her aunt and her grandmother had introduced Danielle to them when she was little.

"It's because you've refused to join me in to shul on Shabbat, neither of our children attend synagogue, even with Gabe's Bar Mitzvah coming in up." Howard snapped, "I'll bet Danielle knows more Indian words than Hebrew or Russian, and you're Russian-born, for God's sake."

"It's Hindi, Bengali, or Guajarati—"

"What is?" Howard demanded.

"There's no Indian language, there are many different languages and dialects—" She stopped, took in a fresh breath, and added, "but that's beside the point. I don't see how a man who goes to synagogue and then stuffs his face with pork at the local rib place can feel so self-righteous, refusing to meet a boy just because he's not Jewish."

"Don't you dare talk to my son like that. I should have stopped Howard from marrying you. If it hadn't been for my mother...you of all people running around with—" Suddenly Lia feared Grace's next words.

Did Howard and even his parents know about her first love?

But with a quick glance at her grandchildren, Grace clamped her thin lips shut.

"Absolutely right." Howard said. "You're lucky I came and saved you."

Stunned for a moment, Lia fumbled for the car keys, giving them to Danielle. "You and Gabe can wait in the car for a minute."

As soon as the main door closed, ignoring her mother-in-law, she faced Howard. A sigh reverberated within her almost air-starved lungs. "Please be reasonable. Would you risk losing our daughter over this?"

"I'm not going to lose my daughter." He barked. " *You* better go and talk some sense into her. I'll be home...later." Checking his watch again, he started to retreat. "But, no more discussions. I'm not changing my stand on this." He threw the words over his shoulder. "Father," he said as if in after-thought. "I'm borrowing your car until tomorrow, if that's OK." Apparently, his sudden plans had priority over his wife's words and his daughter's happiness.

"You've got to speak to Danielle yourself—now—" But he shut the door on her words.

In the ten-minute drive back home, Danielle had begged Lia to convince her father at least to meet Sanjay. Her promise to her daughter lay heavily on her.

Now in the relative sanctuary of her own home, Lia retreated into the silent living room on spongy legs. Shock and guilty memories settled over her like toxic dust. How could one Indian name shatter everything in mere minutes?

Sitting in the darkness, trying to fight off her past memories, her hands trembled and her knotted insides made her feel nauseous. She was afraid to close her eyes lest the vision of that golden-skinned god, the beautiful Devraj, forced itself into her psyche.

Like a dam refusing to be contained, the clips of her own teenage years crashed over barriers erected and supported by the glue of stale family traditions.

Denial and self-talk that she was relatively content with her lot in life had finally caught up with her. To give her children the security of traditional family dynamics, she'd made the best of her marriage. But now as she tried to decipher the consequences of her daughter's news, everything was unraveling like a wool sweater that had seen better centuries.

Lia would fight whoever got in the way of Danielle's happiness. Unlike her mother, Danielle *would* get her chance to find out if her first love was her true soul mate.

The young couple would make their own decisions.

Be strong and brave, she reminded herself, just as she had when she'd been Danielle's age, in the same—but hugely different—predicament. Because Danielle had her mother on her side, who now vowed history would not repeat itself.

Chapter Two

FINALLY, AFTER WEAVING through the dense Saturday traffic and getting almost all the red lights down prestigious Baker Street on the way to Howard's medical clinic, Lia parked outside the impressive, old building. Taking in a deep breath and exhaling, she focused on calming herself before facing him.

She'd hardly slept last night but had made sure she was awake before Howard left for synagogue and then the office. True to his stubborn nature, refusing to listen or discuss Danielle's news he'd rushed out as soon as she'd confronted him. What else was new?

Now at nearly one o'clock, Lia was certain she'd find him at his quiet desk, where he preferred to catch up with his paperwork on the weekends.

With her worsening headache, she wasn't sure she'd be up to meeting her girlfriends. She'd let them know after speaking with her husband.

Entering the eerily silent reception area, Lia's heart beat

faster. Distant female laughter coming from one of the consultation rooms propelled her on unsteady legs.

Stop! Go back! But her legs wouldn't obey.

Her shaking hand hovered near the door, which was slightly ajar. Through the small opening, she saw her husband's unmistakable pale, flabby butt cheeks do a small gyrating dance above a reclining unfamiliar, young redhead.

They were laughing softly, whispering sexual encouragements. With his trousers around his knees, Howard pounded himself into her on the large, white medical chair.

Neither noticed Lia in their quest to quench their animal lust.

Revulsion like she'd never experienced made her back away. Her other hand slapped itself against her mouth, as she fought uncontrollable nausea.

She didn't know how she ended up on a bench in the park, outside Howard's clinic. Tearless, she sat in the April breeze, the sun shamelessly proving that once again, life went on; just like after Mr. Amit Shah's visit to her college, or after she'd lost both her grandparents within a short time of each other.

So, Howard had lied. She'd seen no subtle signs in the past thirteen years since the night she'd conceived Gabe, when too much hurt and disappointment, on both their parts, had blown the truth open about Howard's affair. Blaming her cough and cold and his snoring, Lia had moved into the fifth bedroom. But though she'd believed him when he'd sworn it was a singular extramarital slip, and it was over, she never returned to their marriage bed.

All these years trying, but failing to be a loving wife, Lia had opted to respect her workaholic husband, while he'd made her feel solely responsible for her aloofness and lack of connection between them.

But had she known on a deeper level, that because of her low interest in sex, Howard could justify his adulterous behaviour?

Lia's head slumped, tears leached down her face. Why had she stayed with a man who'd called her "as responsive as a cold, limp fish" on their wedding night?

How she'd cried, yearning to be in Devraj's arms.

Only Danielle's birth, nine months after the wedding, had transformed her life. Being a dutiful wife, daughter-in-law and granddaughter had become bearable in her absolute adoration of her perfect, little baby. The same child she was afraid of losing, and why she was here.

Finally, she had to admit defeat. The marriage was dead.

But she couldn't let anyone interfere in her daughter's happiness. Somehow, she'd find a way out of this mess; she'd become financially independent, and stop escaping reality.

This was the last straw that broke this coward's inactivity. Lia had no choice but to take action and fast.

Taking in the first deep breaths since yesterday she briskly wiped away the tears with the back of her hand.

She reached for her bag and with shaking fingers called Patricia, who said, "Hello darling, we were wondering where you've got to—"

"Patricia," Lia's voice croaked. "I-I'm outside Howard's

office. I s-saw him...they were—" She bit her trembling lip.

The short silence was palpable through the phone line. "We'll be there as soon as we can, Lia. Don't move."

"I swear I'll castrate that pig." The blonde Maxine said in her lilting French-accent, her Rubenesque curves quivering. Beside her, the ebony longhaired Patricia scrutinized Lia. Concern marred her Modigliani-model-like angular features and her vibrant grey eyes held patent anger.

Lia wiped her eyes with the tissue Patricia handed her, as they sat in a dim corner of the busy pub around the corner from Howard's clinic. The smell of beer and cheese-and-pickle sandwiches surrounded them.

Gingerly, Lia accepted Maxine's offered glass, and took a sip of the searing brandy.

She forced herself to talk. "I've not been a good wife, only a dutiful one. It's not only Howard's fault."

"Don't you dare blame yourself, Lia." Patricia said. The multifaceted entrepreneur with acres of land all over Europe, with fingers in many enterprising pies, looked ready to help Maxine with her threat to do Howard bodily harm.

"Well, *chérie*, you know how I've felt about that *cochon*," Maxine said, "I'm glad now it's no longer a secret. You've been the best wife. He didn't have to jump into bed with all those—"

"Stop it Maxi." Patricia gave her friend and business partner her head-mistress glare. Then softly said to Lia, "Talk, get it out of your system. Together we'll get you through this."

Lia sighed, beginning to breathe without it hurting too

much.

Patricia held her hand as Lia said, "I came to see Howard to talk about Danielle. Last night she told us she's in love with a non-Jewish guy."

"Last night, at your in-laws'? Oh, *chérie*, you've had an eventful twenty-four hours, eh?" Maxine shook her head, making her blonde curls bounce.

"What happened?" Patricia asked.

Slowly, she recounted the conversation, through the ever-present lump in her larynx. "She seems quite serious about him, and I had no idea about any of this. I haven't been there for her."

"You're always there for everyone," Maxine said indignantly. "You're a marvellous mother, and you're always running around, organizing those business dinner parties for that scumbag, and I'd have strangled your snooty mother-in-law." Maxine said. "And what about your volunteer stuff at Gabe's school?'"

"All this in addition to helping out at our art gallery." Patricia added.

Lia looked at them. "I'm afraid we'll lose Danielle, because Howard will never accept Sanjay."

Maxine nodded. "Indian?"

When Lia nodded, Maxine shook her head, "Global warming will be solved before he'll allow that." She folded her arms over her buxom bosom.

"I'll change his mind somehow. I won't stand by and let history repeat itself."

Her friends shot concerned glances at one another.

Her loyal confidantes didn't know about Devraj.

No one in her new life knew. It had been her only way of forging on.

"Are we at last going to hear about the real Lia who's hidden behind the perfect housewife all these years?" Maxine's tension eased, her eyes wide as she smiled.

"One day I'll tell you all about it, but not now." She absently massaged her temple with shaking fingers for a moment.

From the corner of her eye, Lia noticed a young couple taking the intimate corner table in the booth next to them. As if to ram home her sleepless night's thoughts, she saw how Danielle probably looked beside a handsome dark haired, tawny skinned man. Again, she wondered if by osmosis, her daughter preferred exotic, dark men because of her. Did Sanjay resemble this tall, enigmatic man? Did he look like a Bollywood actor, virile and larger than life?

Seeing this man's dimples, her heart played a staccato beat against her chest, at how Devraj's sensuous mouth had made her feel, how easily she'd brought out that amused expression and those dimples.

For the first time in years, her fingers itched to capture that masculine aura onto a sketchpad.

As always, attuned to each other, knowing how emotionally bled dry Lia was, Maxine hugged her, while Patricia held her hand, studying her with those kind soulful eyes. "How can we help?"

"I don't know." Lia said, "First I have to sway Howard's

mind. Even if Sanjay isn't her Mr. Right, I'll be damned if in years to come, she'll be wondering, what if?" Lia's lips trembled again.

"You can divorce his ass." Maxine said vehemently.

"Maxi, please." Patricia said, turning to Lia. "Don't think about practical or financial constraints, what do *you* want to do? What does your heart say?"

Filled with fear yet feeling empowered, Lia said, "I can't stay with Howard." She shook her head. "I've been a fool for too long, and no one's going to dictate my life again. I'll support Danielle and Gabe on my own. I want nothing from Howard."

"That's the spirit." Patricia said, respect shining in her eyes.

"And you've got us, *chérie*."

"Thank God for you." She hugged her soul sisters. "I don't know how I'd have managed all these years without you."

The three had become even closer over the years, sharing the ups and downs of Maxine's three divorces, the births of Lia's children and Patricia's only son, and when losing the love of her life, Patricia had become a thirty-five year-old widow.

"Maxi, what do you think about offering her the curator position?"

"At the new Soho art gallery? Hmm."

"All these years she's been learning the ropes, and you said how you'd hoped she'd join us..." Patricia raised her brows.

"Well," Maxine looked at Lia, "if you think you can manage, we'll train you. But you know the position is extremely busy and involves much travel." Then she smiled. "And of course it comes with an obligatory make-over and new sexy wardrobe."

The shopaholic Maxine obviously saw a ripe opportunity to play fairy-god-sister. Her old friend, Ella came to mind. How she'd helped transform the shy, geeky Lia for her first date. But again, she buried that away to the place she wouldn't visit.

Patricia smiled for the first time today. "After all you'll be a spokesperson for our company."

Replacing her earlier desolation hope blossomed within Lia. "You're the best. I'll let you talk this over. Right now, I can't think straight. Thanks for coming for me, but now," she sighed shakily, putting down her nearly empty brandy glass. "I have to get home, to do some over-due spring cleaning." She tried to smile but it wouldn't come.

"No more regrets, *chérie.*" Maxine smiled.

Lia swallowed hard, fear and exhilaration intermingled. "But... it'll be hard for Gabe. He's quite sensitive to any change. And Danielle won't like it."

"She's a teenager," Patricia said, "She'll see that she can't have her cake and eat it, too. This could be the only way she may have a relationship with Sanjay. She has to choose."

"I wish she didn't have to."

"Stay strong, darling." The sympathy in Patricia's eyes nearly started Lia's tear reflexes. But she fought them away.

"And maybe now you'll have that hot long overdue affair, eh, *chérie?*"

"All in good time, Maxine." Lia gave her a wavy smile. It was the furthest thing from her mind and she wasn't the affair type.

Right now, she'd learn to survive out of her comfort zone, without the safety of the gilded cage. The close bond with her children was strong enough to get them through this, she prayed. Somehow, she'd learn to rediscover that sense of excitement and joy in their new life.

Her children were her priority, but eventually, she could travel to exotic places like Tibet and India and paint... Her heart did a staccato gallop. Suddenly it was a possibility.

It would feel strange to reach into the personal fund in her own account, which held the money left to her by her grandparents. But she'd do whatever she could to move forward.

She couldn't wait to put her much-overdue plan into action. This year, instead of cleaning up for Passover as she always did, she'd also declutter a very important, neglected part of her life.

The change would be so swift, Howard would suffer whiplash.

Chapter Three

"WE HAVE TO talk." Lia said to Howard who had come through the door and was walking away from her down the hallway. She had returned home two hours earlier, having been fortified by her soul sisters. After she'd served a quick Nicosia salad, Gabe had gone back upstairs with his friends and Danielle had rushed out, yet again, without telling Lia where she was going.

"I'm tired."

"This can't wait, Howard." After procrastinating for years, she couldn't muster up a minute's patience.

His strides faltered. "If this is about Danielle's nonsense—"

"I'm filing for divorce on Monday."

"What?" Turning to her, he frowned as if she had spoken in Swahili.

Her heart thumped painfully as she retreated into the living room. Aware that Howard wasn't following her, she sat waiting.

"What the hell are you going on about?" Howard came into the dimly lit room, reaching for the light switch.

"Leave the lights off. It's simple; I'm divorcing you."

"Here we go. And if I refuse?" He almost sounded amused now, as if she was a lead-footed teenager demanding to drive his brand new Maserati.

She kept her gaze on his moon shaped face as he stood above her. "For the children's sake don't make me dig up the dirt about your... extracurricular activities. No, don't bother denying it."

Howard closed his mouth, his eyes wide.

"Did those witches you call friends put you up to this?"

"No, I saw you today with the redhead." Even in her state, it hadn't escaped her that her friends hadn't seemed surprised. Had she been the last one to know about her husband's affair? Was that why Miss Jenkins, Howard's prim and proper receptionist, always treated her with a mixture of disregard and pity?

Lia no longer cared.

"I packed your bags, and you're moving out of this house. I want my life back."

"Now wait just a minute –" Howard turned puce from the effort of keeping his voice low. "You may be angry, but you'd better not be suggesting I leave for good."

"That's exactly what I'm suggesting." He paled at her words.

"Why now?" He loosened his already loose tie, the vigour of his attempts made his paunch jiggle slightly above his belted trousers.

"It seems you've wanted to be caught with your trousers down for a long time."

"I don't know what—"

"Stop it, Howard. I've had enough."

"This isn't the same as what happened with Shirley. Carmel doesn't mean a thing to me, it's just that a man's got needs, and you sure as hell have never—"

Lia balled her fists, keeping quiet.

"They make me feel like a man... And if I hadn't been that angry with you that night when you called out that ... that guy's name, I'd have never told you about Shirley. And you'd have never known about it. And I did stop seeing her like I promised, didn't I?"

Lia closed her eyes. How could he be bringing this up? Why had she tried so hard to maintain a calm façade in this marriage? She'd felt guilty at her discontentment, pushing away memories of an intense young man, who probably never existed the way he did in her mind.

Now she let herself remember that night, when deeply asleep, she'd dreamed and relived once again the one and only time they'd made love in that abandoned college hall. Whether it had been the warmth of two glasses of wine she'd had at dinner or her need to quench her emotional hunger, she'd been transported to another base world. And she'd cried out Devraj's name. Waking up in Howard's arms, she'd felt him freeze on top of her. Self-disgust and the sheer power of loss had made her push him roughly away.

With that thunderous expression, Howard had accused her, "You still harbor feelings for that bastard you gave your virginity to. Or have you been screwing him all along?" Then he'd hurled his ten-month affair with Shirley at her, but instantly had seemed to regret it.

Apparently, seeing nothing wrong with his past and present behaviour Howard must have continued justifying his sexual urges. After all, thirteen years ago hadn't Lia been the one to move out of their bedroom, cutting what little sexual contact had existed between them?

"Stop talking about any of them. You're making it worse."

Now she felt no guilt, just disgust at the recurrent vision of her husband and the redhead. Had it really only happened six hours earlier?

He swallowed hard. "I'm sorry, Lia." His voice was closer, making her cringe. She refused to open her eyes. "But, but this is my house." He growled, grabbing her by both arms. She finally looked up at her soon-to-be-ex-husband to find the same explosive expression in his eyes boring into hers in the dim lamplight.

She shook herself out of his painful grip.

"It's my home too, and don't raise your voice at me."

"Before you get carried away with another one of your delusional fairy tales, like your art career, if anyone goes, it'll be you."

"You'll stay with the children while I leave?" Lia reiterated slowly.

"You're serious about this." Howard let her go.

"I can leave and the lawyers can tell you how much of this house—and your business assets—I'm entitled to. We can sell the house for whatever the agents can get for it, and I'll get a settlement and you can take care of the children's financial needs. At last I'll travel on my own—"

"Don't be an idiot. I have a business to run. Let's talk about this when you're rational and calm."

"I'm always rational and calm."

"This isn't like you, Lia." He donned a charming magician's tact.

"What do you know about the real me?" Her voice rose. "All these years I've listened to you about your work, your family, your friends, but you never bothered to get to know me." She leaned towards him.

"What's there to know? You're the one who pushed me away. And I've provided for you and—"

"You won't have to anymore."

"Yeah, right." He snorted, his confidence making her grit her teeth. "Have you got someone stashed away somewhere?" His eyes narrowed, as he impatiently wiped away the sweat off his forehead into his thinning hair.

She was too appalled to validate the question. "I'm going to be independent and it's none of your business how."

"Hah!" He barked. "What are you capable of doing, some running around for those friends of yours, putting up some stupid waste-of-space pictures?" That showed how little he knew of her capabilities outside her housewife persona. "Or are you going to paint for a living?" He laughed, his complexion turning slightly pink.

That hurt but she refused to catch the bait.

"You won't last a week without me, phoning me, 'Hello,

Howard'," he mimicked some high voice, "'I'm sorry, but I can't pay the bills. Sorry, I don't know where this and that is...'"

"Well, you'll never have to worry about any of that. Just promise you'll spend quality time with the children—especially with Gabe at a time like this, with his Bar Mitzvah coming up. And don't get in the way of Danielle's future. Give me a quick divorce. I'll be happy to stay in the house and not get the lawyers involved if you take care of the costs for the Bar Mitzvah in September, and Danielle's studies until next year, I'll take care of them and everything else."

"All this so you can let Danielle make the same mistake you nearly made."

"This has nothing to do with Danielle, apart from the fact that she was the reason I wanted to talk to you... But I suggest you seriously reconsider meeting Sanjay. If you refuse, well, you've always done whatever you wanted, but I won't be part of your hypocrisy."

"Will you stop going on about this divorce bull if I agree to meet the boy?"

"No, Howard that's a separate issue, and I know how your mind works. But as her father, drop this stubborn, archaic attitude about Sanjay."

"Don't dictate to me. And I can refuse to pay for anything if you go ahead with the divorce." He raised a brow. "My lawyers can prove I'm not as solvent as you think."

She sighed, feeling the slow thudding pain worsen in her temples and back of her head. Even though her insides shook, knowing she would work in three different jobs if she had to, she said, "Then I'll manage somehow."

"You can't wait to get rid of me, can you?"

"What do you expect after I saw you with that...? You animal." She swallowed down the bile threatening to choke her.

"Carmel doesn't feel disgusted by me." He smiled tightly.

She got up. "So are you leaving?"

"You know what? I'll leave tomorrow, for a while." He rose, his eyes suddenly bright, before he turned away.

"No, Howard, you're leaving right now and for good."

The door slammed downstairs. Howard was gone. It had been a long day, and it was only after eight on the longest Saturday of Lia's life. Apart from that day when she'd finally broken up with Devraj when he'd barged in on her and her grandparents, and her wedding day...

Stop it.

It was the end of her marriage. Now that Howard had finally left, she suddenly felt exhausted. Avoiding the haunted gaze in her bathroom mirror, she splashed her face with warm water.

She'd talk to Gabe and Danielle as soon as possible.

From the voices downstairs, Danielle was back, sounding upbeat and excited. Lia stopped in mid splash, not recognizing the male voice. Had her daughter hoped to force Howard to face Sanjay in his own house?

Excitement warred with a familiar sense of foreboding at meeting Danielle's young man.

Her trembling fingers grabbed the soft hand towel when the doorbell rang urgently. Maybe the memories that had assailed her over the past twenty-four hours were playing with her mind, but she couldn't shake off the memory of Devraj forcing his way into her grandparents' house.

She began down the stairs.

The doorbell rang again, joined by urgent thuds threatening to break down the door.

Half way down the stairs, almost paralysed, Lia gripped the banister and gawked at the young man following Danielle towards the door. Her heart drummed harder. Apart from the blond streaks in his short, fashionably mussed hair, he could have been the twenty-one-year-old Devraj's clone. The youth was as tall and rugged as her first love had been.

Now Devraj was probably bald, sporting a paunch and jowls where a strong, kissable jaw used to be.

Dizziness made her wobble, a shiver rippled through her. Neither her daughter nor the young man saw her stop at the foot of the stairs on the last step.

As Danielle opened the door, although Lia couldn't see who'd caused the ruckus, she heard the gorgeous baritone voice she'd remember until she died.

"What the hell are you playing at, Sanjay? Your mother's worried sick."

Chapter Four

LIA GRASPED THE banister even harder as Devraj entered her hallway. She watched him stare at Danielle, unaware of her own presence. Did he notice the resemblance, despite Danielle's lighter hair and blue eyes instead of her mother's dark brown ones?

As if feeling Lia's eyes on him, he slowly swiveled towards her. As did Danielle and Sanjay.

In a haze, Lia heard her blood whooshing through her overtaxed veins and gripped her chest with a shaking hand.

Everything but Devraj vanished from her vision, drinking in the way his eyes lit up.

Within seconds, she registered every detail about him. His jet-black hair, with a hint of silver at the temples, still looked silken, although not quite reaching his crisp blue shirt under his perfectly tailored, dark suit. He'd filled out even more, making her remember how comforting those powerful shoulders had been.

She couldn't have been more wrong about how he'd have aged. He was more handsome, his presence even stronger than she remembered. But the expression in his eyes made her continue gawking at him. The unmistakable pleasure in them made her chest muscles constrict, making her knees quiver.

"Lia." His deep voice held the disbelief she understood too well.

"Devraj." She breathed out the name. His wide gaze devoured her face, resting on her mouth, as if he was about to bridge the few steps dividing them.

As if against his will, he gazed at Danielle for a moment, and then gaped back at Lia, "Oh. My. God...No!"

His demeanor changing, his poker-face expression erased all tenderness.

Was Sanjay Devraj's son? Was Mrs. Shah waiting in the car like a good Indian wife? How could this thought burn deeper than her whole day's nightmare?

Devraj's accusing eyes settled on Sanjay. "You can't be serious. Is this what you got me on the plane for, the life and death matter?"

"Yes, this is Danielle, but Ma and Aunt Surita wouldn't understand—"

"No, Sanjay. You're all we have left. I won't let you ruin your life like this. Over my dead body." Devraj's broad shoulders squared and as he turned back towards the door.

"No, uncle, I'm fed up of being emotionally blackmailed by everyone. I thought with your modern thinking you'd understand that I can't give Danielle up."

"Why didn't you come and talk to me about all this before it got serious? Let's discuss it at my place. *Chalo.* Let's go."

Lia found her voice, "Stop, Devraj." She took small steps closer to him.

He glanced at her, his eyes unfathomable. The nerve pulsed in his strong jaw.

"Don't let our past interfere in their future."

"Your past?" Both Danielle and Sanjay echoed.

Devraj's eyes narrowed, burning with volcanic fury. Just as quickly, an enigmatic mask veiled his face again. "But you know the saying, 'like mother like daughter'. Why would she be any different from you and not do exactly—"

"Mum, what's he talking about? What's going on?" Danielle demanded.

As if a spell had been broken, Lia focused on the younger couple. Sanjay extended his hand.

"I'm glad to meet you, Mrs. Goldman. I'm Sanjay Dutt and you seem to know my Uncle Dev." He glanced over his shoulder at Devraj.

That was why his name had been familiar; Lia remembered Devraj telling her about his sister's baby, and the namesake after Malika's love of the young actor from the 1991 film "Saajan".

Disoriented with her thoughts, Lia shook his hand, studying his dark eyes. "Nice to meet you, Sanjay."

"Don't get your hopes up, Lia. I don't have time for games." Devraj said.

Could this day get any worse?

Forcing herself to look away from Devraj, Lia addressed Sanjay, "Your uncle and I need to have a talk, alone."

Devraj neared her. "Don't bother. Nothing you say will change my mind." Wasn't that what she'd promised *him* when he'd first pursued her? Days later she'd become besotted with him and his dance skills on the college stage.

She shook herself mentally. "Stop being stubborn, Devraj. I've had a nightmare of a day, just give us five minutes." She was surprised at her level of energy when she'd felt so shattered only minutes earlier.

"Where's Daddy? I didn't see his car." Danielle started towards the stairs.

"Your father's gone. We'll talk about it later."

"What do you mean 'gone'? What's happened, Mum?" Danielle's face turned pale.

"Later, Danielle, don't worry, I'll take care of everything." At her words, Danielle's brows lifted.

Turning to Sanjay Lia said, "Why don't you take Danielle out for coffee, and we'll call you later." Forcing a smile, she dismissed the nodding young couple who looked hesitant. Danielle seemed ready to burst with questions, but seemed to trust her mother's alien take-charge attitude.

Chapter Five

LIA WAS ALONE with Devraj. The heavy tick of the grandfather clock sounded ominously slow as they stood in the large, bright foyer, so different from the stuffy corridor at her grandparents' old house, where they'd last seen each other.

He looked down at her like a Maharaja about to claim his bride.

Stop fantasizing, she ordered herself.

Just like on their first meeting, when he'd caught her sketching him, again, she couldn't take her eyes off him.

At this proximity, his new, subtle, sophisticated cologne surrounded her. His striking features had matured flawlessly, though the resolute tightness in his jaw line was new. Where was that ready grin, that gregarious, warm, fun-loving spirit? Gone was the light in those eyes of the idealist.

He returned her frank gaze. Her eyes stopped on his sculpted lips. Biting the inner flesh of her lip, she fought the sudden, familiar lurch of sexual hunger for him.

"Do I meet with your approval?" He seemed amused. Raising a brow, he appraised her, too. The reserved air around him sparkled with potent passion she remembered too well.

Her hands balled into fists, feeling the heat in her flushing cheeks. To put distance between them, to regain her composure, she walked away.

Entering the quiet, antique filled living room she sat on the sofa, reminding herself now was *not* the time to get distracted. She was on a life-changing mission.

Devraj sat in the armchair opposite her. "So, talk, Lia."

How could her name sound so much more sensuous on his lips? Like when he'd called her his angel in the passionate throes of their lovemaking. She groped for normalcy, averting her eyes. "Until last night Danielle hadn't mentioned Sanjay at all."

"He'd told me about a girl, but not how serious it had got. After today's crazy message, I flew back to see Malika. She was distraught about his threats of eloping."

"Danielle mentioned eloping too, but her father wouldn't budge..."

"History repeating itself, hah? Only now it's not your grandparents, is it? And this time *I* won't let this go on."

Even after all these years, the resentment, which should have fled upon losing her grandparents, resurfaced. She wouldn't allow her deep sorrow to drag her down. "Why don't you ask your father what really happened on that day after we..."

"My father died almost eighteen years ago."

Lia must have paled, because the fire of retribution dimmed in Devraj's eyes, but only slightly. "He died in a plane crash over India, along with my brother, brother-in-law and uncle." Devraj seemed to regain his calm now.

"I'm sorry. Your poor sister, and your mother with her heart condition... That must have been so horrendous." Questions piled up in her mind.

He inclined his head, sitting up straight. "How did you know about my mother's heart condition? I never told you."

She shook her head. "It really doesn't matter." What was the use of rehashing the past? Mr. Shah had been right to bring her down to reality.

"More importantly, Howard won't be involved in this." Then added, "I'm divorcing him. But Danielle doesn't know yet. It just happened this afternoon."

"I'm sorry." The impersonal tone masked the underlying bitterness she recognized. Then his mouth softened as his eyes scoured her face. "You've gone through a lot, it seems. So, was it brought on by Danielle and Sanjay's news?"

"In a way, yes. But I won't let him—or anyone else—stand in their way."

There was a twitch in the corners of his mouth, "Are you warning *me*, too?" It reminded her of Howard's earlier expression. Only this one warmed the pit of her abdomen.

Oh, those dimples... His closeness and his scent, reminded her of their rain-soaked first kiss, which had blown their friendship into all consuming love.

Concentrate! "Absolutely. Danielle and Sanjay are old

enough to make decisions—"

"Like you made your decision nineteen years ago? Strange how things work out, isn't it?" Devraj's tone was conversational, but his eyes mocked her.

Feeling like an ensnared criminal in her own territory, she sighed. "If it'll make any difference at this late stage, I want to apologize for…hurting you all those years ago…Let's put all this behind us for Danielle's and Sanjay's sakes—"

The intensity in his eyes cut her off. "I personally would like to have some things cleared up before we get on to that." He said, like the easygoing charmer he used to be before their growing attraction and intense words of love had complicated everything.

"Why? Let's talk about their future, and help them."

"That's very grown-up of you. I'm glad you seem to have better judgment in your…"

Lia winced. What was he seeing? An overdressed, suburban housewife pretending to be younger than her thirty-six years? She deserved his disdain, this hostility. But she had to get through to him, to bridge over their past.

Especially if there was any chance of them becoming related. God help her.

Surprised at the velocity of her mounting frustration, she got up. She stared down at him as he put one calf over his other muscled thigh, looking as if he'd always been around in this suddenly pompous and cluttered looking room.

"If you refuse to be reasonable and civil, please leave. We'll manage without you."

He made no move, showed no reaction. She was aware of that glint in his eyes. Then he smiled, "Sending me away again?"

About to react like a child, she reminded herself that she was an adult on the verge of independence and that her own children were her number one priority now. "You know, they'll do whatever they please, and I don't want them to make the wrong decision because of overwhelming opposition. So either think it over or go."

Lia was no longer a confused, manipulated teenager. She'd stand her ground. Starting to count, to calm herself, she wished she could slap that half-grin off his face. "Now, do you want a drink, or are you leaving?

Seconds ticked by.

"A scotch would be nice." He said at the count of thirteen. "On the rocks. Please."

Head held high she escaped towards the kitchen, hoping he'd stay where he was.

No such luck. She felt his energy close behind her as she switched on the lights and crossed the expanse of the kitchen to fill the stainless steel kettle in the gleaming sink. Dropping pieces of ice in a tumbler, she turned to Devraj. "Make yourself—" She'd nearly said 'at home.' "The Scotch is in the drinks cabinet in the living room."

Go away. I need to regroup.

She averted her eyes, and waiting for his footsteps to recede, she prepared a peppermint tea.

God was cruel sometimes. Why send Devraj into her life today of all days? Why had Devraj not aged badly? And why was he here dragging her into the past on the eve of forging into her freedom?

She was no closer to enlightenment when Devraj sauntered back in. Even concentrating on her daughter's happiness seemed impossible right now.

He leaned one slim hip against the dark granite counter, and Lia summoned her self-control to overcome the effect he had on her body and heart. Her skin tingled from him standing so close. Her mouth was arid as if filled with sawdust. His mocking amusement seemed almost dangerous.

Why should he make it easy for me, when at last he has me alone? They'd never been alone like this.

"You have a beautiful home, but I always knew you had good taste."

The lump in her throat lifted, as Devraj seemed to change tact and backed off from his rejected-Rick-from-Casablanca moodiness. He was admiring the dark cherry wood cabinets and running a hand over the polished seaweed-colored countertops. "You seem to have got everything you wanted." As she opened her mouth to protest, he added, "and Danielle seems determined. Have sparks been flying with your two spirited personalities, an artistic mother and a feisty teenager? Or have you given in to her as easily as you did to your grandparents' wishes?"

"I'm quite different from the girl you knew back then."

"Did I ever know you?"

She heard the volatility behind the outwardly unaccusing words. He put down his drink, not taking his eyes off her.

Inhaling another deep breath, she put down her steaming mug. "Obviously you haven't forgiven me, but I refuse to dwell down memory lane. I'm telling you again—"

"Just humor me." He folded his arms over his impressive torso. "Tell me what happened after the day we made love—"

That deep place within her abdomen melted, her throat threatened to close up as he added, "for you to break up with me." Within his eyes, she saw the passionate young man was alive and well.

"I had no choice." She couldn't find the right words to eradicate his disbelieving expression. "It wasn't just my grandparents, but your father, too."

As if about to lunge for her he said, "Yes, let's hide behind our families and traditions!"

She held her tears at bay by digging her nails into her palms, readying herself for the inevitable roller coaster ride.

"If you'd loved me you'd have believed in me, in us." He hit his chest, afire with the same fervour as the last time they'd faced each other in her grandparents' kitchen.

She'd done this to him. She couldn't bear to see the bitterness and resentment in those eyes. Her heart crashed against her ribs, the growing pain hindering her breathing.

"How long did it take you to fall in love with the plastic surgeon's money and all he had to offer you? And did he take you travelling and encourage your art? Hadn't I warned you, Mrs. Howard Goldman?" He emphasized the 'gold' as if about to hurl a shovel at the gold-digger.

Guilt singed her insides, hearing that name on his lips.

"At least admit what you really are." A frown marred his features and he broke their eye contact. Was that guilt? Although unable to pry, she wanted to know so much about him. Like did he still dance the way he had in college? That classic, yet sexy dance...

She stomped at the nostalgia. It could be dangerous for her children's future.

Remember that!

Devraj picked up his drink, downed the rest of the amber liquid, and smacked the crystal tumbler on the counter. Surprisingly it stayed in one piece.

"Dragging up the past won't change it." She said. "I repeat, let's concentrate on Danielle's and Sanjay's relationship. Surely, you must know they're in love. You can't stand in their way. They can give it time—"

"What if this is a passing fancy? What if Danielle changes her mind and decides Daddy's right, and then marries a Jewish guy?"

"You sound so bitter—" He narrowed his eyes, but she couldn't shut up. "I don't think you're ready to hear anything right now. I really understand your anger but—"

"I don't give a damn if you understand or not." He said as if through gritted teeth. "You never—if you'd just met me once more..."

She glanced away, looking for an escape, but he continued, "Did you ever really love me?" His chest rose and fell as he waited. "Or was I just the guy who took your virginity?"

She closed her eyes at the bittersweet realization that he still harboured feelings for her.

Her eyes shot open. No. Her romance-starved brain was playing tricks on her.

His bruised male ego needed justice.

All he needed was closure.

He need never know about her inner suffering. How on her wedding day she'd yearned for Devraj to grab her and run off with her.

She recognized they both needed closure. Maybe fate had brought them together now to set the record straight, to put this behind them and move on. Other people's happiness depended on her dealing with this maturely.

"I did love you." She paused through the lump in her throat, taking another deep breath to steady her breath. "But I honoured my commitments..." She looked away from his eyes. She hadn't kept her promises under the wedding canopy to be the best wife. Now she admitted it was because of Devraj's long shadow over her.

Brooding resignation marred Devraj's features.

Maybe she should have stayed silent. The pain deep inside her resurfaced. She was damned if she did, and she was damned if she didn't—*hadn't* loved him.

He looked down at the cream porcelain floor like a defeated man. When he finally glanced at her, he appeared to have regrouped. Had her words penetrated through his male pride? Was it sufficient to know she had loved him?

She'd have to quash her attraction to him. Her own husband seemed to belong in the past more than Devraj ever had.

"Can we move on now?" As she scanned his eyes, something changed in his demeanor and a plummeting sensation in her stomach told her she'd betrayed herself.

That astute gaze brought her flight reflexes to full alert.

Then she made another mistake. She looked at his mouth, craving to bring back the happy-go-lucky grin and his dimples.

Looking away, she stepped back to put space between them.

"Let's give them the chance to find out if they have what it takes. OK? Would you please call Danielle and Sanjay now?" Even though she sounded calm, she felt her betraying pulse in her throat beating against her gold chain. Safety in numbers; she prayed to be saved from her crazy illusions and teenage fantasies.

"I don't think we're finished...yet." His voice was hoarse. The fire in his eyes had a new vitality, as he swiftly bridged the remaining gap between them.

Instantly, she retreated again, but the cold granite trapped her. Her elbow caught the cake plate. Hearing it crash she knew it had exploded into small shards by their feet. But she didn't care, and Devraj seemed oblivious to everything but her.

Unable to breathe, she saw her own need reflected in his probing gaze. Her heart pounded faster as Devraj pulled her unresisting body into himself.

How could she have forgotten how powerful he was? Instead of regaining control of the situation, she felt desire overload and was mesmerized, as he brought his lips hard against hers.

And she was home at last.

What the hell are you doing, Dev?

But he couldn't help himself.

Ridiculous, he thought as he devoured her mouth, inhaling and tasting the familiar vanilla and apples of her silky skin and lips. He'd only intended to prove to himself that he'd feel nothing when he touched her, kissed her. He was no longer that young fool, he reminded himself, yet he couldn't move away. Lia glared at him with those large expressive eyes before her lids fluttered shut. Her lush curves moulded against him, breathing into him.

His impulsive act had backfired.

He resented Lia for how perfectly they fit together, and how the electric charge between them was even more potent. All these years this girl-woman had been the yard stick by which he'd measured all others. She'd left him commitment phobic, burying notions of romantic love years ago. No woman—and he'd met and bedded many, and even convinced himself he'd loved some—had ever brought out this ferocious sexual hunger.

He'd been incapable of love. But now he understood that harbouring passion for the young Lia, had overshadowed all else.

A rough sound escaped his chest as she put her arms around his neck, matching his fervor.

She'd blossomed into an even more beautiful woman, sexy in her elegant, sheer, blue blouse and figure-hugging slacks.

He buried his hands in her silky brown shoulder-length hair, which framed her angelic features. Even now, she turned him inside out, that deep soul-searching stare sending scorching heat through him when she'd admitted she had loved him.

How he'd missed this luscious mouth, the color of red poppies and as addictive.

She kissed him back. He moulded her sweet curves into him, her back against the counter. Now there was no escaping. Their lips and tongues explored in perfect harmony.

What a sap. You're no better than your infatuated nephew. He started to pull away, but Lia's pleasure ridden face came into focus, turning him on to hell.

She moaned and he wanted her even more.

She whispered something inaudible, between urgent kisses she planted on his face. He felt her tears against his face. Or were they his? Did it matter?

God he wanted her. The kiss went on.

"Mum!" An indignant voice screeched from somewhere close.

Dev almost lost his balance as Lia fiercely pushed him away from her.

Chapter Six

"GABE," LIA'S HARD breathing made Dev observe closely, as she fumbled for an explanation. The thin boy glared at them with a thunderous expression, his chest rising and falling fast.

"This is Devraj, Danielle's boyfriend's uncle..." She clasped her hands together. "This is my son, Gabriel." Then with another steadying breath, she added, "Please call Danielle and Sanjay."

Speed dialling Sanjay's number on his mobile he watched Lia clean up the cake mess. Forcing himself to unglue his attention from her, Dev looked at her son who stood at the doorway regarding him suspiciously. Dev said, "Danielle and Sanjay are getting some doughnuts."

"I'm t-twelve, I'm not a b-baby you can b-bribe with a doughnut."

"Gabe, that's rude." Lia said firmly.

Dev didn't doubt that instead of doughnuts the boy would have preferred a box of hand-grenades to put to good use in very close vicinity of the interloper Dev obviously was. He refrained from smiling at the boy's admirable trait of defending his mother's honour.

"Are—are your friends still here?" The pink-cheeked Lia asked through plump lips, studying her son's face as she tore another couple of paper towels off the roll.

"I heard something crashing..." The boy gaped at the mess on the floor, then at them. "Never mind." His dark brown hair fell over one delicate eyebrow above large brown eyes. He rushed noisily back upstairs.

Ten minutes later Danielle and Sanjay returned. Reeling from their kiss, Dev focused on shaking off the sexual undercurrents between Lia and himself. Silently, she glanced at them in turn around the large kitchen table.

"I think you two should get to know each other better before thinking about getting engaged." Dev said. "Because you'll have to convince me you're ready, otherwise I won't stand by-"

"What do you mean?" Sanjay's chest rose as if about to attack an evil power. "We want to get married immediately."

"We're not stopping you, and I won't let anyone get in your way," Lia continued to avoid looking at Dev. "But please don't rush into this big decision."

"We've thought about this very seriously." Sanjay insisted.

"Dad will never accept Sanjay, so why wait?" Danielle asked. "We love each other and we might as well as marry in a few weeks, with a small gathering of friends."

"Why don't you give it time? Dad may come around." Lia averted her eyes from her daughter.

"That's as likely as him converting to Buddhism." Danielle rolled her eyes like Lia used to back in college. But behind her bravado, Dev saw the hurt.

"I know we can't stop you," Devraj said to Sanjay, "but start with an engagement, and I'm not saying I'm going along with this, but we can first introduce Danielle to Mum and Aunt Surita, and give them time to adjust. And what about your other relations, Danielle, like your great Aunt Eliza, or your great-grandparents...?"

Danielle shook her head. "My great-grandparents died when I was six."

Devraj looked at his cup for a moment. Even if they'd been the sole antagonists in his and Lia's love story, their loss must have devastated her.

He wanted to know so much about her.

"Only Great Aunt Eliza would come." Danielle absently served Sanjay with a sugary confection ball on a gold-rimmed white plate. "My grandparents are even worse than Dad about...this." Danielle sighed, trying to keep her chin up.

"Let's give it a few weeks for the dust to settle, it may help them come round to the idea." Dev offered.

Dev enjoyed Lia's grateful smile, and hope and confusion warring within her pretty eyes. Averting her attention, she poured the coffee into cups. Its scent mingled with the fresh, yeasty doughnuts and her new, elegant perfume. Prizing his gaze off her Dev added, "remember, you have to show me—us— you're fully committed." Dev sent a meaningful glance to Danielle and then Lia.

"Fair enough," Then Sanjay narrowed his eyes, "why are you being so helpful?"

Leaning towards Sanjay, Danielle's gaze veered from Dev to her mother. "You aren't hoping that if we aren't up against any family opposition that our love will fizzle or something?"

"Will it?" Dev asked.

"Of course not." Sanjay and Danielle said in unison.

Sanjay's eyebrows furrowed together. "This isn't a silly, rebellious act."

"Then you've got nothing to worry about, with us on your side." Dev said. Instead of feeling like a pushover, Lia's wavering smile made him want to have her all to himself.

"In the meantime, let's go out for dinner to talk next weekend and I'll speak with Malika and Surita to arrange for us all to meet at the shah house the following weekend. You think Gabe would like to join us?"

Blushing Lia's looked like an errant teen.

"I'll let you know." She offered him a steaming gold-rimmed cup, not looking at him. He discreetly prolonged the contact of their fingers accepting the cup.

"Cool, thanks Uncle Dev. I knew you'd come through for us."

"I'm just making sure you pace yourselves and think this through. Marriage isn't—"

"Yes, I know how you feel about marriage, Uncle Dev. You'd rather have root canal with no drugs than get hitched." Sanjay interrupted, digging into a second doughy sugar ball.

Lia was almost shaking at the prospect of seeing Devraj again, and so soon after that fateful night last week. Mortification burned her face and travelled throughout her tingling body whenever she thought of her wanton response to her first love.

As if she hadn't been touched by a man in forever. Well, she hadn't. But she *should* have practiced a little self-control.

It hadn't been easy telling Danielle and Gabe about the news of the impending changes. Gabe had stayed stoically quiet while Danielle had started blaming Lia, then turning on herself, for causing the death of her parents' marriage.

Lia had listened, reassured, and comforted Danielle this had been an overdue decision with no one to blame.

Scrutinising her sheer cream silk top under her dark-chocolate two-piece trouser suit, she blushed at last week's memories. How would Devraj like her appearance today?

She could no longer enter her kitchen without those sensuous emotions erupting through her. But there'd be no more kissing.

She went to check on Gabe and fussed with his shirt cuff and then collar. "I know you'd rather be with your friends, but this is important for Danielle. So please no sulking."

Danielle stood by the door. "Yes, GB, and maybe you'll get a nice Bar-Mitzvah present and get rid of me permanently."

"I'm—I'm not a geek." Gabe flushed at the nickname short for Geeky Brother.

"Danielle, stop." Lia said.

Giggling, Danielle ignored her, fluffed her hair. "You *know* I mean it in the most affectionate way." She kissed the top of his head and mussed up his hair, knowing how much he hated it.

Lia knew her daughter was miserably missing her father, but she braved on. Looking like a lanky model about to strut her stuff Danielle asked, "Are we ready?"

"N-No!" Gabe shrugged away from them both.

Lia worried her lower lip at Gabe's returning stutter. The excellent student had backtracked overnight. He seemed invisible to Howard, with the longest conversations between father and son being about the upcoming Bar Mitzvah in September. Howard seemed more concerned about appearances and Gabe doing well at reading the *parsha.*

On top of having to deal with sudden changes at home, Gabe had witnessed his mother in a hot embrace, kissing a stranger in their kitchen. Instead of concentrating on how she looked, Lia ought to think about the damage all this could cause to her son's self-esteem.

Chapter Seven

"NO THANKS." GABE said to Dev who'd offered him the bread-basket. The lanky boy looked like a hermit yearning to be alone, instead of eating Indian food with the enemy. Dev reasoned it couldn't be easy to see his still married mother in a stranger's arms. Even though it would probably be a lengthy and painful process, in an effort to give the family time to adjust to the impending divorce, Dev hadn't even phoned Lia, in the past week, waiting to speak to her tonight.

"I'm sorry, honey, I thought you loved tandoori chicken and pilaf rice and naan—"

"Well I d-don't anymore. OK?" Gabe interrupted her. "Don't w-worry about me. As long as you and D-Danielle are h-h-happy."

When the waiter placed another dish on the wooden trivet and Lia took her shy gaze off Dev, and absently reached her spoon towards it, Gabe said urgently, "Mum, don't touch that, that's the Madras curry."

"Oh, my gosh. Thank you, Gaby." Lia flushed, pulling away if it was on fire. "I'd have soon known my mistake."

"Yeah, you'd end up in hospital." Gabe grumbled.

"You have allergies, Mrs. Goldman?" Sanjay asked.

Dev racked his brain to remember if she'd had any allergies in her teens. How could he forget such a thing? He wanted to know so much about her.

But not here.

Lia nodded, "Yes, chili and cayenne pepper. And please call me Lia. I feel old enough without the 'Mrs.' part."

"You're not old at all, and you look beauti—" At Danielle's delicate uplifted eyebrow Sanjay busied himself with refilling his plate with more rice and Aloo Gobi.

Dev grinned. The young couple were so reminiscent of how he remembered feeling about Lia it should have made him sad. Instead, he accepted God was having more fun with him.

"Danielle tells me your Intergalactic Planetary project's been chosen to represent your school. That's cool, Gabe." Sanjay smiled.

Gabe shrugged, making no attempt at eye contact.

Dev took advantage of the quiet moment. "Danielle and Sanjay want to take you to a movie. I'd like to talk to your mother alone."

Lia felt Gabe's gaze, before he confronted Devraj's eyes.

"Let's talk another time, Devraj." Lia said, covering Gabe's cold hand on his lap with hers.

"The sooner we discuss the strategy before next week's dinner with Malika and Surita, the better, no?" His cool, calm logic made her envy him.

"I don't want to go anywhere." Gabe pursed his lips. "I want to s-stay with Mum."

"What's with you, GB? It isn't our fault Dad's not here." Danielle's bright eyes lost some of their luster, but she added, "And you're lucky you're only twelve and don't have a girlfriend yet. Because she'd have to be Jewish for Dad to approve."

Gabe's face flushed pink, as he lowered his gaze to his almost full plate. "You don't know anything, so just sh-sh—"

"Can we have a word, Gaby, honey?" Lia interrupted, rising.

She was aware of Devraj's eyes following her as if she was Salome.

Gabe followed her to the front of the busy restaurant with exotic bronze and mahogany idols and curvy statues in every dimly lit corner. "I know everything's different, and you refused to discuss the other night, and I know it was a shock to see me—But it won't happen again. But tonight we're discussing Danielle and Sanjay's plans to marry."

"Why can't you talk about it here, now?"

"Because this is adult stuff, and I really thought you liked the food. Please help your sister. I promise we'll spend more time together once all this is settled."

"Then you'll be busy with your new job and your art stuff, I know it." Gabe kicked at the carved table leg, nearly dislodging the meditating, smiling Buddha off its top.

Pulling him in gently, she was glad he let her hold him. He was growing up, she marvelled, as she kissed his head, remembering the baby smell of his hair, his skin. "Many things may change, but one thing that will never change. You and Danielle will always be the most important people in my life. You understand?"

She must have reached that special place where they'd always had a bond. He nodded, breathing in against her shoulder, and like a wise soul, sighing in acceptance.

"I love you Gaby and I'm proud of you. Now can you be the polite, wonderful boy I know and love?" He shrugged but without the heavy weight of the world on his shoulders.

Now she had to strengthen her resolutions against the terrifying and tantalizing thought of being alone with Devraj.

Her heart beat like a cartoon throbbing red mess inside her chest, as she slid into the cool, soft seat of Devraj's sumptuous black sports car. The smell of luxurious leather and his intoxicating cologne made her fully aware of how far he'd come in the world. The convertible Jaguar was the perfect bachelor car.

He obviously continued enjoying the luxuries life afforded. He exuded a confidence she yearned for, the kind that came with a sense of self-accomplished success and independence.

"Shall we go for a drink?" Disappointment plunged down to her naval. What had she been thinking?

She nodded. For all she knew about the new Devraj, he could be involved with someone.

"Are you with anyone?" Had she just asked that question?

Glancing at her sideways with a lift of an eyebrow, he said, "Not right now."

Relief and something else mingled within her.

His physical pull took over the interior of the car. She asked about his work. He talked about his business expansions, and about Jim who was his business partner. Jim was divorced from his second wife. It made Lia wistful listening about her once best friend, Ella, whom Jim had divorced four years after their baby girl was born.

"They tried to make it work, but he was too young after all, for all that." Devraj said, easily manoeuvring the car with the ease of being in control of great power.

"I think they both were. I never stayed in touch with... anyone, I'm afraid."

Devraj said nothing.

She was hardly aware of where they were when he parked in an underground car park.

Within minutes, they were walking on glinting dark marble, through a plush hotel lobby. He then ushered her into the dimly elegant nautical-theme-inspired pub, overlooking the beautifully lit Tower Bridge in the inky night.

She remembered those hidden memories of her second double date with Jim and Ella, walking with Devraj beside the grand old bridge. They'd never been inside the elegant bars or buildings around this area and she hadn't been back all these years.

As if reliving the same past weekend, and the shaking, excited Lia, Devraj smiled at her and said, "I see you wear high heels very confidently these days."

"I've had a few years practice." She didn't add that she

hadn't worn heels as often because of her husband's medium height.

They lounged at a cozy, dark table overlooking the bridge and the shimmering Thames River. How different life looked from here.

Had he deliberately brought her here to jog her memory? Or did he bring all his dates here?

You're not on a date, dummy.

"What would you like?" He raised a dark eyebrow.

You. "Irish coffee," She glanced around the dimly lit, understated surroundings and the elegant clientele. The unassuming background music added to the romantic ambiance.

"So how do you suggest we go about this?" She started.

"Straight to business, as usual." Devraj glanced at her from the panoramic night view. "Let's get to know each other first. There's plenty of time to talk about Danielle and Sanjay."

"We're here to talk about them." Relax, for goodness' sake.

"I'd like to catch up on old times."

"We did that the other night." She stopped. "Let's forget about what happened before, let's leave it with the past..." She tried to sound more menial.

The smoky haze coming into Devraj's eyes wasn't a good sign.

Not again.

"I don't think I want to." His words were so soft, she wondered if she'd imagined them, as his probing eyes sought something within hers.

Swallowing hard, she was glad of the waitress's interruption. When they were alone again, Lia didn't trust her suddenly clammy hands not to betray her unsteadiness. She left her drink untouched for now. "How do you plan to break the news to your sister and the other relatives?"

Was Devraj contemplating her question, or whether he should let her ignore his words? "The three of you are invited to come for dinner next Saturday evening at the house."

"Is that where you live?"

"No." It gave nothing away. She tried not to gawk. His immaculate, black jacket looked smooth as peach-skin, moulding against his considerable torso. The crisp mustard colored shirt brought out the tan of his flesh so perfectly she had to unglue her gaze from his and forced herself to concentrate on the beautiful vista outside.

"I live alone in my flat in Swiss Cottage and I'm not married or otherwise attached."

"Not that it has anything to do with us—me." She reached for her dark laced coffee topped with cream. "We'll be ready for next Saturday. Is there anything else you've got planned?" Then not liking the enigmatic light in his eyes, she added, "Because I'd feel comfortable if we convince Danielle and Sanjay to have a longer engagement and then marry after they're both finished studying."

He responded with a non-committal nod.

"I'll be busy over the next few months setting up my new career and with the divorce proceedings. So I'd appreciate your help with Danielle and Sanjay." Again, when he nodded, she said, "If there's nothing else for now, I'd like to go home." She wished she had her own car, to be in control.

Unwavering, Devraj stayed silent, not moving a muscle. His smooth shaven jaw was steely, as he brought the crystal tumbler to his lips, took a slow lingering sip of his Scotch.

Was that lust or anger shining in his eyes? "There's nowhere to rush. We've just begun, Lia."

Chapter Eight

Trying to keep her breath even, Lia said, "No, we haven't, Devraj. We haven't begun anything."

"You're right. More correctly, we have some unfinished business." His expression left no room for doubt.

She sighed, feeling lightheaded; she wasn't used to drinking much alcohol apart from Patricia's wines at the French villa, and that was very rare. She wished she were there right now. Alone, safe. "Please stop looking at me like that."

"Why?

"Because you know it's inappropriate. If the kids get married, we're going to be related"

"There's no 'if' about it, it's probably very likely, if I don't decide to put a stop to it. But what's that got to do with us?"

"Don't threaten to put a stop to it. And there's no 'us'." Lia blinked rapidly, embarrassed at her passionate words. Putting down her drink, she sat up in her chair. "Will you please take me home? Or I can get a taxi." She said quietly.

He continued his frank gaze and said, "We both know what's going on here—that kiss says it all—don't waste time pretending you don't feel the same, and that you don't think about how it really was between us."

"You're not listening to me." Her throat constricted, her heart jumped up to her throat.

He gradually leaned over the tiny table between them until there was a whisper of space left. Raising his free hand, he gently stroked her cheek and she thought she'd melt all over again.

Get a grip. Get up.

But instead, she returned his naked gaze. "I'm listening to much more than your words, Lia."

"Don't." Her voice was no longer audible. The chills caressed her body, puckering her nipples under her lacy bra, and clothing.

His eyes told her everything she'd always dreamed of and more.

"This time we won't stop at making love just once. And it won't be rushed in a college hall, against a wall. You deserve better. Like I'd promised you. It'll be between cool, silky sheets..."

She inhaled sharply, desperate to untangle herself from his trance. She nearly hiccupped, drawing back against her seat. The warmth of his fingers on her flushed cheek left a disappointing trail of nothingness behind.

Pulling her towards him by simply tugging at her arm, he closed the space between their lips and kissed her.

Her eyes shut of their own volition at the heavenly kiss. She was disgusted at how much she wanted him.

His small groan reminded her of their surroundings.

Opening her eyes, leaning back in her bucket seat, she took a dazed look around. Life went on and no one stared at her as if she was easy.

Devraj said softly. "I'm not that young romantic anymore, but I want what I want."

"And I have no inclination to relive the past. I'm starting a new life. Now, I've got a lot to do, as I'm going away this week."

"So you'll have time to think about us. Good. I'm away until Friday, too." He looked at her as if he had all the time in the world, to wait for her to come to the forgone conclusion.

We'll see about that.

"Lia. We're here." She jumped at Devraj's fingers on her arm bringing her back to the present.

"Thank you." She sat up and breathed broadly. The song 'These Eyes' played softly in the background of the car—or was it in her imagination?—sent shivers up and down her spine. She unbuckled her seat belt, evading Devraj's knowing eyes.

She swallowed her melancholy.

No regrets about the past or not ending up in Devraj's bed.

Embarking on a future of independence, both as a woman and as an artist, she had to control every aspect of her life.

"What's on your mind, Lia?"

She prayed he couldn't read her confused thoughts. "Is it necessary for me and Gabe to come to dinner at your sisters' next weekend?"

"Meaning you don't want any more contact with me than necessary?"

"Devraj—"

"You may be tossing Danielle into the lion's den with no moral support. She's that tough?"

"Why would she need to be tough? I was hoping your sister and sister-in-law are the more 'live and let live' type."

With a slight, cynical grunt, he said, "Malika would warm to the alliance. But Surita? I think you should meet her and make up your own mind."

"Fine. Sanjay can give Danielle the address, we'll meet you there."

His chuckle made her sound like a scared, immature child. She was about to thank him and make her escape when he stroked her forearm. Her heart skittered again as she straightened in her seat.

"Can't leave me fast enough, can you, Lia?" he sounded amused. Reaching for her hand, he brought it slowly to his mouth. She gently pulled away, unable to bear the delicious, inevitable heat between them.

He seemed to misunderstand her reticence, freezing at her withdrawal. Releasing her, he scanned her face but she glanced away, picking up her clutch bag. Forming a polite smile, one that didn't give away her lustful thoughts of wanting desperately to kiss him, she thanked him.

"Thank you? Is that the best you can do?" As he reached for her, the sexual attraction smouldered again.

She welcomed his mouth on hers. Her betraying sigh mortified her. Heat warmed her cheeks and with great effort, she vied to put much-needed space between them.

"Bye, Devraj." It sounded more as if she was about to pounce on him.

"OK, run away little girl." He smiled, finally letting her go. "I'll see you Saturday. Think about me, my Lia."

Chapter Nine

ON MONDAY AFTER work, Lia drove home, thinking about her new position. She couldn't wait to get to France tomorrow.

She'd be working in Paris at La Galerie Chevalier Noir. Her friends' newest brainchild was situated in Old Paris, in the quaint part of her favorite neighbourhood. The new hip gallery would be rubbing shoulders with centuries-old buildings, museums and the specialty stores Maxine and Patricia had introduced her to a few years ago.

After two days of helping make a few preliminary structural decisions to finalise the footprint and layout of the gallery, Lia would spend a few glorious days alone in Patricia's quiet villa on the sprawling Avignon vineyard.

Introduced to Provence by Maxine earlier in their friendship, Patricia had fallen in love with this piece of paradise in her early thirties, and had bought the lush green land with her husband's legacy. Along with their friendship and the galleries, the widow's son, Peter, was Patricia's only other pride and joy.

Lia could already smell the earthy spring scents and see the serene landscapes of ancient towns of Provence surrounding the quaint village. Her friend's villa was hers to swim and paint in, if the warm weather cooperated on her first break alone. It was going to be the closest thing to heaven, since she'd never allow herself to end up in Devraj's arms.

How she'd face Devraj again on Saturday, after her cowardice two nights ago, she didn't know. She planned to vet his calls and texts and yet was disappointed at the lack of any communication from him. Thank goodness she had enough to keep her occupied, flinging herself into work.

In the past two weeks, Lia's mind kept veering towards what her grandparents would have thought about her impending divorce. They'd have been disgusted and disappointed with her, and hating her sophisticated transformation; ready to blame her two girlfriends for influencing their granddaughter off the straight and narrow. Like they'd put full blame on the pregnant Ella, in their teens.

But the brazen part of her, the one that had been tempted to fall into bed with her first love within days of ending her marriage, now stiffened her resolve not to dwell on anything but the present. She'd focus only on the positives, her freedom and her resurgent art career, even if it inevitably took years to build.

At eighteen she'd promised herself she'd continue painting in her new marriage. That hadn't worked out. Still, she had her two gifts: No one could take away that unique feeling of loving her children, and being loved and needed by them.

Last night she'd finally cleared Howard's remaining belongings for today's collection while she was at work. The detachment from her husband and his stuff left her bemused.

What kind of person was she to feel this little for the man with whom she'd spent almost half her life? She'd believed Howard's accusations of her frigidity until once again she'd responded so hungrily to Devraj's kisses.

The sudden autonomy at home and at work was as intoxicating and frightening as if Lia was about to jump off a plane without knowing how to use a parachute. But she needed time, and she wasn't alone. She had her friends, Aunt Eliza, and endless lists of her personal and professional plans to keep her from being distracted or tempted off her new path.

Patience, Dev repeated to himself on his return flight from Delhi the following Friday night. Otherwise he'd push or even frighten Lia away like he had years ago.

On that day when losing self-control, he'd held her captive, kissing her, moulding her up against the hard wall of the college hall, he'd needed to make her his as if no one could take her away from him after that. Despite the months of their growing lust and emotions they'd both curbed for too long, even in the crazy moment of obsessive love, he'd tried to please her and be gentle with her. But he'd performed badly. Yes, Lia had been yielding and responsive but it had ended too soon, and she'd averted her sparkling eyes like a soiled Cinderella. How often he'd wondered if she'd regretted losing her virginity to such a crass overly enthusiastic guy, in such unceremonious surroundings.

Since last Saturday, he hadn't been able to stop thinking about Lia. He'd make up for his boyish crudeness, and make it good for them both, and this time he wouldn't rush her.

Because despite her words Dev knew she wanted him as much as he wanted her. And he had plenty of tricks up his sleeve, in bed as well as having the upper hand over his nephew's future.

Surely Lia had felt this week had moved at a torturously slow speed, like he'd found it. He'd arranged the family get-together for tomorrow, now he'd see where it all led.

Last Sunday, he'd driven to see his sister and sister-in-law at the large family estate. The two women kept the grounds and the interior as pristine and comfortable as any regal mansion in India or Europe. The ornate antique furnishings, dark wood balustrades and the huge crystal chandeliers were magnificent, but he preferred his modern, spacious flat in Swiss Cottage.

He remembered the two opposite reactions from his sister and sister-in-law at his breaking news about Sanjay's plans.

"Sanjay's getting engaged." Dev had told them as soon as they sat in the large living room with the antiques their grandparents and parents had collected over the past century.

"That's wonderful news, *bahya*," Malika smiled, her large dark eyes shining. Noting Surita's closed expression, she stopped, picking up the end of her dark pink sari.

"Who is she, Devraj?" Surita asked tight-lipped.

"Her name's Danielle, they met in college."

The twin tracks between her dark eyebrows became deeper. "Why have you allowed this, and without our input?" Surita's shrill voice demanded.

"The reason I've called you here is to tell you that Sanjay and Danielle are in love and will be getting engaged soon. If you have any problem with that," he stared at Surita, "as the head of this family, I will have something to say about it. Dad left me in complete charge, and it would serve you well to remember that. Is that understood, Surita?"

"When do we meet...her?" Surita asked as Malika studied him and then their sister-in-law.

"Danielle and her family are coming here for dinner next Saturday night. We will show our generous hospitality and think of Sanjay's happiness."

"What about the Malhotras and the merger?" Surita asked, obviously trying to keep her temper in check.

"The merger's going ahead. This is a love marriage."

"I suppose we'll have to prepare the toned down, bland dishes you always serve your business guests."

"Yes, actually the girl's mother is highly allergic to chili and cayenne pepper. So choose your dishes with that in mind." Dev got up. "No underhanded remarks, Surita, *or* forgetting about the allergies. Understood?"

He couldn't wait to see Lia again. Even if it was across the table, to start with.

Chapter Ten

"I MISSED YOU, Mum. You got home so late last night it was a good thing Sanjay kept me company." Danielle yawned luxuriously.

"I'm sorry. It takes time and hard work to set up a new career and a new life. I appreciated you holding down the fort while I was away." Lia averted her face, busying herself making pancakes they all still enjoyed having on most weekend mornings. Her busy and creative few days in France had recharged her. Now having returned, she'd let voice-mail do its job a few minutes ago when seeing Devraj's name on her mobile's display. But her heart had done that stupid somersault, remembering how she'd turned to mushy putty when he'd kissed her.

Through Sanjay, Danielle had confirmed tonight's dinner at the Shah house. How she wished she didn't have to face those knowing eyes again. But she couldn't let Danielle go alone.

"So, what do you know about... Sanjay's family?"

"His mother, Malika sounds nice, but Sanjay doesn't like his Aunt Surita, much. Apparently, she'd been trying to marry him off to some business tycoon's daughter. Sanjay said Devraj's made sure they leave him alone. They're so close, especially after losing his Dad when he was a baby. Sanjay says Devraj doesn't talk about what happened, as if there's some kind of mystery regarding the plane crash. Can you imagine how hard it must have been losing so many male members of his family?" She shook her head, pouring herself a mug of freshly brewed coffee.

"I know." Lia ladled the creamy batter into the sizzling pan, trying to enjoy the delicate vanilla-and-cinnamon-infused scent, and not be dragged by the memories of her own losses of both her beloved grandparents. Dedda had passed away from a heart attack before the fifth Passover of Lia's marriage, and ten months after that, a year before Gabe was born, Baboola seemed to have lost all will to go on living without the love of her life.

Her grandparents' love for each other and for her, like their constant beliefs and prejudices, never changed.

"Sanjay said that Devraj had never wanted to go into the family business, but after the accident he had no choice. He developed this new company, Shah Security Industries, starting as a purely security systems company. He added it to the old family import and export business. Now they're into computer security, surveillance, and all that. Devraj and his partner Jim somebody, diversified the company so much."

Lia's heart thumped against her ribcage remembering

Devraj's best friend in college who'd once warned her not to hurt his pal. Last weekend, she'd been too distracted to contemplate Jim's own heartbreak. They must have both hated her so much. She swallowed down her frustration.

No more past, or being tempted into Devraj's sexual net. He was supporting Sanjay and she'd uphold her part of the deal for Danielle. Otherwise, they had no reason to meet outside the obligatory family get-togethers. Over the restful and creative too short stay at the Avignon villa Lia had mulled over all the reasons and justifications, she could about the dangers of succumbing to Devraj's charms.

"So you met Devraj in college too?"

"Yes."

"So what happened?"

"There's nothing to discuss." Her firm tone did the trick, as her daughter dropped it.

"The more pressing subject is, what kind of engagement have you two got in mind?" Lia flipped the perfect gold fluffy disks on to the third plate.

"We hadn't thought that far, we were prepared to elope."

As Lia called Gabe for breakfast and put two plates down on the kitchen table, Danielle covered her hand with hers, "I'm sorry, don't look so hurt. After Dad's reaction to the news, I didn't think it would work out like this. You and Devraj are amazing. But, like... I'm shocked at how overnight it all changed between you and Dad."

"We love you both, and what happened between Dad and me doesn't matter anymore."

How easy it was to be unconcerned about the father of her children. She was more engrossed with how she'd manage to avoid and resist Devraj. She couldn't wait to try on her new sheer underwear and the cherry red dress her friends had helped her pick out in Paris last year. She'd never worn anything as daring. Was it too bold for tonight's occasion? She wasn't sure. But she wanted to feel extra attractive when the two families met to get to know each other.

It had nothing to do with Devraj. Heat rose through her body, thinking of that smile.

How would she feel sitting at the Shah table and how would the Shah matriarchs greet the Goldmans this evening?

Lia was warmly surprised when meeting Sanjay's mother, Malika, whose sweet nature shone through. His Aunt Surita's stoical, cool greeting at the imposing estate didn't fazed Lia. Obviously, the two women adored Sanjay. If there was a subtle undercurrent of disappointment, who could blame them?

Having refused to come, Gabe was at his friend Jordan's, until Sunday morning. Then Howard would pick him up for the day.

She couldn't fault the gracious hospitality, and relished the variety of succulent authentic dishes the women had prepared. Lia complimented the two women as she accepted a second helping of the butter chicken that melted in her mouth.

It felt so natural to sit here, eating at the same table with the few remaining Shahs, feeling that warmth radiating from every glance Devraj sent her way sitting across from her.

Malika smiled with a sweetness that lit her heart-shaped face and large dark-brown eyes, while Surita wasn't fast enough to wipe the real emotions before donning a stiff, polite smile like the one Lia had seen on her mother-in-law's face.

The conversation around the table opened up a different picture of what she'd imagined.

Malika loved to talk about her childhood and youth, even though she was only a year older than Lia.

Surita's strong features lent her an air of being in her later forties. While the Shahs had been in England for two generations, Surita's lilty Indian accent, when she spoke in her low voice at all, revealed she was born and brought up in India. It couldn't be easy to live away from her home.

They talked about India, movies, food. Malika blushed prettily when her son told them about her love of Sanjay's namesake, Sanjay Dutt.

"My husband Ajay didn't mind the idea of the name." That faraway look Lia understood too well tempered the glint in Malika's eyes, before she added with a smile, "Although I've loved Sanjay Dutt's acting, since his role as a poet in love in Saajan, I'm glad *my* Sanjay's not as rebellious as him."

"That's a matter of opinion." Surita mumbled.

Ignoring his aunt, Sanjay asked Lia, "Elle—I mean Danielle—tells me you love Bollywood movies, too."

Now Lia blushed, "I used to watch them with my grandmother and aunt. And I'm getting back into them while I... do other things."

"'Saajan' is one of my aunt's old favorites. Isn't it a loose take on the French 'Cyrano De Bergerac' play?" Danielle asked. This drew Malika into an animated conversation about the film industry, and how it had changed in the past decades.

Devraj sat back and smiled, openly enjoying the easy company and the food.

Then Sanjay asked Lia to tell them about the little Danielle winning the 'Prettiest Princess of the Year' competition, three years in a row in kindergarten; all variations on the royal Indian princess theme.

The atmosphere continued to be jovial and light, until Surita cleared her throat softly, addressing Lia. "Aren't you the Lia that Devraj knew in college?" At Lia's nod Surita added, "I remember my Rav, Sanjay's older uncle, Devraj's older brother, telling me how upset their father was about you two. But like the good son, Devraj had listened to them in the end. It seems that my father-in-law's talk with Lia that day did the trick."

"So you had the same type of father as I do?" Danielle asked Devraj, who sat immobile staring at Surita.

Glancing at Lia, he nodded and picked up his wine glass. Under his gaze, her chiffon dress didn't seem to cover enough skin. Her stomach roiling, she pulled the matching gossamer wrap slightly over her shoulders.

"Someone must be practical and think of the future—" Surita said.

"My future includes Danielle and if we get any opposition, Aunty, we'll elope and you won't have to see us again."

At Sanjay's words, his mother gasped and said gently, "Please don't say that, *mera beta.* Aunt Surita is only trying—

" Malika placated.

Surita interrupted, "Life's not like melodramatic Bollywood films. No one will stop you, unless your uncle sees it's for the best. But I'm not doing my duty as your aunt, and the wife of the first born in this family, if I don't say this—"

"Thanks for bringing it to my attention, Surita. I knew nothing about father's meeting with Lia. Now you've said your piece." Devraj said softly with an unmistakable air of the head of the family, continuing to study Lia. "Now we're moving on to the matter at hand, Sanjay and Danielle."

Lia thought of the contrast of his reaction to Howard's resistance to the subject.

Tight-lipped Surita nodded and the rest of the evening proceeded smoothly, even if it was slightly subdued.

Danielle and Sanjay smiled at each other, but now Devraj refused to acknowledge Lia's existence, even at such close proximity.

Why had Surita unearthed the too painful memories? And was Devraj feeling compromised, being undermined in front of outsiders?

It drove home the once free-spirited, easygoing romantic now had the Shah empire and family legacy to uphold. Memories could weigh down the strongest spirit, as she knew too well.

Chapter Eleven

AS THEY SAID their goodbyes, Devraj walked Lia to her car in the cooling evening, Danielle said, "We're going for a drink. You can join us, if you like." She didn't seem too keen on having her offer accepted.

Before she could answer, Devraj said, "You go ahead, I'll give Lia a ride home."

As she watched the young couple walk down the tree-lined street, the fresh May air was laden with the thrill of new beginnings, and the stars stirred nostalgia and then excitement.

"I can take a taxi, Devraj. Thanks again. This was a good idea. I suppose it'll take them time..." She took out her mobile.

"I'll take you home. We need to talk." He said in a low voice.

"No, Devraj." She glanced back at the two women standing by the open door.

"Come to my place, we'll just talk." As she shook her head, he looked over his shoulder, impatiently. "Wait here, Lia."

A few moments later, a few easy, long strides brought him back to her side, with the door closed and the prying eyes out of sight. "Would you prefer to go for coffee?"

"No. Whatever needs to be arranged for—"

"Let's talk in the car." He opened his passenger door for her.

After a momentary hesitation, she got in.

As he drove away, he glanced at her and said, "Will you continue acting like a teenager or can we talk about what's happening here?"

"Stop it, Devraj."

"Don't fight this, us, it's no use avoiding the inevitable, Lia."

She pulled away in her seat. That confidence again, damn him. "You still sound like the bully you were at twenty-one."

He grinned at her as he manoeuvred the car a bit too fast for her liking. But neither said anything else until she registered he missed the turning for the North Circular.

She swallowed hard. "I-I thought you were taking me home."

"Do you really want to go home right now, Lia?" He glanced at her and then back at the road.

"Let's not complicate—" Devraj's smooth turn into a dim parking lot stopped her words.

Then he looked at her. "I've been thinking about you. I want to be with you." He unbuckled their seat belts and she found herself in his arms.

His hungry kiss left her feeling like a teenager on the verge of something huge she had no control over.

She closed her eyes, drowning deeper into the abyss of their mutual craving.

With a short sigh Devraj nuzzled at her throat, nibbling at her ear lobe, whispering urgently, "I want you, Lia, and you know it's meant to be between us." Those were his precise words in that abandoned college hall, when she'd felt she'd die without him.

Only this time there were no words of love.

"I've missed you, Lia. Will you come with me? Say yes." His eyes bore into hers.

She wanted him so much. All she could do was nod before he kissed her again.

As Devraj opened the door of his flat, ushering her in, Lia paid little attention to the interior of elegant and masculine flat, because she was drawn to him.

Closing the door he pulled her into his arms as he had millions of times in her dreams. She was overtaken by the ravenous need within those amber eyes.

"Let me show you how good it can be between us." He kissed her again.

She fingered the crisp black hair at the nape of his neck, and lowered her hands to roam over his warm, taut shoulders. She breathed in his unique spicy scent and cursed his sexiness and her own weakness.

"I want you, Devraj. Now." Her sigh sounded more like a purr. She knew she'd sold out her soul.

Carrying her to his bed, he wouldn't let his eyes disengage from hers, as if holding on to the magic. Kissing, licking they reacquainted themselves with each other's bodies.

This embrace, his touch, the exploring kisses were different from the past two Saturdays, and from all those years ago. He seemed intent on demonstrating with his hands, mouth, and tongue what she'd craved to feel with him.

This grown man, larger than life, frightened and exhilarated her, as their kisses deepened.

The dim lights in the large mahogany furniture-filled bedroom glowed gently on his intense profile as he shed her clothes with reverent, unhurried expertise. As he unlinked her strapless black bra, she pushed away his shirt from his hot skin. His powerful shoulders and pecs tensed under her first caress. He was broader and more rugged than she remembered. She almost cried from nostalgic happiness, as the satiny dark hairs of his torso felt familiar against her trembling palms, hungry to feel him against her naked flesh. He was so beautiful she wanted to take in every second of every minute she spent with him.

No guilt, no responsibilities outside tonight.

When they were naked, she weaved her arms around his neck and stared up at him. He groaned against her cheek, and taking her mouth, pulled her closer.

His virile confidence of his sexual prowess was new to her.

All remaining thought flew out of her mind as physical, emotional, and sexual desire took over.

God, I love you, Devraj.

She stopped herself from whimpering those words aloud. It was only her sexual starvation talking.

She combed her fingers through his hair as it fell sexy and tousled over his forehead. True to his word, there was no pressure of time and nothing else existed outside his king size bed, between the soft, silky sheets.

Lying beside her, he scanned her face and his dark gaze trailed over the length of her curves. "I can't believe you're really in my arms." His fingertips played havoc wherever they stroked.

She closed her eyes, overwhelmed with the depth of emotion and passion in his eyes.

However, his explorations brought her lids up immediately, catching her breath sharply as his fingers slowly reacquainted themselves with her hungry body.

He handled her carefully as if she was something precious and unique. As his fingers made contact her hot center, she melted into his hand like a hopeless addict.

Biting her lower lip, she surrendered to the kaleidoscope of sensuous need.

As the king of his and her lustful heaven, he explored every millimeter of her sensitized skin and curves. Her secret fantasies were coming true with his Kama Sutra-like knowledge of unique erogenous zones she never knew she had.

Welcoming him inside her as he slowly entered her, she stopped breathing for a moment, lost within his eyes. Slowly, as if through a haze, she felt her breathing meld with his. She let him lead, taking and giving in a natural way she'd never known.

How many times had she woken up from an erotic dream,

her body in the clutches of a wonderful almost satisfying orgasm, alone in bed?

Devraj was in control, on top, deep inside her womb and her mind, united deeper by their obvious obsession with each other.

"Oh, Lia, this feels so perfect. You're so beautiful. I've missed...you." He whispered between deep thrusts that left her feeling fragile and powerful all at once.

As Devraj brought her to her cliff's edge and let her soar, she couldn't compare her dizzying emotions and skyrocketing orgasm to anything she'd ever experienced.

Within the throes of her volcanic, persistent release, she remembered their first time together. He'd seemed intent on proving to them she belonged to him, body and soul.

This felt like the real first time.

As she rode those dizzying waves of ecstasy, tears left a warm trail down her temples. She squeezed her eyes shut and with her legs drew him closer to herself so he could fill her even deeper.

He must have tasted her tears as he kissed her face because, pausing his delicious onslaught he scrutinized her questioningly.

"Don't stop, Devraj, I need you so much." The bittersweet awareness of how connected they still were intensified her need for him. He was sweeping through her lonely soul as if he belonged there.

Dev was in awe of Lia as he took her delicious mouth, reacquainting himself with her glowing skin and delectable curves. He loved those sounds of delight, her soft breath catching in her throat. He revelled in her butterfly-light caresses trailing his flexing muscles and skin.

As he felt her body respond, nearing another climax, her demanding fingers through his hair pulled his face closer to plant hungry kisses over his eyes, cheeks, jaw, and Adam's apple. He closed his eyes to savor every moment.

"Come with me, again, Lia." He whispered gruffly staring into her glistening eyes.

How could he have tried to substitute this magnificent perfection in any other woman's arms?

Lia loved seeing that pleasure on his intense, desire-filled features. In poetic synchronicity, his sure strokes plunging into her were in perfect correlation with her desperate hunger. His burning caresses were healing, revitalizing.

Crying out, she prayed this sweet torture would never end. And as she floated above the realm of reality, Devraj took her to the next level of climax with his connoisseur's hands and mouth, until she knew she couldn't survive this bliss.

Nor could she bear it to end.

With his name on her lips, the earth shattered into millions of psychedelic colors behind her eyelids.

Keeping the momentum, she drew him with her, willing him to accompany her. Devraj grew rigid above her, his spine arching backwards. Then he joined her in their temporary nirvana.

His rasping low sounds into the curve of her throat made her clasp him tighter.

Panting and catching their breaths, Lia held onto him like a lifeline, welcoming his heavy, sated body on top of her. Then lying beside her, he drew her into him, holding her protectively.

Chapter Twelve

THROUGH HEAVY LIDDED eyes Dev smiled hearing Lia's breathy sighs and enjoyed how her breasts rose and fell against him.

But her salty tears, he'd tasted earlier, worried him.

Did she have regrets; was she concerned about their impending family connection?

He knew how hard it had been for her to succumb to her needs tonight. Whether she was here because of sex, or reliving their past, now wasn't the time to probe or push. His ego was ready to believe that she'd never felt this attraction with anyone else, and her hunger for him was enough for now.

"I never knew it could be like this, Devraj. I don't know how to describe it." She sighed.

"Amazing would just about cover it for me." He kissed her damp forehead and her peony pink cheek. She nuzzled her face into his shoulder. She smelled of apples, cinnamon, and lust.

Kissing her again, he closed his eyes. He hadn't kidded

himself that making love with Lia would exorcise her out of his system. No longer that desperate twenty-one-year-old in love with love, all he wanted now was to have her in his bed for as long as he could; even if it was a few weeks or months.

He'd learned to live for the moment and not plan too much.

But was she already mentally shrouding herself away from him? As she tried to pull away from him, adjusting the warm silky sheet around her breasts, he held her firm with a lazy arm.

"Do you want me to get a taxi?" She whispered.

"Why?"

"You look so peaceful."

"I wasn't sleeping, Lia. I'm just...content." He gently brought her head back to rest on his shoulder. She relaxed into him.

"I have to go, Devraj." She sighed regretfully. That was a good sign.

She got up, obviously self-conscious under his amused gaze. "Still as shy and unaware of how beautiful you are. Trust me, you're absolutely perfect."

She looked at him over her bare shoulder. "Trust you, because you've got lots to compare with?"

A cold chill prickled his skin. "If you mean other women, yes. I'm no saint. But as I told you, I'm not—"

"That's all right," Lia interrupted, putting on her sexy, lacy black underwear, hiding away those lush breasts. "You owe me no explanations."

He rose from the bed, which had felt like heaven moments ago. "I know. But I want you to know how much..."

"I've enjoyed it too, Devraj." She said.

Feeling slightly used, he pushed one leg through his trouser leg and then the other. He was gratified to see she was having trouble keeping her darting eyes off his body, as he donned his shirt, not bothering to button it.

Again, she looked the lady, and he wanted to rip the slinky red dress that accentuated every delectable curve, and kiss her until she begged him to take her again.

God he wanted her in his bed, again. It felt empty and cold without her, while she was convinced he saw this as a one-night-stand.

As Devraj drove her home, Lia wondered if his sudden aloofness was a man thing. He'd had his fun...

No negative thinking to detract from their time together. She shouldn't have shown her jealousy; he wasn't beholden to her. They had to tread softly for Danielle and Sanjay's sakes.

Why hadn't she thought about that before falling into bed with him the moment he'd touched her? What about her promise to Gabe?

Weak and sexually deprived fool!

Even the thought of other women he may have been with wasn't cooling her ardor. She couldn't blame them for wanting him. He was the perfect lover.

He was so addictive, so persuasive she wanted to lean in to him right now, smell his sweat-sheened cooling skin, and lick that mouth that had played sweet music with her body and mind.

She cleared her throat to let out the involuntary moan. Glancing away from the object of her hunger, she concentrated on practical things, like putting a stop to this madness. She was in danger of drowning in this sexual and emotional quicksand.

As he brought the car to a smooth stop outside her dark and lonely house, she faced him and said, "Thanks, Devraj." As she reached for the door she added, "We can never...do anything like this again."

The slight narrowing of his eyes in the dim confines of his car made her heart lurch again. "We both know you don't mean that, because all I have to do is touch you and you feel just like I feel."

She was tempted to slap that lopsided grin off his face. Dimples and glinting eyes be damned. "Maybe that was a one-off for old times' sake." She couldn't help sounding annoyed.

"You were never a good liar." He unbuckled his seatbelt.

She said, "It was good for both of us. But now let's get back to the real reason we've been—"

"Thrown together?" He offered. She hated that tone.

"Let's not complicate things anymore than they are. I love...loved our time together," she heard the tremor in her voice, "but I can't do this. I told you about my plans to help my children over the divorce and concentrate on my career. Nothing else can interfere, Devraj. Nothing."

Maybe it was her passion or anxiety that made the subtle difference, as Devraj appeared to consider her words.

Defensiveness seemed to dissipate from him. "All right, so it's not that you don't want to see me, but that you don't have the energy to put into a relationship right now."

"Well..." That wasn't all, "I'm just getting out of a marriage."

"I understand, and you deserve to have fun. So why not see each other—discreetly—and enjoy each other? No strings attached."

"That sounds very calculated."

"Sounds to me it's what *you'd* prefer. And it's fine with *me*."

Spoken like a true bachelor. A small part of her was disappointed to hear him say it.

OK, a big part of her felt let down. But, what did she expect?

He valued and enjoyed his freedom and was used to the lifestyle he'd built for himself.

Her first instincts had been right after all.

"No, thanks." She opened the car door when Devraj's arm stopped her from exiting.

"Give it some thought, my Lia. You can text or call anytime and I'll be here."

What annoyed her more than the logic and patience in his voice was his confidence that she'd reconsider his offer, and be back in his arms whenever he wanted her.

Finally free to make her own decisions, as a red-blooded woman who hadn't allowed herself to feel or enjoy much for far too long, being in his bed tonight had been cathartic. Now that she'd relived the sexual fantasy, it was time to move on with the present. Get out now, and nip it in the bud.

Yeah, how had that worked out years ago? It seemed Lia hadn't gained an ounce of wisdom with age.

Chapter Thirteen

"HOW ARE YOU managing with the pace so far, Lia?" Patricia asked at the ten o'clock Monday meeting with Maxine and their young assistant in the small, beautifully designed office.

"I'm managing." She nodded with a smile. "I'm glad we got the confirmation from Bella Ricci for September and Jazzy Carrington for the Paris gallery for next April. Now I can fully concentrate on the next exhibition in London—"

"I know, don't worry about the details, we trust you implicitly. Maxi and I were making sure you're not over-worked. I know how you can be."

"I'm enjoying all the challenges so far, and if I'm not sure of anything, don't I ask you? That's the advantage of being friends with the bosses."

Maxine nodded. "Good and how are Danielle and Gabe settling into the new routine?"

"So far so good, and Howard's being surprisingly civil. Well, up to now, anyway. Although he hasn't signed the papers yet."

Feeling the niggling annoyance of talking about her soon-to-be ex, she changed the subject to work.

Patricia said, "As your insights at the Paris gallery were so helpful, we wondered if you're up for going in August and overseeing the Bella Ricci solo exhibition in for September showing."

Maxine added, "We can help you with the rest of the plans for Gabe's Bar Mitzvah, of course. So it won't add more stress."

Her spine tingled from the top of her neck down to her soles. "If you're sure I can oversee it on my own, it would be an amazing experience."

"If we weren't, we wouldn't suggest it, friend or no friend!" Maxine waved a dismissive, pristinely manicured hand.

Lia appreciated being taught by her friends, the best in the industry, guiding her on all aspects of running an art business. Art curating was a varied and fun job, although it was exacting and demanding and she had to be ultra organized.

But so far, she loved every minute of it.

If she missed actually creating art, she reminded herself no one had stopped her from pursuing her painting in her married years. Now she was free to create art in her spare hours, and she was making up for lost time. When she wasn't working or spending time with the kids, she planned to spend every free moment painting.

The creative dam was unleashed.

The only prickle of apprehension about this new opportunity to go to Paris was how to broach the subject with her kids, who were going through enough change. Even if it were not until the end of summer, Gabe and Danielle would be upset to hear of her plans.

She'd have to cross that bridge when she came to it; maybe broach it in a few weeks. She worried her lower lip.

"Lia, it's Devraj." She knew bloody well who was at the other end of the line. Why had she answered the phone on this quiet Sunday morning, anyway?

She tried to stay immobile in the steamy bubble bath filled to her chin. The lavender scent added to her erotic image of Devraj's expression if he was here.

"I know. What can I do for you?"

"Why have you been avoiding my calls? I know you've been busy, but it's been over two weeks—" He paused as she swirled a leg up into a different position in the suddenly too warm water. "Where are you?"

She stopped in mid motion. "I have to go. I'll call you later."

"Are you in the bathtub, Lia?" Amusement tinged his soft, low voice.

She closed her eyes, and indolent hunger danced within her body and mind. Why didn't his question sound dirty and interfering? Was his mind roaming over her curves, like his tantalizing mouth, tongue, and expert fingers had fifteen long days ago?

"I have to go."

"Lia." His breath caught with unmistakable lust. "I haven't been able to stop thinking about you..." She imagined him raking the dark hair back, almost hating himself for admitting this. "I'll be there in half hour."

"No, Devraj." But, the line was dead. Tempted to hurl the betraying phone against the bathroom wall, she reminded herself she was in control of her new life. She dropped the receiver onto the pile of bath towels on the floor by the edge of the tub, and with a gruff sigh, she splashed two fists into the water. All her reminders of staying focused at work and at home were fraying.

Would she ever breathe freely?

When Lia answered the ringing doorbell, she was prepared to lay into the sexy devil that was causing her sleepless nights, sabotaging her dreams with even more hot, vivid images.

"Howard." Surprise made her step away from the doorway, as her soon-to-be-ex-husband stood frowning.

"You remember me, good." He said curtly. "I'm picking up Gabe, it's eleven o'clock. Is he ready?"

"I'm sure he is. But before he comes down, have you got the signed papers for me?"

"I'll get to them."

"I'd like them right now. Don't string this out."

"Or else? What if I don't?" Howard grunted with a nasty smirk.

She'd been afraid of this. She sighed. "I'm sure the courts will be intrigued by your business ethics, especially about those floozies you've hired and fired during our so-called marriage. Thanks to your cooperative receptionist, I have the latest girl's details, before you replaced her with your current redhead 'intern'. I plan to do whatever I have to, to get the divorce processed as fast as possible. If I were you I'd cooperate and sign the documents this week."

Howard's frown deepened. Before he could respond, Lia called up for Gabe and heard his "I'm c-coming."

Following Howard's distracted gaze she noticed a familiar black open-topped Jaguar smoothly gliding to a stop on her driveway next to Howard's unfamiliar sleek, silver sports Mercedes.

"Who the hell's that?" Howard asked staring at Devraj sauntering up the path.

"Sanjay's uncle."

Devraj reached them and extended a hand out in greeting. "I'm Devraj Shah."

Ignoring his hand, Howard glared up at him. The puce shade of his face betrayed his recognition.

Lia's heart careened against her tightening rib cage.

"So you're the guy. How morbid of fate to play such tricks on you two." The venomous, gloating smirk suddenly disappeared. "Or has this been going on during our so-called marriage?"

"Unfortunately I don't believe in 'what's good for the goose is good for the gander.' Devraj is here on behalf of Sanjay."

"Ha!" Howard snorted. "As if I'd believe *that!* If you've come back sniffing around Lia—"

The split second of rage in Devraj's eyes was replaced with the poker face expression that must have contributed to his immense business success. "Then it's no longer your business."

The contrast between the two men struck Lia. Being a few years younger than her husband, Devraj looked like a dashing movie star in his prime, while Howard appeared like an overindulged executive on top of his midlife crisis hill.

With an accusing glare, Howard turned away. This arrogance was nothing new from him or his family. He glanced back and said, "Don't you dare do anything to embarrass me or my family, you hear? Tell Gabe I'm waiting in the car."

Then almost knocking Devraj back, Howard ran down the three steps. Lia placed her fists on her hips.

"Charming man." Devraj muttered. The only betrayal of his emotions was the clenching of his jaw and the slight flaring of his regal nose. Then studying her, he asked, "Are you going somewhere?"

As she shook her head, Gabe ran towards them.

"Dad, I'm—I'm c-coming." He skidded to a near halt by the door. "W-What's *he* d-doing here? Is he s-staying?"

"Gabe, that's enough." Lia demanded, but he rushed away and didn't look back. There was a delay between Gabe getting in the Mercedes and it purring off the driveway. Was Howard grilling the poor boy about Devraj, and what had been going on in the past few weeks?

She sighed and averted her eyes, leaning against the doorframe. "I'm sorry for my family's bad manners. But I asked you not to come."

"I was compelled."

When she looked at him, his eyes scoured her face. She moved back, considering shutting this Bollywood Adonis out of her house. But, she wouldn't be fast enough, from the animal expression in his eyes, and in her betraying heart she didn't want to run away from him.

She wanted more of him, and not because Howard was livid about it. She'd missed Devraj even in the crazy-busy two weeks.

Despite having felt conspicuous when leaving Devraj's flat in the early hours that Sunday, now she didn't care. She wanted him even more, to explore his every sinewy muscle...

She stopped herself from getting carried away, as she shivered in the warm, sunny morning. Maybe he was here as the loving dutiful uncle, like she ought to be concentrating on her daughter's happiness.

"Come in." She retreated into the quiet house. "I take it you'd like to discuss Danielle and Sanjay's engagement." She was bound for the kitchen but hesitated. Changing course, she entered the living room.

He followed. "Stop it, Lia. We're good together."

She widened the gap between them. "It's easy for you, but I'm not cut out for this sort of thing."

"Don't, Lia. You know you enjoy being—"

"What? A divorcee with an insatiable sexual appetite?"

Dev sighed. Having enjoyed her unbridled hunger, their explorative lovemaking he hadn't been able to stop thinking about her. "I was going to say, being with me. We're grown, responsible adults who are rediscovering each other, and you're deliberately undermining it, tarring it. What's really bothering you, Lia?"

"You know what's bothering me. What if Danielle and Gabe

find out?"

"So? Why are you so sure Gabe hasn't told Danielle about...our kiss on that first night?"

"Because she'd have confronted me. She won't like it."

"Is she the mother, or are you?"

She shook her head tension obvious on her lovely, soft features. The pain in her eyes before she turned away made him feel guilty for a split second, and then he grabbed her arm to face him.

Like someone in limbo, half on earth and half in heaven, she stared up at him. He wanted her on any terms.

Was she shaking? "You don't look well, Lia, is there anything I can do?"

Yes, Lia thought, *get out of my life, and stop complicating it further.*

The confines of the large room became claustrophobic. Lia refrained from rubbing her throbbing temples. Her headache hadn't improved with the bath or painkillers.

Shaking her head, she hurried towards the hall. "I need some fresh air."

He stood next to her by the cloak cupboard. "Good idea, I'll join you. Unless you'll be rude and shun me, too?" He said lightly.

She tried to smile.

They meandered through the beautiful Oaklands Park, the nostalgia of their many walks through the city parks near their college reawakened her melancholy.

God, give me strength and wisdom to understand why this

is happening now, she prayed as they strolled in silence for a few minutes.

Gradually the silence was interspersed with his undemanding conversation that left her strangely grateful for his company. He talked more about his business, his travels, and Jim's escapades since his last ex-girl-friend.

When she told him about her girlfriends, how Maxine had married twice on the rebound over her first love, and Patricia becoming a young widow at thirty-five, Lia hesitated and then added, "Although my friend Maxine would understand what he'd gone through, I'd think my other friend, Patricia would be a much better match for him. On the other hand, it's the worst idea. Either way I'm not interfering." She smiled.

"Neither am I. Only he prefers to be married, for some reason."

"Spoken like a true bachelor." She stopped walking and gave him a sideways glance. "At least your life style and choice in cars give that impression."

"I *was* married once." The shock at his words made her freeze momentarily in mid-step. The bitter taste in her mouth nearly choked her.

"I—I never knew," she peered at him. "When? Do you have children?"

"No. It lasted twenty-seven hours. One month after you got married. But it didn't work out. I forget it ever happened." She could tell he'd have preferred to change the subject.

She yearned to ask, *'Did you love her?'* but instead asked, "Do you mind talking about it?"

"Not anymore." He studied the foaming fountain a few feet away, a faraway mist in his eyes. "My family arranged my marriage to an old family friend's daughter from India, the one I'd refused to meet. She was only seventeen and seemed so frail when she came here. She cried throughout the ceremony. In our hotel room, I asked her what was wrong. First, she wouldn't say anything, as if petrified. Eventually she confessed about being in love with a boy back home. She was inconsolable. The next day I arranged for an annulment, I took her back home and reunited her with her true love."

"Wow, Devraj, you're such a romantic... I'm sorry." The lump in her throat expanded into her chest. She added, "What a gallant gesture... So now you're leery of any woman who wants to snare you. From what Sanjay said on that first night."

"Depends on who the woman is." His raised brow and the playful smile didn't detract from his meaning. Her sweater and jeans suddenly felt too warm against her skin.

"Admit it, it's because I'm not flinging myself at you that attracts you."

"Is that what you think?"

"Stop answering my questions with more questions. Maybe you're used to women becoming obsessed with you, and you'd run a mile if I turn into a clinging vine." She challenged.

"Try me, and see." His challenging, enigmatic smile and the intensity in his eyes would have frightened a wiser person.

Her breath caught in her suddenly parched throat, as she felt their sexual attraction entwined them closer to each other.

They walked on and Devraj changed the subject, relaxing

somewhat. They smiled at the throng of children suddenly catching up to them from behind, some on tricycles, with their harassed but evidently happy parents in tow.

Lia wondered what it would have been like if she *had* stood up to her grandparents and turned her back on family traditions she'd believed she couldn't live without. Would she have married Devraj and had his children?

Stop daydreaming and playing 'what if'. It couldn't have worked between them. It was different for Danielle and Sanjay. Life had moved on and they had her and Devraj as allies.

Apart from those family obligations, she contemplated if God was now gifting her this chance for what she'd yearned. Now that she'd tasted what making love was really like with Devraj, she'd be a bigger coward and fool to turn away from this opportunity.

She wanted to enjoy more of that passion.

Yes, it *would* complicate things, but after all the years of planning and keeping within the lines of conformity, she was tired of it all.

Despite her inner voice of warning, she refused to dwell on the repercussions of them being together. It would hurt no one if they were discreet. She wouldn't contemplate how her children would feel if they did find out.

Instead, she focused on Devraj's face. It was obvious he was game. He wanted to be with her.

And now she knew what she wanted, craved, deserved.

Just for herself.

A fresh beginning, a new career, and being with the only

man she'd ever wanted.

Lia raised her face toward the sun, breathing in the smells of fresh grass and jasmine. She'd been hankering after this moment when she'd sat at her last supper at her in-laws, weeks ago.

The song "At Last" sounded within her brain. This could be just what the doctor—or in her case Maxine—had ordered.

A hot steamy affair, with her in charge of her own life. Guilt free.

Something was changing in Lia's demeanor, Dev could tell through their uncanny connection. Was she starting to relax, to trust in him and in the undeniable bond between them?

As they sat on the sun-warmed bench, the May day felt more like a tropical, romantic summer day.

Don't be a sap. Sitting close to her, he rested a casual arm on the bench back behind her, not quite touching her. Like he'd done so often in their sneaked movie excursions in their college friendship/romance.

With her pretty blush, she looked twenty-seven instead of having turned thirty-seven last month. "How could you have changed so little in all these years?" He asked softly.

"I've changed. Everything and everyone changes."

"Inside you're still that gregarious, beautiful girl." He had to bring her closer to him, to kiss her forehead. He waited for her to raise her face to let their lips meet.

She did. It felt so right, he sighed as she relaxed further into him.

"I want you, Devraj." She whispered shyly against his mouth. He took in a sharp breath.

Was she also remembering their recent intimacy, the night he couldn't get out of his mind? The passion igniting within her dark, expressive eyes drove him crazy. His heart thumped and thudded, as their lips and tongues danced in delicious prelude of what could be. Turning fully she put her arms around his neck.

A giggle or two made them end their kiss.

"Maybe we shouldn't indoctrinate young children about the birds and the bees quite yet." Slowly Devraj let her go. "Would it be all right to go to your place, or would you rather...?"

As if not wanting to wait to drive to his place, she shook her head. "My house will be fine." A shadow crossed her face. "I want you to know, I just want what you want, a no strings attached— "

"Affair." He said gently, smirking.

He wanted her so much it tore at his insides.

Patience. With time, she'd see this was more than just sex. He ached to have all of her, yet he'd pretend she meant as little as any other beautiful woman in his life. He hated his lonely bed without her.

Go with the flow, giving and taking mutual pleasure.

Until *he* got bored or tired of all this and was ready to move on.

Chapter Fourteen

LIA LOVED SUMMER, especially enjoying this swelteringly hot and humid June. She felt reawakened, going through a myriad of new emotions in this glorious, sexually liberating, secret affair. She took the plunge by asking her two girlfriends for lunch at her home on Saturday instead of meeting at the restaurant. She was ready for their inevitable questions and possible recriminations of her secretiveness. The extra surprise at dessert was a delicious bonus.

As she flung the door open to let them in, one astute glance at her smiling face must have told Patricia and Maxine something was different. "You look more gorgeous every time I see you, Lia." Patricia smiled as Maxine nodded like a proud sophisticated fairy-god-mother.

"So what have you been up to that's kept you too busy to see us these past few weekends, *chérie*?" Maxine asked.

"Are we working you too hard and you're sleeping them away?" Patricia's arched eyebrows rose.

Oh, she was sleeping all right, but mostly not alone. Lia shook her head. "No, of course not. You know I love you both and I love my work. But I have a surprise to show you." The curious friends glanced at each other. "After lunch."

As the three enjoyed Lia's Indian dishes she'd refrained from making for so long (because of Howard's aversion to anything spicy or pungent), they chatted and laughed at Maxine's latest escapades with Derek, her first husband whom she'd divorced nearly fifteen years ago. He seemed intent on etching his presence in her life once more. But Maxine was playing it cool with the repentant, forty-something Mamma's boy.

"And don't you dare say one word related to business, *chérie*." Maxine pointed a ringed manicured index finger at Patricia. "Until Monday."

"Yes, there's more to life than business." Lia agreed, trying but unable to wipe away her self-satisfied I've-got-a-delicious-secret grin. Her facial muscles, like the rest of her body and mind, seemed to have their own ideas.

"You're right." Patricia sighed. "Did you hear about Bella Ricci?"

"What about her?" Lia filed away her envy. She loved the prolific artist's quirky style, the paintings of voluptuous women against surreal backgrounds. Her exhibitions were always a great success, which was excellent news for her friends' La Galerie Chevalier Noir for this coming September. Thanks to FaceTime and Skype Lia was comfortably staying up-to-date with all the developments she was in charge of until she'd fly there for two weeks in August.

Patricia looked at Maxine and said, "Bella's cancelled her show. She was diagnosed with rare blood disease. Her agent explained she'll be out of commission for a while, having treatments and recuperating."

Suddenly the jovial summer air was filled with a dense fog of the uncertainty of life.

"I don't want to get morbid—"

"Oh, you surprise me, Morticia." Maxine smiled at Patricia. "But I know where she's going with this." As business partners, her friends often reflected one another's ideas, often finishing each other's sentences.

Patricia nodded, "I'm not just mentioning this because she won't be exhibiting in September, we'll sort that out later. There's another artist we'd like you to vet for us, but right now I'm talking about how fragile and short life is. We all have to live by that advice, but you have some catching up to do, Lia."

Maxine said, "grab every opportunity and enjoy every moment. Look at how young and beautiful you look. No one would believe your age." Smiling, Patricia and Lia gently clinked their wine glasses to Maxine's proffered glass.

"I owe you both so much, especially to my personal fairy-god-sister for the makeover and wardrobe update." She winked at Maxine. Unable to hold back her happiness of the past revitalizing month in Devraj's arms she added, "We have to try and find Patricia the perfect man, Maxine. Are you game?"

Her eyes widening, Patricia shook her head. "I was talking about *you*."

"Don't worry, I'm doing fabulously." She was tempted to burst out with her secret.

Her pulse quickened. If they met, Maxine would probably drool at the 'superb' or 'magnificent' specimen the charismatic Devraj was, while Patricia would admire his regal bone structure—like she herself had when she'd first met him, at the college cafeteria. Her eyes misted over again and for a moment she couldn't see clearly. Carly Simon's 'You're So Vain' drifted into her mind. But he was far from vain. Just supremely confident, which she found extremely sexy.

Maxine frowned, "Fabulously, hah? I can smell something's going on."

"All in good time, my dear. First, let's have coffee." Lia smiled broadly.

She smiled a lot these days, despite all the juggling, and sneaking time to be with Devraj.

Sipping their espressos and tea, discussing more artists and art, Patricia peered at Lia. "I've always wondered why you stopped painting those fabulous seascapes and landscapes." Patricia said, "You were so good."

Lia averted her eyes. The evening art classes the three women had met in almost twenty years ago had left Lia frustrated and bored.

For years, she'd tried to recapture her passion, loving painting so desperately her pores dilated with anticipation, but it had constantly conjured up Devraj in her mind. She'd packed and locked away her art materials, sketches, and silly daydream-filled journals in the new sewing room in her marital home. Torture and pleasure had dueled within her for years.

"I didn't really enjoy the subject and there wasn't enough time after I had Danielle. But I'm very excited about getting back to...my painting. I'm exploring so much right now."

"May I see some? I always liked your bold strokes with so much intricate detail in your painting."

"Yes." Lia smiled. For the first time since her teens, she was enjoying creating and painting. Proving herself capable of taking a grip of her new life; running her friends' art gallery, spending quality time with her children and mooning over— and enjoying—her affair with her first love. She was in control of most of her bills; her temporary financial arrangement with Howard was that he take care of Gabe's Bar Mitzvah expenses coming up in the end of September. She wouldn't feel badly about that, he was her children's father. This way guilt didn't affect her, as she wouldn't yet use the money her grandparents left to her.

Becoming increasingly independent she was determined to take care of Danielle and Sanjay's engagement party this November and the wedding next June all by herself. She had to be careful, a year would come and go before she woke out of her sexual reverie. She couldn't afford that.

She frowned, a sudden familiar feeling of claustrophobia pushing on her chest. She concentrated on Maxine's words.

"I saw great potential, but somehow you seemed to hold back." Maxine said. "If you like, *chérie*, I could help you with your technical know-how, composition, presentation, framing—anything at all."

Guilt burned in her heart at their generosity. "It's the perfect time to share something very important with you. I can't wait any longer..." She rose from the table with her empty plate.

As she led them upstairs, Maxine asked, "So, at last you're going to show us where the kinky stuff happens?"

"Not quite." Little did they know what had been taking place in her bedroom, and in Devraj's flat over the nights they could steal away together. She blushed, her pulse quickening at the memories, and at the impending revelation of her new artwork, and the long hidden sketches.

Opening the door of the large, newly renovated art room, they were greeted by an array of matted sketches propped up against six easels, and against the walls, all of one model.

Maxine's intake of breath and Patricia's gaze travelling over the various sized paintings said it all.

"He's the one, isn't he?" Patricia said gently, sympathy shining in her gray eyes.

"This is Devraj, we'd met in college."

Maxine's mouth gaped open. "You mean this model is the one you knew before you met Howard?" Her indignation at Lia's obviously inferior taste in mates was shaming. "You sly dog." She added in a slightly accusing tone, picking up loose sketches stacked by the tall window.

Patricia neared the largest, most evocative oil painting of Devraj, her own favorite, and considered it intently, with the eye of an art connoisseur.

His intense charisma was abundant in every brush stroke.

He was the embodiment of all the heroes of love stories in books and movies throughout the civilized world. She'd painted through many hours of tears putting her heart into these earlier works after their breakup, before her marriage.

But filled with joy and hugging her secret affair to herself, in the past weeks Lia had been enjoying painting again, while running Bollywood movies in the background on the new TV screen. It was so liberating to revisit some of the old classics like Satyam Shivam Sundaram with Shashi Kapoor and the luscious Zeenat Aman, singing along with the evocative music, while sketching or painting for uninterrupted hours. These days, in addition to catching up on all the Shah Rukh Khan movies, with Kajol and other beauties, her new favourite idol was the young star, Kris Darshan. When he came on the screen with his mesmerizing green eyes and sexy smile, she was smitten. Not only did he look dreamy, he danced better than any other actors she'd ever loved.

When Danielle had come in late one night and seen one of these movies on the screen, she'd smiled, "Kris Darshan's so hot. Since his first movie in 2000 he's adored, like, by millions, and Aunt Eliza and I have seen every one of his films."

She'd have loved to paint the star. Now Lia couldn't help grinning, thinking about her own idol, and personal model who was, to her, even sexier than Kris Darshan.

She blushed, excited at seeing him tonight.

Maxine gasped as she focused on the same painting that mesmerized Patricia. It reminded Lia of her own visceral reaction to Devraj when she'd first set eyes on him. Even now whenever she heard 'The First Time Ever I Saw Your Face' it transported Lia back to that moment. Heat prickled her sensitive skin.

"Now this is a man I could sink my teeth into." Maxine smacked her lips.

Lia thought of how she'd sunk her own teeth into Devraj's...

"Just don't tell me if he wasn't as hunky in real life. I couldn't bear that, *chérie*." Maxine fanned herself dramatically.

He still is, if not more so.

"Why hadn't you shown these to us before?" Patricia asked.

"I showed them to no one." She was still keeping secrets. "These are my newer ones I've been working on for the past few weeks." She picked out the latest sketches.

"You must have been lonely all those years..." Patricia nodded. "You certainly have kept this side of you a secret. Who knew? You're one hell of a talented artist. Are you thinking what I'm thinking, Maxi?"

"Absolutement!" Maxine's eyes riveted to the picture she was studying. "We have to show these at the new gallery.

"I think you've got enough pieces here for the September show, don't you agree?" Patricia asked. "We'll develop a marketing strategy ASAP and..."

"You'll be very easy to promote." Maxi finished her sentence. "And here I thought you'd need technical help. This is magnifique."

Lia hadn't expected this. She'd planned to paint without putting any pressure of selling or exhibiting, but this was a gift. And a huge compliment from the caliber of artists they represented in their galleries. Fear and excitement interweaved through Lia. Her relief of having opened her artistic Pandora's box was immense. "This means so much to me coming from my friends."

"Now will you tell us about the hunk?" Maxine asked.

She sighed. "I'm sorry I wasn't ready before. But now, absolutely, what would you like to know?" How different her reaction was on that day her friends had saved her, and she'd changed the course of her future.

"None of us will ever see you the same way again." Maxine gave a conspiratorial smirk.

"That person's gone forever." Lia promised.

"Now," Maxine nearly stomped her elegantly clad foot. "You tell us every single thing, *chérie*, even if I have to hand-cuff you and find that whip—"

The doorbell rang and Lia stiffened, not expecting anyone. Maybe Devraj had sent another beautiful bouquet of red roses. That had been hard to explain to Danielle and Gabe.

She descended the stairs while her awe-struck friends continued admiring her other babies. Opening the door, she inhaled sharply, pleasant surprise and sexual hunger flaring at the site of her art's inspiration in the flesh.

"I couldn't wait until tonight, my Lia. And I was passing." Devraj said softly. His smile was her undoing as he stepped over the threshold and immediately she was in his arms kissing him thoroughly.

The instant spark ignited. He certainly knew how to seduce a woman, she marvelled.

Tonight Gabe was sleeping over at his friend's house and Danielle had planned to see Sanjay at a late night gig at the local comedy club. She couldn't wait to spend another romantic evening alone with Devraj.

The familiar delicate clearing of Maxine's throat brought Lia out of Devraj's arms, to face her friends' self-satisfied smiles.

"We've just been admiring the artwork upstairs, never imagining that we'd meet—" Maxine started, her voice and demeanor in top flirtatious gear, as Lia urgently interrupted her words and introduced the three to each other.

Patricia smiled, her eyes following every line of the man's face as directly as she had the paintings, while Maxine oozed charm.

Devraj smirked at Lia's obvious discomfort at having her secret lover revealed.

"I'm glad to be finally meeting you face to face. From her descriptions, you must be Patricia, and you, Maxine." He shook hands with them. "I wonder if you'd like to join us tonight. My nephew Sanjay..." at the instantaneous sharp reaction from Maxine he paused, then continued, as Lia avoided her friend's yet another accusing glare, "I like to support his love of stand-up comedy. He's quite good. You may enjoy the show. You don't mind, do you, darling?" He asked Lia, placing a casual yet unmistakably protective arm around her suddenly rigid shoulders.

Chapter Fifteen

DEV WAS WELL aware of the pride and fear warring within Lia's beautiful eyes. Throughout his years in business, he'd learned to take opportunities wherever and whenever they arose. Getting to know her two good friends—and bosses—was the beginning. She had to get used to being with him in the real world. Where better to start than to get her friends on his side? His instincts confirmed that they cared about her a great deal, from their concerned, curious glances as they spoke over dessert in the kitchen. He loved this kitchen, especially the counter where he'd first reacquainted himself with Lia's kisses.

In the past month, he'd taken more time off work and travelled far less than he had in the past two decades. He was utilising FaceTime and video conferencing whereas before face-to-face negotiations had been his preference. But work held no challenge the way seducing and satisfying Lia's smouldering passion did. He loved seeing the glorious rapture on her face when she was in his arms. Intuitively he knew he was the only man who brought her such pleasure, as she always did to him. He wanted her every moment of the day and night, in bed and out.

On the weekends when he knew Gabe was out with his friends, or his father, Dev didn't even try to resist the temptation to surprise her in the middle of the day.

As they sat and laughed together, he found out more about Lia's career aspirations and talents from the grave elegant widow Patricia, and the bubbly voluptuous Maxine, than Lia had divulged to him in the past weeks. Maybe it was because their days and nights together entailed romantic outings and decadent meals that were always preceded by or ended with great sex.

He didn't care to discuss his work much because there were so many other things they could be talking about; light, fun, and non-committal stuff. They both upheld the unspoken rule from that first walk in the park. No strings attached even if he wondered if he was merely her rebound reconnection to sate her needs and nothing more. So far: win-win.

But he wasn't used to being distracted and sitting at meetings trying not to let his smile betray his thoughts of a delicious moment in Lia's arms, or something she'd said or done that made him wonder where this could go.

She was still keeping secrets. He could tell that from whenever either of her friends mentioned art, Lia would become alert, and she would change the subject. He saw her flush at the mention of a Jean-Pierre at the Villa. At this Lia got up to refill the coffee pot.

Fine, he'd continue working at their relationship, such as it was, without triggering her flight reflexes. She'd have all the freedom and independence she sought to forge her career, but he'd be damned if he gave any other man a chance to enjoy her as a woman.

Whoa!

Where did that archaic stuff come from? His chauvinistic thoughts distracted him from Maxine's words. Sanjay or Jim wouldn't believe him capable of such crap, especially after Jim had helped him pick up the remnants of his life in those months after Lia had left him. He had to curb his caveman impulses, and no matter how long it took, he'd prove to her that they were meant to be together.

In the meantime, he'd pave the way for Sanjay's marriage to Danielle, if they continued on the right track. He'd also find a way to get to know Gabe and help him, even if it was only through Sanjay.

Dev would show the boy he wouldn't hurt his mother, take her for granted, or betray her like Gabe's father had obviously done.

Gabe was coolly responding to his attempts at not impinging on the mother-son time. He remembered how precious his own time had been with his own gentle, romantic mother, how protective he'd been over her in that year after the loss of his male family members before Ma had died of a broken heart. And Gabe was much younger and more vulnerable with his stutter and a father who could learn a few lessons in manners.

"Now I'll leave you ladies to catch up." Her friends protested while Lia, almost relieved, saw him to the door. "Thank you for letting me stay. They're genuinely good friends. You're lucky."

"Like you're lucky to have Jim, too."

He leaned to kiss her on her sweet mouth. He loved the way she clung to him for a moment longer, feeling possessive and proud that he was the man she was giving herself *almost* completely to.

Chapter Sixteen

"I HAVE AN announcement to make." The excitement and anticipation illuminating Lia's lovely face gave Dev renewed hope. Had she decided to announce their relationship to her children? Maybe his inner confidence, which she said she loved, was rubbing off on her.

With the hottest consecutive days of this July, it wasn't just the weather keeping things exciting and sweat inducing between them.

Dev never seemed to have enough of Lia, no matter how often they were together. He appreciated the multifaceted and generous woman she now was. Yet, over the past couple of months, she refused to stay the night at his flat. And even when Danielle or Gabe weren't around, Lia didn't invite him to sleep over.

He was certain Lia was under the same love spell, and soon her denial wouldn't be much of a shield. Maybe they could go away for a few days. He knew she'd accept his invitation.

Maybe then she'd open up to him further.

But he wouldn't push her, or risk losing her again because of impatience.

Dev focused on her animated face, noticing how Danielle prised her smiling gaze away from Sanjay, in the suddenly quiet dining room. Gabe didn't seem sure he wanted to be in the room. He'd hardly eaten or spoken all evening. Dev sighed inwardly, his heart going out to the boy.

"Maxine and Patricia asked me to oversee their newest Art Gallery in Paris and many of my own pieces will be exhibited, too. They want me there in the last three weeks of August to launch the September show."

Someone's cutlery hit the hardwood floor. Was it his own?

Dev didn't break contact with Lia's cautious eyes. Where had this come from? She'd mentioned nothing about it.

"And you already accepted?" Gabe shot up from his seat, his chair crashing behind him drowned out Dev's words.

"P-Paris? W-why are you d-doing this, Mum? I won't stay at Dad's, or Grandmas." Gabe's voice screeched as he glared at his mother.

"You're not. I'll be at the villa for a while and so that you wouldn't get bored, I registered you for August in this amazing summer camp in Provence. It'll help your French and they have a fantastic science program and lots of water sports on their own huge lake. Jordan's Mum said he may go too—"

"How c-convenient! You d-didn't even tell me, but I'll b-bet you t-told Danielle and even D-Devraj. I'll bet you'll take him with you to the villa." Gabe's nostrils flared, breathing like an asthmatic.

"What do you mean?" Danielle sounded confused, but Dev continued to scan Lia's suddenly pale face.

"Why should Mum take—"

"You d-d-don't know a-anything." Gabe shouted down at his sister sitting across from him.

"That's enough, Gabe." Lia started.

"Why? So Danielle doesn't know what's b-been going on since that first night you k-kissed D-Devraj?"

"What?" Danielle said hoarsely, standing up.

"Don't get excited, Elle." Sanjay said calmly, stroking her arm. She shook him off, glaring at her mother, and then at Dev.

It wasn't Dev's place to say anything but he started, "Danielle, Gabe..."

But Gabe focused his wrath on *him*. "Don't t-talk to me, you're n-nobody. It's all your fault." He screamed and ran out of the room as if he was on fire, his fast footsteps echoing up the stairs.

Sanjay got up just as a door slammed somewhere above them. Lia seemed torn between following Gabe and staying. She frowned at Danielle, "Devraj and I had known each other from college, you know that."

"But why would you—you haven't known each other while you and Dad were still—"

"Of course not. We met that night I met Sanjay, but..."

"So you've been having a torrid affair all these months, while I thought you were helping Sanjay and me?" Danielle accused.

"This isn't any of our business." Sanjay said. "Your Mum and

Uncle Dev are adults—"

"None of my business? Did you know about this, too? Am I the only one who didn't know what was going right under my nose?"

"That hardly matters, Elle," Sanjay's voice had a steely warning she seemed oblivious to.

"How could you do this to me, Mum?"

"I've done nothing to you, Danielle." Lia sounded annoyed, defensive.

"Will you come up and talk to Gabe with me? Please, Elle?" Sanjay took her hand, but again she pushed it away.

"I'm talking to my mother right now."

"Fine, but remember what I said." Sanjay looked disappointed as he left.

Dev wasn't sure if he ought to leave too. He got up and picked up some plates, when Danielle said, "It's creepy. Why couldn't you have found someone else to get your rocks off with?"

As he started for the kitchen, he heard Lia say, "How dare you speak to me like that!"

He blinked, disappointment cooling his insides. In the past few months while he was finding it increasingly difficult to keep his promise to stay cool, being drawn into the same volcanic depths from their youth, Lia had been in a different place.

While she was getting into his blood—and he wasn't minding it one bit—while he was falling deeper in love with her, Lia was planning to go her own way.

Chapter Seventeen

HER MUM LOOKED pale clutching at the edge of the table, but Danielle held on to her disgust.

Seeing she wouldn't get any reply she demanded, "Have you only been helping Sanjay and me, so you can get closer to Devraj?"

Surprise then fury ignited Mum's eyes, and her usually calm demeanor vanished.

Appearing to grow a couple of inches taller, Mum stood up too. "Don't think that because Dad talked to me like that, I'd let *you* get away with it. I'm *your mother.*"

"Well, obviously that hasn't been your priority in the past months." She felt justified in hurting her mother. It didn't matter that Mum didn't know how often she'd spent nights with Sanjay in his flat in Islington in the beginning, when she'd told her parents she was with her various girlfriends. Mum had believed her. She couldn't hold her mother's gaze.

"It's just not right, not with Devraj, for God's sake—"

"Don't lecture me about right and wrong." Mum looked like a teenager caught in a lie.

"Well, maybe someone should. Dad was right, after all. You never loved him and you never wanted to be with him."

"What? When did he say this?"

Her and her big mouth. What was the use of repeating that Dad had never felt appreciated or cared for, that her mother was "cold" and that was why he went out so often? "I was fourteen and my friends and I saw Dad kissing this woman in the Brent Cross car park." That day had shattered her young, romantic illusions.

Devraj returned from the kitchen, studying Mum as if he was afraid she'd faint or something. "You want me to go?"

"No, Devraj, please stay." Her mother insisted, without taking her eyes off Danielle.

Devraj sat in an armchair in the living room a few feet away.

"Go on," Mum's lips were a thin line.

"He told me that you had an understanding, that it wasn't a real marriage since before Gabe was born. But I'd known that already."

"And you never asked *me* about my side of it?"

"I saw that you were going along with it, or I reckoned you'd leave if you weren't happy."

Would things have been different between mother and daughter if she'd confided in her then, instead of growing to despise her for staying in a loveless marriage? She'd pegged Mum as a weak coward, although she was always affectionate and constantly there for everyone, especially her, Gabe and even Dad.

Hadn't Mum always tried in the past hellish years, to convince her and herself that the teenage hormones were to blame for the friction between them; that eventually it would pass? How could she have believed that this one-sided 'arrangement' would have been something Mum had accepted?

"Aunt Eliza had explained you just weren't one of those women who went after what you wanted. All I knew was that I'd never accept such an arrangement if *I* ever married." She thanked God for her Mr. Wonderful.

She felt a heavy lunge between her ribcage and abdomen, feeling sick and ashamed at how selfish she must have come across to Sanjay, never mind to Devraj. "Anyway, this isn't about you and Dad—and the past."

"Yes, it is." Mum turned away from her, retreating into the kitchen. "In a very big way."

"How?" She followed her.

"When I decided to take my life back, and asked your Dad for a divorce, I also decided that no one would ever make me feel like a second-class citizen again. I owe you no explanations about my relationship with Devraj or anything else. But I'd have told you, if you hadn't jumped down my throat."

"You could have told me yourself."

"I'm sorry, you're right." Mum sighed, the tension in her features lessening somewhat, "but from now on I'd appreciate a little more respect. I don't interfere with your relationship with Sanjay, do I?"

"No, you're the only one who's helping, with Devraj... You'd be happier if I left altogether, wouldn't you?" Mum shook her head but she added, "and I'd move in with Dad, if he wasn't so bull-headed and such a hypocrite."

"Danielle," Devraj re-entered the kitchen, "you know your Mum loves you and we're—"

"Now, it's 'we'. Stop acting all fatherly, I don't need another father."

"Danielle, " Mum warned.

"How *is* your father helping you with your plans to marry Sanjay?"

"You know bloody well Dad won't even meet him."

"Exactly." Devraj's calm answer shook her.

"I know it's a shock for you right now, I didn't think things would get this..."

"Spare me, mother." She knew she sounded like the self-centred Vida, Joan Crawford's daughter in the old Mildred Pearce movie, she'd once seen with Great-Baboola, but she couldn't stop herself. "I don't want to know any details about this—this torrid affair."

"There's nothing torrid about it." Mum said patiently, blushing, peering sideways at Devraj, who put his arm around her as if they belonged together. As he smiled at her mother, Danielle couldn't shake off her revulsion.

Devraj looked at her, "Your mother and I go back a long way, and if you weren't so shocked, you of all people would understand. Can you imagine your life without Sanjay?"

Taking a deep breath, Danielle straightened and said, "Talking about Sanjay, can you tell him that I've gone for a walk. I need to be alone." And she refused to glance back.

Chapter Eighteen

LIA SAGGED INTO the dining chair, the remaining mess on the table forgotten. A trembling hand covering her eyes she whispered, "This is exactly what I was afraid of."

"Danielle will come round, Lia. At least it's all out in the open." Devraj's fingers on her arm made her look at him. "What I'm disappointed about is why you didn't discuss, not even a mention, about going to Paris, before making your decision."

Smarting from the revelation her talk with Danielle had brought, she pulled away from his hand. "I can't talk about this right now, Devraj."

"Is that fair, Lia?"

She shook her head, sighing. He was open to discussing anything with her, as opposed to Howard, who used to say what she'd just told Devraj. "I'm sorry." Then added, "But *you* don't discuss your business travel decisions with me, and I don't expect you to."

"When's the last time I've travelled?"

"Are you saying you've stopped travelling because of me?" She felt her cheeks warm.

"Maybe. What's wrong with that?"

"This wasn't supposed to get serious, Devraj." She glanced away for a moment from the vulnerable expression in his eyes, "I love my work, and this is an amazing opportunity. I was looking forwarding to going... I thought you'd be happy for me."

"I am, but this isn't about Paris, Lia. You didn't mention it to me, or your children."

"I suppose this is all new territory for me—which you've always taken for granted—real independence for the first time in my life. And we had an agreement. No strings attached."

"At the beginning, yes. But now you're running scared, pushing me away, again."

She shook her head. "I'm not. I wanted you to come to Paris with me."

"Not true, otherwise you'd have given me notice to plan my business around your schedule. But over the past few weeks you've become busier with your art thing..."

"Art thing!" Her rising fury and disappointment made her stand up. "You condescending—Just because I fell into your arms, doesn't mean I'm without a backbone or the guts to go after my dreams. You male chauvinist! And I thought you'd matured. I'm not some Indian subservient woman or like I'd been in my marriage; I'm determined to make my dreams come true this time."

He stood up, too, studying her face. "Admirable, but we can

make this work together. Let me take care of you. Please rethink my offer. I'll take care of the engagement and wedding expenses."

"No. You're not listening." Frustrated, she added, "I won't accept money from anyone. Not only have I been unfair on the kids—they've both gone through their parents' break up, for God's sake—I've been selfish, needing to prove to myself that I was attractive and desirable. But no more gallivanting." She gingerly touched her throbbing temples.

"Whatever this has been between us, Devraj it's over."

"No, Lia." He neared her, shaking his head.

"Don't make this harder for me." She took a step back.

"Making what harder? You running away again? Bloody right, I will."

They were too different from each other. She had to be realistic. This grown man with intense feelings outmatched even her own. As an independent, free spirit, she'd hoped Devraj would understand. But he didn't.

She could no longer digress from her responsibilities. She could never go back to being the quiet dreamer of four months ago. And whether this was love or lust, or reliving her youth, now she'd focus only on holding on to her newly found identity. She'd forge ahead with her career and be fully engaged with her children. "I'm sorry, I'm getting proper perspective for the first time ever, and I'm taking my life by the horns ." She took in another fortifying breath before exhaling, "I need space."

She looked away as he frowned. When would she stop feeling like a heel for having used Devraj in her need to grow up?

"You know we're more than mere lovers, Lia. I love you."

"Stop it. We're going to be related through Danielle and Sanjay's marriage and that's it."

"What if I put a stop to their wedding plans?" Devraj asked.

She clamped her lips. Taking a deep breath and letting it out, she said, "I'll take my chances, though I know you're not that selfish. This is about what *I* need. Now please go." She started out of the kitchen, but Devraj followed her and blocked her way.

"I'm laying it on the line, being transparent about wanting you on whatever terms you dictate, not caring about my pride or ego, but you're sending me away again?" When she wouldn't look at him he slowly said, "OK, I'll go." But then added, "But where was that determination when your husband was cheating on you?"

Lia's face paled. Her shoulders rose and stiffened, the tender pulse beating in the delicate hollow of her throat tempted him to take her in his arms and kiss away the hurt in her eyes.

Her jaw set, she said, "I won't discuss anything about—"

Squeezing his shaking hands into fists, he asked, "Why? Because he's the father of the children you could have given *me*?" The pain in her eyes made him hate himself but he forged on, "More importantly, where was that will when you capitulated to your grandparents' wishes? And even if my father had come to warn you off, you could have trusted me to take care of everything. Instead you... you walked down the aisle with that bankbook...you coward." He saw her flinch but couldn't stop.

Taking in another deep breath and sighing out, Lia said, "Why are you digging up the past? This confirms that you'll always feel I've cheated you, and I've had enough of compromise in my life. And when I'm ready for a relationship it'll be with someone who'll be happy for me, and not put more obstacles in my way."

"Of course I'm happy for you, Lia, I just won't share you." A horrible thought stomped on his heart. "Or maybe you want freedom to go and *paint* that French sculptor your girlfriends mentioned."

Lia's cheeks filled with colour. Anger shone in her eyes. Her hands on her hips, she looked like a flamenco dancer who was about to throttle him.

As if finally finding the right words she said, "And there's your answer to why we're ending the affair."

"For the hundredth time, it's not an affair; we're in love. Even if you can't admit it in our most heated love making, at least admit it to yourself."

"Keep your voice down." She peered over his shoulder up the stairs and then back at him.

"At first the grandparents, and now you've got your career and the children to help you hide." Defeat coiled his insides.

"Leaving behind a nineteen-year marriage isn't the same as turning away from your two-minute marriage—" She stopped abruptly, "I'm sorry, now *I'm* doing it."

"Independence isn't all it's cut out to be." He thought of all those years of loneliness and losing his members of his family within a short time. The duties he'd performed as the head of the Shah empire and the years he'd put into the family business that had nothing to do with autonomy or freedom. While Lia believed he'd had full control of his life, doing whatever he wanted.

A part of him understood her yearning to break out, yet he couldn't accept how ready she was to throw away their relationship. The damned freedom above all else.

"This happening tonight showed me we're not as compatible...outside the bedroom." She blushed so prettily it nearly threw Dev's anger off track. "You need to be in complete control and command of your relationships."

"Me?" His laugh dripped with sarcasm. "Just like in college, *you've* been in complete control of where, when, what we do and how."

She blushed again. Was she also thinking of their hot sessions in bed in the past few months, on his couch and in the large bathtub, and the shower? He had to stop dwelling on those memories before he'd need a cold shower.

With one step and with gentle but urgent hands, he pulled her into himself, forcing her to stare up at him. "How can you calmly talk about stopping seeing each other, while I go crazy? I'm a horny, walking cliché." What was it about Lia, the only woman who could turn him inside out, that made him say and do things beyond his own control?

She was so stubborn. Well, so was he!

He recognized the challenge and fear intermingled in her eyes. Her plea-like moan made him wonder if she really knew what she wanted. "I can make you melt in my arms with one stroke. I won't make this easy for you, this time."

Her gasp turned him on further, as he refused to let her break eye contact. Imprisoning her in his arms again, he dipped his head to devour her soft, full lips. He willed her to stop trembling.

In her eyes he saw her warring confusion. Her dilated pupils and yielding body gave him hope this would end happily after all.

As if aware of his thoughts, she franticly pushed against him.

He allowed some space between them.

"It's finished, Devraj, and if your ego needs it, then I admit I loved these months together. It was wonderfully freeing sex-"

"Don't." He stopped her infuriating words, holding her forearms. "There's no past tense, you know this relationship's very much alive."

Desperation taking over her sweet features, she said, "No, I need my freedom, and my family needs me much more than I need *you*."

Silence. He let her go.

"Your family needs you more than you need me." Eyes wide, Devraj shook his head. "Well, that says it all. I hope you enjoy your...freedom."

He slowly swivelled away from her, like on that night he'd confronted her grandparents and, once again, had to give up.

Before he could act on his urge to grab her and kiss her until she begged him to stay, again he strode out of her house and out of her life.

Chapter Nineteen

"WHAT THE HELL'S got into you, Dev? Are you trying to kill your best mate?" Jim jogged toward Dev, panting, his mop of reddish blonde hair plastered to his square shaped skull.

"I'm sorry."

"OK, out with it. Is it true, what Sanjay told me? Why didn't you tell me you'd met Lia again? Never mind get involved with her again?" Jim followed him, wiping his neck and face with a towel.

Dev strode away toward the squash court exit. Gripping the racquet until it hurt, he couldn't talk about Lia, especially with Jim. "Would you have approved?" Dev glanced at him as they walked toward the changing rooms. He hardly paid attention to the sleek luxury of the gym in the heart of London.

"Would you have cared?" Jim's steady gaze increased Dev's frustration with himself, feeling like that squash ball he'd pounded against that wall.

What was he doing with his dead-end life, going nowhere,

achieving nothing but a numbing sense of welcome exhaustion? What was he getting from all his professional successes? How smart could he be if, with eyes wide open, he'd fallen in love with the same woman who killed him spiritually, yet again?

"Lia will be Sanjay's mother-in-law, for Pete's Sake. What were you thinking?"

"I don't want to talk about it. Anyway it's finished."

"Is it? You were always a complete imbecile where that girl's concerned, Dev."

"Lia isn't a girl, she's a woman."

"God, you're still under her spell."

"I swear if you say another word ..." Gritting his teeth made his head and jaw ache harder.

"What will you do? Smash that racquet in your best friend's face? Need I remind you who helped you pick up the pieces years ago?"

"No, Jim, you don't." He sighed, unable to look his friend in the eye. Yet again, Lia had run away from him and the truth she couldn't—wouldn't—face. "I don't know how to stop thinking about her. She's so obstinate." It was under two weeks since they'd last seen each other and just like outside that synagogue on her wedding day, he'd hoped Lia would come running back to him. And as if it had been a dream, an illusion, he'd lost her just as suddenly then, too. And now, it seemed as unlikely they'd ever make a go of it. Missing her again brought back those crazy, lonely months after her marriage.

But he'd never go back to her, not even if she begged, *if* she came to her senses. God, how would he survive it either way?

Because despite his strongest resolutions he knew he couldn't resist her if she wanted him.

Where was she right now? The thought of another man near her luscious body made his insides coil.

"Pushing yourself and planning all these upcoming trips like the devil's after you, won't do you or the business any good. As your friend and partner, I'm warning you; stop bullying everyone. There's only so much employees will take before they quit. We've put too much into this company to risk it now, and with the growing competition I'd rather you get your stress playing more tennis and squash, but without nearly killing me. You *know* I get it, Dev."

Dev felt like a heel, knowing what Jim had gone through with Ella, and the rest of his loves.

"First love always screws you up." Jim said with that faraway expression. "Anyway, anything I can do to help?"

Dev didn't deserve an empathetic pal like Jim. "No. But thanks." He squeezed Jim's shoulder.

"So, friend or no friend, one more complaint about the boss, and I'll sock you in the jaw. Control yourself, or you'll lose me as your partner, on and off the squash court." Jim shook his head, again wiping his forehead with a towel.

"OK, point taken." Devraj grinned for the first time in days.

"About bloody time, too." Grinning back Jim walked toward the showers.

Dev reminded himself to stop being obstinate and immature. But how could he stop the images of Lia, smiling, laughing, caressing him, her bliss-ridden features...

He shook his head. How the hell could he face seeing her across the family dining tables or at the banquet hall at Sanjay's engagement and wedding? He'd make a fool of himself. Working almost round the clock obviously wasn't helping. He needed to regroup.

Forget Lia. What an oxymoron. It was like saying forget your culture, forget love. Forget breathing.

But look at what happened to you the last time?

He couldn't afford to get derailed again. He had to move forward. In slow motion he dialed his sister's number on his mobile. On the second ring, Malika answered. He heard himself say, "Malika? I'm sorry about my rudeness the other night. I've thought about your suggestion. About meeting the...the woman you'd mentioned. We can try it again, if you like."

"I'm sorry about Uncle Dev." Sanjay peeked at Lia sheepishly across the dinner table on the first Friday night dinner in September.

"What do you mean, Sanjay?" Lia held her fork tightly as if it held magical powers. She needed sanity whenever she heard or thought about Devraj. And it shook her every time she looked at the younger version of her ex-lover.

Keeping extremely busy hadn't helped drive Devraj out of her mind for the past excruciating five weeks.

"The way Uncle Dev looked at you, I thought this was quite different. Until now he's been allergic to any talk of commitment or relationships, but he seemed so gung-ho about you." Sanjay said.

Maybe that's the problem. But Lia stayed silent.

"But then to break it off again..." Sanjay shook his head.

"I hope that's not genetic." Danielle said breaking open a crispy bread roll and slathering butter on it. "Don't get any ideas, Sanjay."

"I'm in this for the long haul." He grinned and was about to kiss her.

Gabe grunted, "G—get a room, you t-two." But as if they didn't hear him, their simple kiss made Lia want to cry. From happiness, of course. *Their* union was meant to be.

She *had* needed to relive her own youth and exorcise her romantic daydreams with Devraj. But not having thought it through, it had backfired.

Now back on track, she didn't regret their few months together. Her art and new position at the Soho gallery and her exciting new responsibilities at La Galerie Chevalier Noir, were gathering momentum. She was even becoming more comfortable with crowds, which used to bring out her hives. What a difference a new lover and a backbone could do.

The trip to Paris had opened up many creative doors within her, shooting her with renewed zeal for her artistic self-expression.

But despite the dragging weekends, she was accomplishing more, and during the ten days at the villa, she'd produced some good art pieces.

Even Gabe seemed to have forgiven her for 'fobbing him off' at the summer camp in Provence.

What was Sanjay saying about Devraj?

"Jim called me asking if I knew why Uncle Dev was biting everyone's head off, causing friction with the managers and directors. And he nearly lost his secretary, who's been with the firm forever. Even Mum told him off for being unreasonable the other night, walking out in the middle of dinner. But," Sanjay shook his head again, "arranging another blind date for him, was begging for trouble. Mothers." He rolled his eyes and grinned at Gabe.

Lia wouldn't think of how she'd feel seeing him with another woman at the inevitable family gatherings. What about him travelling, like the intense Draper from Mad Men, making deals with beautiful female executives across boardroom tables?

Bile threatened to make her lose her dinner.

"I just don't get why he broke it off." Sanjay said.

Inhaling and exhaling slowly Lia said, "He didn't. *I* did."

"What?" Both Danielle and Sanjay asked.

Gabe's flushed face distracted Lia for a moment. She was glad for their togetherness before camp, and in the past week since their return to reality and back to school, had helped bridge the gap between them. But now the furrowing of his delicate brow confused her.

Danielle asked. "Was it because of me?"

Gabe gazed up, studying his sister then her.

"No. You had some valid points, and I'm not that easily swayed by anyone, anymore. It had to end—"

"Ah! Now it makes sense." Sanjay's expression cleared, then disappointment clouded his light brown eyes, so like those of his uncle. "He's in love with you, he'd never let you go. I should have known. You're each other's first loves, after all."

"How d-do you know h-he loves M-mum?" Gabe demanded.

"I know my uncle."

"You're such a romantic, Sanjay, which is great for you both. But meeting Devraj gave us a chance to put some closure—"

"Closure's obviously not what's on his mind, Lia."

What's the difference? She asked her still flattered heart. Surely, it was natural to miss the one man who'd reawakened her, as he had in her teens.

Some days she could keep her mind off Devraj for an hour or two. But on those long, sleepless nights thinking about him, then dreaming about him, she'd ask herself, like right now, what did she really want out of life?

Then she'd quell any foolhardy notions of calling his mobile or driving to his flat and begging him to hold her.

Time would help.

"Trust me, he'll be all right. It's just his ego that's bruised."

"You know in your heart, that's bull. It's clear he's never loved anyone else, and now I know why he's never had long term relationships."

Feeling cold in the still warm evening, Lia wanted to escape to her art room and cry.

This wasn't helping her move on with her life.

After successfully selling the few paintings of Devraj—the few she'd forced herself to part with—she'd arranged to transport the rest to the London gallery, until the next show in Paris. She definitely couldn't have produced the new landscapes and commissioned portraits in the past weeks, if they had stayed in her art room. Devraj's eyes and memories seemingly following her, impregnating her with longing: His and hers, mingling in an unfinished dance.

No, it was over!

Instead of mooning over her first love, she'd concentrate on the excitement of the next Paris exhibition. She'd create more pieces for the prestigious show in October, and the contest, while planning her very first solo art show next spring.

The only way she could repay her friends' faith and encouragement was by producing the best damn art she could.

Yes, she'd concentrate on the positives: Think about the things in her control, like the Bar Mitzvah in three weeks, and the engagement in November.

She wouldn't consider how she'd deal with seeing Devraj again. She prayed time *would* help her.

Realizing everyone was waiting for her response, she sighed, "I don't like you upset, but you two have nothing to worry about. You're different from us, and we're still your advocates, no matter what."

She saw her daughter biting her lower lip, while Sanjay frowned again. But she couldn't decipher Gabe's accusing glare.

"Now no more glumness at this table." She gave her brightest smile to bring back the easy atmosphere in the dining room. "So, are you two going to the cricket match tomorrow?" She looked at Sanjay and then Gabe.

As Sanjay answered her, talking about their favorite sport, she smiled, finding it hard to swallow her small forkful of the now cold salmon.

When she was tempted to ask if Devraj would be there too, she reminded herself to shut up and grow up.

Chapter Twenty

"WHAT ARE YOU up to this weekend?" Devraj asked Gabe who sat in the back of his cool convertible Jaguar XKR, on their way to the cricket match. Gabe loved the paddle gearshift and the effect it had on the pitch of the subdued roar from the engine. He'd have liked to ask more about this catlike supercar. If this was the latest model, and if the top came up or down in under twenty-five seconds. If its supercharged V8 engine was really as dazzling as the adverts said.

But he didn't want to seem too easily impressed. Especially as Devraj seemed to take the car for granted.

He'd ask Sanjay about it later. He didn't want to be rude to Devraj, especially after what Sanjay had said about him acting like a bear with a sore...everything. Although he didn't seem too bad right now.

"Nothing much." Gabe noticed how Devraj's ebony convertible with its caramel interior caught and held people's interest. Female and male drivers as well as passengers in the passing traffic glanced at the car and its driver. Gabe supposed that was why Devraj had such a sleek car. Why he could get any woman—even his quiet Mum—to kiss him.

He wished he had just a tiny bit of that confidence with girls.

But Devraj didn't seem to care about the attention. Almost brooding in his own world. He was glad he could come with Sanjay and Devraj today. Mum had been distracted as usual with her artwork, between phone calls and emails in Dad's redecorated old home office.

"Aren't you going to your Dad after the match?" Sanjay asked from the front seat. He wished he could sit in the front.

Gabe shrugged, "Yeah." He wished he could sit in the front.

"Not looking forward to it much, hah?" Sanjay grinned sympathetically.

"You wouldn't either, if you'd d-do the same things every single time."

"Like what?" Devraj asked.

Gabe didn't want to talk to Devraj. But he replied with a sigh, "We play games on the Xbox, and I always win, and then I feel bad."

"So it's not fun, huh?" Sanjay said glancing round at him.

"If Dad paid more attention he'd learn what it's all about. I sometimes think I should let him win or something."

"Sounds the kind of stuff we did, Uncle Dev. And I became a better chess player than you. And you're the one who taught me the game." Sanjay's laugh made Gabe want to join in.

"Don't spread that rumor around, Sanjay. I'm still the chess king." Devraj said, grinning sideways at his nephew.

"Yeah, we believe him, don't we, Gabe?"

He saw Devraj's eyes in the small mirror, "Then what else do you do, Gabe?"

"We order a pizza and watch a movie Dad's chosen, never over PG13."

"So you don't talk or go out much? *We* used to, a lot." Sanjay said.

"What do you mean, 'used to'?" Devraj glanced at him and then back at the crowded road. "You're the busy one these days." Devraj said.

Although Gabe felt sad thinking about Sanjay not having a father, he wished he were as close to Dad as Sanjay was to his uncle.

"I know we still do, Uncle." Sanjay grinned. "I mean in those days when I had all those questions I couldn't ask Mum or anyone, we'd go on outings and you'd answer them, or we'd look them up in books and then later, on the net."

"Dad and I talk sometimes, sort of." He hated it when Dad asked about Mum, because it would always lead to tense silence.

"You know I'm here if you've got any questions. If you think Uncle Dev's too old and not really with it..." Sanjay's lopsided grin reminded him of how Devraj used to smile at his Mum. It made him feel sick inside.

"Hey, don't be ageist. And I intend to beat you in our next match, so we'll see who's not with it."

Was Sanjay exaggerating about Devraj being broken up about Mum?

He seemed OK to him.

Gabe took another deep breath, wondering if he'd stopped Mum from having a chance at a relationship. Was he selfish like Dad? "It's just that Dad asks these questions about Mum..." Seeing Devraj's back stiffen and his curious eyes in the mirror, Gabe knew he shouldn't have said anything.

"You're like a spy, huh?" Sanjay asked.

"Of-of course not."

"I hope you play both sides and get paid well." Sanjay smirked, and Devraj threw him a stern expression Gabe knew too well.

"What do you mean?" Gabe asked.

"I'm kidding, Gabe. So you want Dad to stop asking about Mum?"

"Yeah." Duh. He rolled his eyes. Did Devraj just grin at him in the mirror? No, he was too serious a guy.

"Does he have a girlfriend?" Devraj asked.

"I don't know. Maybe."

"Does your Mum ask you anything personal about *Dad?*"

"No." Gabe said defensively.

"Uncle Dev's saying, tell Dad you don't feel comfortable talking about any private stuff."

"What if he gets annoyed?" He felt like a coward, his cheeks and ears feeling prickly warm.

"You could tell him to ask Mum directly about anything he wants to know." Devraj offered.

"That's good advice, Uncle Dev. You see, Gabe, that's why I keep him around. Sometimes he knows what he's talking about."

"You're asking for trouble, young man, just watch me kick your behind. Let's go." Devraj parked smoothly.

Gabe wished he hadn't been so rude to Devraj when he'd told him those things at their last dinner together. He'd broken Devraj and his Mum up. She hardly ever smiled anymore.

He sighed, staring on to the sunny green cricket grounds. Even though he'd rather have not had any advice from Devraj, Gabe would try it.

It was worth a shot. He had nothing to lose, well, apart from the bit of closeness he did have with Dad.

Chapter Twenty One

"SANJAY, I'M WORRIED about my Mum." Danielle knew it wasn't the right moment to talk about what had been eating away at her since Friday night, but she'd make up for it later. She wasn't used to carrying this guilt or keeping everything bottled up, like Gabe.

Kissing Sanjay on his full lips, she sat up in his bed and covered her nakedness. "She's been acting like one of those Stepford Wives."

"She seems happy enough."

"It's an act. She works, she cooks, she's there for Gabe and me, but when I've come in late, I've heard her crying. It's because of me and my big mouth that she's miserable." She wanted to cry. "I think she's always loved Devraj."

"But she said it's over." Sanjay propped up his pillow against the headboard. She got distracted for a moment by his muscular shoulders and arms, her fingers itching to caress his smooth pecs.

She shook her head and said, "She's in denial. Mum's really enjoying her new art career and her freedom means even more than I'd realized. But I think she's also terrified about love and everything. I can't imagine how she could have given Devraj up all those years ago, and now she gave him up because of Gabe and me. I'd never be able to survive losing you for anything."

"I know, gorgeous." He smiled, caressing her exposed upper arm.

"After Jim spoke to him, Uncle Dev doesn't talk about the breakup either," he frowned. "But he's walking around like a crossed thunder god. Mum and Aunt Surita are giving him the silent treatment and the only person he's civil with is Gabe."

"And of course, his favorite nephew."

"But of course." Sanjay's fingers crept under her sheet.

"Stop it, Sanjay." She laughed, as he pulled her towards him.

"Don't fight your future husband, woman. Remember I'm your god." He nuzzled his mouth into her throat eliciting more gurgles of laughter from her. "I'm glad to see this empathetic side to my near-fiancée. I do believe you're growing up."

Was it his words or his fingers that spread warmth in the pit of her stomach? She loved him so much she could die.

"But, how do you expect me to concentrate on anything while you sit as proud as a naked goddess, giving me that adorable look? Kiss me."

"I'm serious. I've screwed this up and I have to come up with a way to get them back together."

As he crossed his arms against that bare bronze chest she adored so much, she wondered if he was sulking.

Then he gave her that cheeky dimpled grin. "I've got an idea."

"It's over, Mum. I'm finished with Sanjay. And no one can do anything to help. Maybe Dad was right." Danielle looked too pale for Lia's liking.

Her daughter ran up the stairs and with her heart pounding against her chest, Lia followed her.

Entering Danielle's ultra feminine room, she saw her sprawled on her stomach on her bed.

She sat next to her. "What happened?"

"He's listening to Devraj," she sniffed into her pillow, "who's encouraging him to go after his dream and do comedy!"

"That doesn't sound like Devraj." Lia shook her head in bewilderment. "I thought he'd want his only nephew to join the family business."

"I can't believe how easily he takes his uncle's advice, while I hardly matter."

"I'm surprised, but you can't let anyone interfere with your plans."

Danielle raised her tear-stained face, her pink-lidded eyes full of accusation. "What do *you* know about making decisions and not letting others interfere or influence you?"

"Exactly. I didn't marry for the right reasons, but you're very different from me, and you love Sanjay so much that you've even risked your bond to your Dad."

Danielle sighed, "I never even wanted to go into medicine. I just wanted to get Dad's...But I do love Sanjay so much, I wanted to spend the rest of my life with him." Her voice cracked and Lia's heart nearly shattered.

"Nothing matters more than love; real, lasting love, Danielle. Come here." She gathered up her sniffing daughter into her arms. Remembering how Aunt Eliza's hugs had saved her so many times. "Learn from my mistakes," she admitted quietly. Shame buried from deep wounds prickled her.

"You love Devraj, don't you? And that didn't last. So what chance have *we* got? Or was it just to get back at Dad?"

Looking into her daughter's challenging eyes, Lia was speechless for a moment. Shaking her head, she said, "You don't know anything about it."

"So what happened? Did you break up because of Gabe and me?" She paused for a moment. "Or did you use Devraj on the rebound?"

Lia hardly recognized herself in this animalistic indignation. "No!" Then breathing in deeply, she added, "That's not important. This is about you. If you want to take it slower, fine, get to know each other better. If you want to live an independent life first, that's up to you, too. You decide and I'll help. This isn't as bad as it may feel right now."

"You're such a romantic, even after how unworthy Dad's made you feel. So why *did* you break up with Devraj?"

"Let's not dwell on that."

"But I'm confused. I mean, what if I grow out of this relationship in let's say five years, or if Sanjay starts seeing other women like Dad has. What if it fizzles out like it did with you and Devraj?"

"It didn't fizzle out..." Lia felt interrogated by the worst type of torture, her own kind.

"So you do love Devraj, but you broke it off because of me."

"Just stop, Danielle. Concentrate on *your* relationship. Sanjay's very different from your father. He adores you, but listen to your gut instinct. If you have any doubts, maybe destiny's telling you not to jump into an early marriage, and regret not being independent in your own right."

"No. I'm not like you." The renewed challenge in Danielle's eyes would have made Lia doubly proud of her, if she didn't feel so goaded.

"I'm glad you're not, you're tougher and smarter than I ever was. But sometimes it pays to slow down and make decisions with your mind, not just with your heart."

Danielle scoffed, "Is that what you've done with Devraj? The first time as well as now?"

"For the last time, Danielle, my relationship with Devraj has nothing to do with yours. I wasn't as worldly..."

"I saw those paintings you'd locked away in your sewing/art room. You must have really loved him. And thinking back, the way you looked at each other, makes me wonder if Sanjay and I feel as strongly as you two do. What chance do we have if you two couldn't make it?" Danielle snatched a tissue from the box on her creamy antique-finished bedside cabinet, and blew her nose. She inclined back into Lia's outstretched arms.

"Shh, let's look forward, not back. We're strong now. If you love each other, we'll make this work."

"It's bad enough Dad won't budge," Danielle sniveled like a

toddler in her arms, "or answer my calls, but now with this interfering... Please, Mum, will you talk to Devraj?"

Lia wished he'd also get the hell out of her mind. The fresh memories of their recent steamy months together, haunted her. She had to do something and soon for the sake of her sanity.

But right now, once again, she had to prioritise the young couple's future.

Chapter Twenty Two

AS LIA OPENED the door early that evening, she was unprepared for the delicious relief of seeing the man she hadn't expected to see until the engagement in November.

"Why are you doing this to them?" He walked in past her, obviously not bothering to curb his thunderous mood.

"What am *I* doing?" Lia was confused.

Commanding her pulse to stop galloping, she closed the door and followed him into the kitchen. What was it with him and the kitchen.

"Can't you bear other people being happy and in love? What did you say to Danielle that she's having second thoughts about marrying Sanjay? And I warned you I won't let anyone hurt him."

"What are you talking about, barging in here?"

As one dark eyebrow rose, his eyes scanned her stance.

She brought her hands down from her hips, and refused to flinch under his gaze. "Danielle said *you're* the one who's interfering." Turning away, she filled the kettle on automatic pilot. She did her yoga breathing exercises as silently as possible. Like on that night five months ago, she felt him close by.

"It just seems too coincidental that a few weeks ago everything was on track, and now Danielle's cooling, and Sanjay's ready to spontaneously combust."

With her back to him, her tiny smile was bittersweet, sympathising with the young buck. How was the uncle faring after their breakup?

Stop that, Lia. Clearing her face of emotion, she faced him. "I thought they were ready, but facing reality, they're having doubts."

Devraj's frown deepened and his jaw muscles worked overtime.

"How could you make them doubt their relationship?"

"*I* didn't, but there are no guarantees."

"Especially when you and I are in the equation, it appears. I suppose you believe *our* relationship would have fizzled out if my father and your grandparents hadn't stood in our way."

His cynical expression made her want to slap him. "Back to that again. That's what you're really—still—angry about, aren't you, Devraj?" Now she noticed strained lines around his mouth, the tiredness in his eyes. Digging her heels, she said, "Well, *you* stop interfering with *their* lives."

He shook his head, "I'm not. Can't you see how they feel about each other, how they look at each other?"

"Yes, just like Danielle says we look—looked at each other."

Shut up, fool.

It seemed to take some of the wind out of Devraj's sails, but only for a moment. "You're afraid to let anything happen as nature intended." He studied her closely.

"What would you call what we've had? Would you class that as premeditated?"

"For me it was fate." He gazed down at her. "For you? Sex, revenge, living out your youth and sexual fantasy, obviously." That hurt, as truth often did.

"Maybe. Fine. But now I'm where I want to be. But enough. I'm fed up of rehashing all that again. If Danielle and Sanjay are having second thoughts about the marriage—"

"Sanjay has no doubts. *You're* the one having second thoughts."

"How can you say that, when all I keep thinking about is how I'll never know what might have been with my career—with my life—if our elders hadn't interfered?"

"Not to mention 'us'." Devraj added.

"Not just about that—"

"Just?"

"I mean my art meant everything to me then. And my whole life changed when we met. But at eighteen, I didn't know how to stand up for my dreams. Oh, bloody hell, now I'm doing it, digging up the past. We need to move on. And I will, damn it." Tears, hot and unbidden, blurred Lia's vision as she tried to turn away, but he wouldn't let her.

His touch, oh, no, not his touch. She hiccupped, trying to focus. "How can you or anyone think for a moment I'd stand in the way of my own daughter's happiness? Just stop influencing Sanjay, just because you couldn't make your own creative dreams come true. Architecture is different from stand-up comedy. How can you encourage him to make it a serious career if they want to get married next year—?"

"What? I encourage..." After momentary silence, Devraj's unexpected burst of laughter threw her off. Because instead of being sarcastic it sounded like amused laughter of a relieved uncle. His eyes sparkled as if willing her to join him.

"Don't you see what..." Devraj stopped and some of his earlier seriousness returned to his voice, "I'm sorry. Sanjay said Danielle was acting strangely, they'd argued about us, about what chance did they have, if we couldn't make it work..." He brought her gently into himself, holding her so tenderly her resolve started fraying.

Not again, her insides screamed. *You're undoing it all.*

But her body had its own plans. Her eyes closed as more tears heated her cheeks. She'd missed these arms, hearing that sure heartbeat against her ear.

She pulled away and though he loosened his hold, he didn't let her go.

As if words were her only remaining ammunition, she said, "They shouldn't jump into anything if they have any doubts."

She expected his tension to resurface, but he replied, "They're meant for each other. You notice how they finish each other's sentences, like we used to? Their doubts are because of us." He looked into her eyes, searching for something.

"Don't make this about us again, Devraj. We're finished."

She moved back a step staring up at him.

"It's not over—" Devraj said quietly.

"Yes, it is. It broke my heart to send you away again, but I'm moving on with my plans. I can't keep getting distracted."

"I heard you've been quite busy in France and even getting some exciting new social contacts." Even though his tone was soft and factual, patent jealousy burned in his eyes.

Had Maxine and Patricia told Danielle about her mother's painting sessions at the villa with Jean-Pierre? The young sculptor who rented Patricia's small cottage on the vineyard, had modelled for Lia a couple of times.

"None of your business, but yes, and it's all very promising. Anyway, I'll support Danielle the best I can, but as adults, they should work out their own problems. Now if you don't mind I've got some work to finish."

"I can't stop thinking about you." It seemed as if the words were ripped out of him and he hated his demons and admitting his weakness. "I thought the past twenty years had been hell, but I can't go on like this. Until I saw you now, I didn't feel anything was worth bothering with."

She tore her gaze away from those eyes. "I'm sorry, Devraj. Just give it time." At his igniting hopeful expression, she clarified, "For this to heal, and let's be mature about our past, for their sakes."

"Did you feel so little for me that you can stand there as cool as an ice queen and not ache?"

Lia swallowed the lump lodged in her dry throat, languid yearning making her body tingle. It spread into her abdomen and lower...

She turned away from his accusing expression.

"I really need to—" That was as far as she got before being twirled back against Devraj and those familiar firm lips took hers.

This kiss was an urgent demanding one, where he took no prisoners in this battle of wills. Coming up for air, drowning in her need for him, not caring anymore that her eyes probably betrayed her, she whispered through swollen, hungry lips, "I hate you..."

"I know." His gravelly voice became lighter as he held her tighter, crushing her mouth again. And she let herself be drawn under his spell.

Chapter Twenty Three

THROUGH THE SEXUAL haze, Lia heard Danielle descending the stairs, "Mum, we're getting Gabe from Jordan's."

Collecting herself in time, Lia shifted out of Devraj's arms and turned away lest she betray herself.

When she saw Danielle and Sanjay's expectant faces in the kitchen doorway she frowned. Was Sanjay hiding a grin? And why wasn't Danielle furious at seeing her mother with Devraj?

"So, don't worry about Gabe, we'll have him home by nine-forty-five. See you later." Sanjay said, and almost instantly the young couple was gone, with the front door shutting them in a silent house.

"Why would they offer—" Lia asked as Devraj's low chuckle stopped her.

"Did I hear that we're completely alone?" He grinned, enveloping her in his arms, lowering his mouth to her jaw, the crevice of her throat and then nuzzling the heated skin above her breasts. Apparently, his tiredness had evaporated.

His rugged jaw grazed her wherever he stroked, but she didn't care. She was breathless and so aroused she couldn't think beyond this moment.

"Right here, right now? Or... Upstairs? Your call, Lia. But one way or another I mean to have you..." After a long replenishing kiss, she rested her head against him, needing to hear that thud of his heart beating.

His distinctive musk reawakened her senses.

God, give me strength, what am I doing going round this roller coaster again? Her sigh was deep and troubled, "Upstairs, but I think—"

"Oh, no, you don't," he whispered, silencing her with a gentle index finger across her lips. "We don't think, we just be...together."

Mesmerized by his gaze, she let him lead her up the stairs.

They made love as if intent on erasing the past long six weeks they'd been apart; caressing, licking, getting reacquainted, as if they'd been apart for another two decades. Lia felt tears flow as she held on to Devraj as if he was her savior.

"God, I missed you." She whimpered as she caressed his sinewy perfectly chiseled pecs, raking her nails into his shoulders and back. With another sure thrust into her Devraj growled against her ear, "I love you, my sweet Lia." Catching his breath, he smiled down at her, breathing deeply, gazing into her eyes. "Don't ever...punish me like that again. OK?"

She smiled, trembling, winding her legs tighter around his powerful body. How complete she felt. She almost purred. Until she heard Devraj whisper against her breast, "I love you, my Lia. I'll always love you. Tell me... you love me."

Thrusting deeply and deliberately into Lia's softness, Dev repeated, "tell me you love me, Lia. Like you did in college."

But as she opened her eyes, her dilated pupils clouded over. Shaking her head she closed them tight. Lashing her tongue out she explored his lips, his mouth.

Inhaling her scent, enjoying the sweet torture of her fingernails digging into his back, his buttocks, he drove them higher on that Richter scale of delicious insanity. "Lia..."

"This is so... beautiful, Devraj, please... not now. Words... don't mean a thing." Her involuntary groan of exquisite joy was music to his ears.

Chuckling softly against her ear, he said, "Yes, they do. Say it." Driving deeper and more urgently into her sweet center, he kissed her earlobe, her jaw, the hollow of her throat.

In danger of losing himself, he'd thought she'd have surrendered by now. "I—I'll stop."

Her soft laugh made a fool of him. "No...you won't." She replied in her pleasure-tortured voice.

"You underestimate my staying power, my lady." His torso gently grazing against her breasts, he smiled against her lips at her shuddering response. From her erratic, shallow breathing and her swollen lips forming an 'o', he knew she was about to let go.

But curbing his own climbing bliss, he said, "I—I'm waiting—"

"You underestimate my powers of persuasion, my lord." And she trapped him with her limbs.

He was in trouble as she massaged his back, lowering to his buttocks, her gentle fingers now digging into his muscles.

He gritted his teeth, fighting to stay in control for a little longer. When her legs tightened around him even closer and she licked the outer edges of his lips his resolve began to tumble. He chuckled as their sweat-sheened bodies melded perfectly together. The vixen!

"Defeat is only seconds away...for you, my lord," she whispered, panting, as if revelling in her power over him, even though he was on top.

He kissed her deeply. If he was to lose, he'd lose big. For now he recognized he was asking for too much, too soon.

But and soon Lia would be his, body and soul.

He'd make her happy and make certain to be the anchor she'd come to depend on in her career, and by diffusing the simmering opposition from both sets of relatives against Danielle and Sanjay's love match.

As her undemanding but oh-so-satisfying lover, he'd be so embedded in her new life that she wouldn't want to spend a single day without him.

For now, he was glad to have her back, and so close. He sighed and focused on making it good for her, and gave himself completely to the excruciating desire of the moment.

"I love you, honey, and that's plenty for me, for now, Lia. Now, come with me." He softly crooned in her ear, until she relaxed, let their rhythm return to its homely heaven, and surrendered to their perfect haven.

Why did something so sinful feel so perfect with Devraj? Lia couldn't believe how romantic and expressive he was, as she grabbed every crest of every wave of their lovemaking.

Tell him you love him, her heart whispered.

Tell him you'll always want him, her body and soul begged.

Shut up! Her brain ordered, as she sank her teeth into his delectable shoulder muscles.

She'd never make a fool of herself. "Devraj..." She whimpered holding on to him.

"Yes, my Lia, I'm yours."

Pathetically tears stung the backs of her eyes again and she gulped down that same lump she'd experienced when he'd wanted her to say she loved him. She grabbed him tighter, blocking any other thoughts.

His words still haunted her. Surely it was his ego needing to prove his own prowess. Yet she wondered if she really knew what she was doing and where it would all end. Would she repeat her own history and hurt him again?

Later, they lounged against her pillows. Lia's cheek rested on Devraj's relaxed shoulder. The world consisted of only them in this moonlit bedroom.

Devraj sighed, "Imagine how it may have all turned out if we'd had allies on our side."

She could only say, "I suppose Danielle and Sanjay are lucky, they have us."

"Yes. Sanjay said they'd considered eloping, but I wasn't sure if you'd want to see your only daughter marry."

Lia sighed. "Of course I would, but what kind of wedding would it be?"

"Danielle mentioned something about a mix of the two traditional weddings, Jewish and Hindu. Like a combination of the *chuppa* and the traditional Hindu one."

"*Mandap.*" She nodded.

"You've been doing research." He grinned.

"It's from Bollywood movies." She smiled, "But on this website when we were researching about the Rabbi and the Pandit, Danielle and I came across a few couples' stories on the net, where they've coined the phrase Hin-Jew wedding."

"Anything's possible. We'll do it together, Lia. They'll be all right. They've got their heads screwed on right." His arm came round her, drawing her even closer. "And we'd like to hold the engagement party at the family house. If that's OK with you."

"Thank you, but are you sure...?" Lia knew Malika would be happy, having met her and spoken to her a few times over the past few months, but how would Surita feel about that?

"Yes, I'm sure." Was all he said with that determined expression in the dim room. He cupped her face in his hand, staring deeply into her very soul. "But...right now I need you to promise not push me away again, Lia. It takes a lot for me to beg." He grinned that smile making her melt inside like a marshmallow. "Let's be together. I couldn't concentrate on my business, and that's dangerous. But I need you. Even if you just want to use me for my body, go right ahead." He closed his eyes with mock melodramatic tones. "You can even hand-cuff me to your bedpost, I won't complain." He opened one gorgeous eye, watching her with that cheeky grin playing at the corners of his mouth, until she laughed.

"Come here, woman, I've been going crazy without you in my life."

"I've been going crazy without you—"

"In your bed, I know! Don't rub it in, but talking about bed..."

"I wasn't, you were." Another low and contented low giggle escaped from her as Devraj pulled her into his arms in a much-needed bear hug. They kissed and now their hunger had a more sensuous, unhurried edge to it.

"God, I love you." He whispered against her willing lips.

"Mmm." Lia replied. "Shut up, my Prince, just love me."

"Yes, my Rani." His grin was that of a teenager in love and in lust. And that was fine by her.

She wouldn't think beyond the here and now. She wouldn't be practical or a coward or anything else which meant being without Devraj.

Chapter Twenty Four

"GIVE ME A FEW minutes to regroup, woman." Dev chuckled, proud as a king to hear Lia's tinkling laugh, which he'd missed so much. Making this suddenly insatiable woman happy was such a turn on. "I'm only human."

"No, you're a god of Kama Sutra, and you must prove it to me." Lia pulled herself on top of him.

Had she recently tasted any sexual fruit in someone else's arms, like that sculptor? Just imagining her eyes on another man made his fury boil.

But whether she'd admit it or not, she loved only him. And if he'd learned anything about the adult Lia, he'd better let go of the possessive grip.

Circling a lazy finger on Lia's bare belly as they lay in her rumpled bed he heard her say, "I'm sorry I thought you were behind Sanjay and Danielle's doubts."

He was glad she was this relaxed. "I'd never encourage him to concentrate on his comedy and waste his business acumen. I may be a doting uncle but I'm not insane, yet. Neither would I influence him away from Danielle, knowing how much that hurts. Those smart cookies twisted what we said."

Lia raised her head, her mussed up hair falling by her shoulders, "Why would they twist—"

As realization dawned on her, Dev grinned again.

Lia sat up pulling a sheet over her gorgeous curves, shaking her head in disbelief. "The sneaky little... She used those acting lessons—boy is she in trouble!"

"You didn't have to go to all this trouble, you know." Dev hid his smile, drawing the sheet down from her, but she held on. "Concocting this ploy to get me back."

Staring at him, Lia tried to wriggle away from him, as his hands were playing deliberately provocative games over her tingling skin. "Are you serious?" She swallowed down her rising agitation.

"With one phone call, a flick of your finger and a breathy 'I need you, Devraj', I'd be here." He said in languid tones that would have had her laughing if she wasn't furious.

He kissed her bare shoulder, but she turned away. About to escape from within his arms, she wasn't fast enough.

He hauled her struggling body back onto her pillows.

She'd have loved to scratch away that lopsided grin. "Let me go, you arrogant—" She might as well have been a mouse sparring with a tiger.

"Stop bristling, my little porcupine. I'm here, that's all that matters."

"Not if you think... What are you looking for?" She asked as

Devraj searched behind her, mock frisking her, until giggling, she pushed away his hands.

"Your sense of humor."

She wished she could kick him off the bed, even though short minutes ago all she thirsted for was his warmth.

"I realized what they were up to—"

"You knew? Oh." His earlier laughter in the kitchen made sense now. She smiled, shaking her head. "What a turnaround from Danielle. I just wish it would be that easy with other people... like Howard."

"I told you to give her time."

"I don't think it'll be the same with Gabe, though." Regret took the edge off her budding joy.

"Don't worry about Gabe, leave it to Uncle Dev. He's a good kid. He loves his Mum and I can't blame him for feeling possessive. But in the meantime, I want to apologize and I promise to be much more helpful and more supportive from now on. I can't lose you again. And how will *you* make it up to me for keeping away for so long?"

"I know exactly how. Would you come to Paris with me?"

"Try and stop me."

Lia wrapped her arms around him.

Chapter Twenty Five

THE FOLLOWING WEEK Devraj and Lia flew to Paris. With all the plans for Gabe's impending Bar Mitzvah finalised, with her girlfriends' help, she enjoyed this time away guilt-free. She worked a few days, but it felt so right having Devraj with her. He'd booked the Eiffel suite at the Hôtel Plaza Ethénée overlooking the breathtaking view of the Eiffel Tower. The Art Deco splendour fed her soul, and her heart burst with the romance of her lover and gorgeous Paris.

When she was at the gallery, Devraj spent every minute on his own work. The rest of the time was theirs.

They swam in the luxurious hotel pool, oblivious to anyone else, shared their own private sauna or the gym, ending up in the King size bed in their sumptuous suite. They enjoyed the fruits of the well stocked bar hidden behind the ebony Macassar wood in their sitting room, before going out to dinner.

Long walks in the warm September evenings on the chic Avenue Montaigne led them back to bed in each other's arms.

Patricia and Maxine had been confused and then annoyed when Lia told them about her break up five weeks ago, explaining about needing to concentrate on her career. "What a load of rubbish." Maxine had announced. "A man like that's worth anything, including an art career, and he adores you, *chérie*. And why can't you handle both? Hmm?"

So, when she'd asked them for private time at the villa, after Paris, they both congratulated her for coming to her senses. "Now just go and live a little." Patricia had ordered.

"And leave that young sculptor for *me, chérie,* OK?" Maxine had laughed.

She reminded herself to make a note to let Jean-Pierre know she'd be around. That way he'd call before using the swimming pool. Although he lived at the tiny cottage at the foot of the villa grounds, he'd never infringed on her lone hours, or when the three women were together.

After four days in Paris, they drove the rental BMW 760 through the medieval, winding roads of Avignon to the secluded villa. They continued the earlier pattern, into which they fell so naturally.

Between her long painting sessions outdoors or in the midday hours in the cool 'art' room, she loved having the relaxed Devraj around. If she'd feared she'd need some time alone or recharge artistically, she was doubly rewarded with Devraj's sensitivity. Easily accepting their new relationship, letting her paint to her heart's delight while he stayed in contact with the London offices via mobile and email. But he always turned off all his gadgets when she stopped working.

They enjoyed leisurely walks, hand in hand, through the vineyard lanes, talking, sharing. Again, they swam in the large, azure pool overlooking the fragrant and even more beautiful views of Avignon.

The colours of the miles of landscape were awe-inspiring. The earthy lavender and the ripe vines permeated the warm days and cooling nights, making it a magical, perfect week.

The only time Devraj worried her was when the green-eyed monster reared its head.

On the fifth day in nirvana, Devraj brought her a cup of tea into the sunny room she used as a studio. Sometimes he brought her cool drinks on the shaded deck, but he'd never entered this room.

His hesitation made her turn to see what had distracted him. His gaze was on one of her large canvases; Jean-Pierre in semi-naked splendor, dated last month.

Why did the studio seem cramped?

Sighing she waited for his response that could ruin or somehow detract from their perfect togetherness.

Instead, his silence and the tortured expression pierced through her. He put down the glass of iced tea, kissed her lightly on her temple and left.

She appraised the piece from a male perspective. Although he'd admired her college life drawings years ago, Devraj hadn't studied anatomy and the human form as a subject of art: beauty in a non-sexual way. But she saw how Jean-Pierre's paintings could seem too intimate.

Unable to concentrate anymore on her watercolor landscape

that had been going so well, she washed the sable brush in the large water jar and went in search of her lover.

He sat typing at his laptop, eyebrows knitted above his sunglasses under the shade of the courtyard grape vine.

Listening to her favourite sound of birds singing, she inhaled a lungful of delicious air filled with lavender and harvest-ready grapes, and slowly let her breath out.

"It's art, you know. It's nothing sleazy or wrong. And a man of your experience—"

"Don't worry. I'm all right." He continued typing.

"Good. Because there's nothing for you to worry about, ever." She sat next to him, watching him.

The typing stopped but his eyes were on the screen.

Kiss me, she willed him. Slowly she pulled the sunglasses off his healthy, bronze face. "That's better. I like to see those beautiful eyes when I tell you intimate things about myself."

"Such as?" Was that doubt warring with pride in his eyes?

"Such as, I don't go for boys; I like my men to have some experience. Preferably a certain man who makes me feel like I'm the only woman in the world for him." Why did his eyes seem to mist a little? He was a man's man. Or at least when he didn't appear so vulnerable. Like he did right now.

"It's not just my ego, Lia." He bowed his head towards hers, gently fondling the back of her neck. "I never cared about any other woman the way I feel about you, and seeing that guy's picture, imagining him seeing what I see." He shook his head as her lips hovered over his, teasing him. Then she kissed him. He tasted of coffee, oranges and everything spicy and decadent.

"But how do you know when I was painting him I wasn't imagining you? Always wondering where you were, what you're doing and refusing to consider you may be with someone else." The pain stabbed at her heart area.

He broke their gaze, "Actually..."

"No, I don't want to know." She closed her eyes and pulled him closer to kiss him again. She resolved to show him her latest artwork of him, later.

"I feel like a swim, you game?" He asked.

"I don't have my swim suit down here, give me a minute."

"Let's live dangerously."

"In the middle of the afternoon?" She asked, her breath catching in her throat as he cajoled her to sit astride him on the heavy iron, cushion-padded chair.

"The birds in the sky won't tell." He kissed her, his tongue sliding around and in between her lips, pulling her back until his lips were on her now revealed breasts, driving her crazy.

"What about other flying objects like... airplanes, helicopters..." Her voice sounded shaky.

"I don't care right now, do you?" He breathed against her lips.

She groaned, her eyes closing, she whispered, "No."

In the deep end of the sun-warmed pool, as they made unhurried love Lia gripped his shoulders and forearms, as she heard the gate hinges squeak. A familiar low male voice intruded on their nirvana.

Again, the unmistakable French accent asked, "Maxine, Patricia? Lia...is that you?"

Devraj stilled. Woozy and in agony of desire Lia couldn't find her words.

Finally gazing in the direction of the hidden gate, she let go of Devraj's shoulders, grated her back against the concrete pool wall, and lost her equilibrium.

She tasted chlorine and felt Devraj arms support her straight away.

Spluttering and splashing, she grabbed him, too aware how exposed she was at this angle to the elements and the uninvited guest.

"Stop, Jean-Pierre. Don't come nearer." She squeezed her burning eyes and tried hard to focus. "I forgot to let you know I—we're here. I'll call later. Now please go."

"OK, Lia. No problem." Came the sexy French reply from a few yards away. Then after the retreating footsteps and the singing hinge, silence.

Feeling Devraj's gaze she blinked and saw his expression change. Mirth filled his eyes and his laughter rang out in the peaceful silence. Soon the humor in the situation made her smile until she was laughing, too.

"You should've seen your face, hiding like we're teenagers." His glistening pecs hardened against her bare breasts as he hugged her. She was glad his hard-on was alive and well.

"I *felt* like a teen." She kissed his clean-shaven jaw, nibbling on his ear, pulling his wet hair back from those amused eyes. "I'm sorry about that. What lousy timing. Jean-Pierre rents the small cottage on the grounds. Patricia and Maxine let him use this pool whenever he wishes, when we're not here. Anyway, it's all your fault."

"What is?" He grinned at her, the droplets of water on his face making her thirsty.

"You've distracted me and I forgot to call him, and *you* wanted to make love in the pool in broad daylight."

He whispered into her ear. "He sounded disappointed he wasn't in my place."

When she nipped at his lower lip he said, "Ouch, you vixen." Then smiling again he said, "Now where were we?" His hands massaged her back through the smooth cool water, lowering to her buttocks, pulling her closer to himself until they were as one.

Chapter Twenty Six

HERE IN THE cocoon of privacy, they spent further hours together, laughing, slow dancing, and sometimes making love into the early hours. On their last night before returning to reality and London, drinking their wine on the patio, they'd watched the sun set.

Each day and night was bringing them closer. Since she'd shared some of her earlier paintings of him, and her new sketches, their bond seemed even stronger. Patently moved, Devraj seemed to comprehend how much he meant to her. "This is how you see me, even now?" He'd asked in disbelief. Her modest lover, who was beautiful inside and out, had then smirked, "I'm a pretty handsome hunk, huh?"

She mock thumped him, remembering Maxine's similar words.

They were embroiled in the romance of the villa, talking about how easy it was to exist here without missing the rest of the world. "I never knew how romantic you were." Holding his face with both hands, she kissed him deeply.

"There are many things you don't know." He watched her lips for a moment. "Like I saw you on your wedding day."

"What?" Lia's heart constricted, palpitating. "I didn't know."

"Your aunt said if I loved you I should let you go, but I couldn't stay away. I overheard Ella tell Jim you hadn't been allowed to invite her to the wedding, and I found out when you were getting married. On your wedding day I waited to see you outside your house, I followed you."

"I didn't have the courage to run away." She closed her eyes, leaning against his torso, wondering how she'd managed to live without Devraj.

"Then I followed your Rolls Royce." His eyes glazed with tears, like she knew he'd been crying on her rainy, grey, miserable wedding day.

"It made it real for me. I couldn't believe you loved anyone else, that you'd actually go through with it. I thought, *any minute now she'll run like hell, towards me.* And then when you did... but still turned back... I knew one day you'd regret this, that you'd remember me." He brought his shoulders up, as if straightening his resolve.

She could never listen to Michael Jackson's song, 'One Day in Your Life' without every inch of her skin prickling in an automatic response.

"I'd wanted you so badly. I'm so sorry, I really felt convinced it was for your best interest, remembering your father's words." She grasped his hand against her chest. "But twenty-

twenty hindsight..." She wouldn't tell him how she'd kept seeing him in all the dark haired men. Even her art hadn't been her saving grace.

Then within months, her baby, Danielle had come along.

"I don't know how I managed to survive the following weeks. Then after my own mistake of a wedding, I left home and travelled for what seemed like years." He told her how his great aunt had tried to find him when his mother had turned ill, slowly giving up on life, and he'd returned home from his trek to India and Thailand two days too late. "I'd been trying to run away from myself, and as they say, wherever I went, there I was. Or more to the point, here you were." He tapped his chest.

Staring, he said, "I saw you again a few years later, you were," he inhaled and exhaled deeply, "you were quite pregnant, with a little girl walking with you. You looked so luscious it nearly killed me. I never went shopping to Brent Cross after that."

Her prickling tears behind her eyes hurt. She pulled him to herself. She could never admit the secret about the night she'd conceived Gabe when, blinded by grief over her recently deceased grandparents and her loneliness, she'd closed her eyes and instead of Howard had imagined she was in Devraj's arms. Shame burned even now, at how she'd called out his name. It had opened her eyes to her husband's true nature.

Filing these memories with the past, she held him even tighter, focusing on his pain. "We're together now and that's all that matters."

"Yes, my Lia, my angel." As if needing to shake off the

melancholy he held her and brushed a gentle knuckle against her cheek. He grinned. "How's that for a romantic sap for you?"

Would he always feel such passion for her? She had the answer within her own heart. Their mirrored love.

"There's room for improvement." She breathed in. "Want to try something new tonight?"

"I'm game, babe." His eyebrows lifted in challenge.

"Give me five minutes and then come up."

"I like it already."

"You're so easily pleased." She got up.

He made a grab for her wrist. He missed. "Don't kid yourself, woman." His playful voice was gruff.

"We'll see, lover-boy." Throwing him her best cheeky grin, she ran naked up the stairs.

A few moments passed and a few items of his clothing flew by him, landing in the narrow corridor floors. "And put these on, will you?"

"But, I thought we were going to bed—" Dev's heart lightened at Lia's lack of shyness and playfulness.

"No questions. Five minutes." Her dancing eyes sparkled down at him. Then she vanished with another impish smile.

As he entered their low ceilinged bedroom, his senses alerted him to the enticing essence of lavender and other exotic smelling candles.

His breath caught at the sight of the naked nymph in the center of the high bed.

Her dark emerald satin negligee draped loosely around her

shoulders accentuated her lush, creamy curves, her head propped up against multicolored pillows. The soft jazz music built up the sexy ambiance, with candlelight playing with the mood of the room and her inviting smile and delicious contours.

"That was the longest five minutes of my life." He grinned, starting to undress.

"Not so fast, sailor. I want you to strip, like your life depends on it."

"The slow or fast version?" His smirk broadened at her slight gasp.

"I'll leave it to your expert judgment. See this as a modern version of Salome..." Lia's breathy voice lowered and slowed. "Your mission is to titillate the queen...otherwise you may lose your head."

"You think I haven't lost it already, a long time ago?" He protested, opting for the slower, more tortuous route for them both. "But one must obey his sexy Rani."

As he pulled the shirt-tails out of his already uncomfortably tight trousers, his audience seemed ready too; the hard pink nipples jutting towards him invited distraction.

Deliberately prolonging his queen's agony, he made slow work of unbuttoning and taking his shirt off, revealing small amounts of torso and abs. "This is going to be one long night. Can you handle it?"

"Your impertinence is going to cost you." She whispered, licking her lips.

Eventually he removed his shirt, deliberately tensing and flexing his shoulder and upper arm muscles and then pecs, enjoying her eyes on him, he slowly sauntered to the stereo.

He chose a racier CD that would kick up the stakes in his favor. "I'm too Sexy for my Shirt" made Lia giggle and laugh, and then one of her favourite sexy Barry White soulful numbers made her cheeks glow pink and her lips opened in that cute 'o'. She licked them and shifted slightly.

"Getting hot and bothered, my lady?"

"Less sass, more action."

As Devraj had turned a five-minute strip into a meltingly hot and agonizing twenty minutes Lia swore to take revenge. Moving slightly, she parted her legs to pay back the favor.

From his inhalation and the fire igniting in his narrowing eyes, she was succeeding. But then he turned his back to her and unhurriedly started to lower his trousers and work those perfect butt cheeks.

As he glanced back at her, she wondered who'd give in first. Should she just jump him now?

No, she had to finish what she'd started.

She swallowed a sigh.

The soulful sounds of 'Sexual Healing' enveloped the room, making her hungry for the teasing Devraj who moved to the music, tantalizing her, hypnotizing her, until she was ready to burst.

She almost surrendered when seeing his hard-on fighting against his blue silk boxers. He sauntered toward her, his smiling eyes never leaving her.

He came close enough for her to feel his muscled heat.

Her fingers itched to reach out. She moved her head up

slowly, her hair tickling her already over sensitized skin on her throat, jaw, and shoulders.

"Would Queenie like to do the honours?" He glanced at his boxers, the protruding bulge daring her.

"As you did such a great job, so far," she said breathily, "I'll do the rest." Her voice was betraying her, she knew, but she was so wet and turned on she couldn't think clearly.

Seconds later, he was lying next to her reaching out as if she was a long awaited gift.

Outmaneuvering him, she got on top. Straddling him, she looked down her nose at her resplendently naked god. She stroked his jaw, those arrogant features she could draw even if she was blind. Her breasts teasing his torso felt fuller and more sensitized. His jaw clenched against her cheek, and she knew she had him.

"How do you feel being completely at my mercy?" She asked huskily against his mouth.

"I pray to survive the night." She studied those mysterious eyes in the semi-darkness. The music slowed to a languorous tune, the soft sax sounds pulling at her insides, as she felt his penis effortlessly finding her wet center. Her hands travelled in slow motion down his considerable shoulders, down to his forearms and wrists. With all her strength, she cajoled his arms to rest above his head, to the heavy brass antique headboard.

As he stared at her mouth she feared all would be lost if she didn't take full control.

"Don't touch, yet...Leave your arms up." She whispered and rewarded that hunger with teasing feather-light strokes over his lips with her own ravenous ones.

Pulling out two red silk scarves from under her pillow Devraj swallowed, seeming to recognize her intent. He gripped the brass rails above him as if to stop himself from disobeying her.

"Red silk," he said hoarsely, grinning unsteadily. "I like red on *you.*"

As she raised a haughty brow, he added, "but I'm your humble servant, to do your bidding, my Rani."

Her voice unsteady, she asked, "Do you trust me?"

"Implicitly, I'd walk through fire for you." He said gruffly as she rose above him.

Her nipples hardened, her lower abdomen constricted with lava-like heat. *Concentrate.* She focused on loosely tying the swishing silk first around one muscular wrist and then the other to the brass bars. The sheerness was no match to Devraj's might but she felt dizzy with power.

Settling back on him, she enjoyed how his dark nipples pebbled under her gaze. Hungrily she took in every nuance of his physique, stroking that beautiful golden skin contrasting against her own alabaster paleness. "You're so beautiful, Devraj. Even more glorious than Michael Angelo's David sculpture."

"I love...the way you look at me. You're the only one who really sees me, Lia."

She held his intense gaze, while running slow fingers over the length of his broad shoulder muscles, hovering above his face until he raised his head to catch one nipple.

"Not yet." She whispered.

"Yes, Rani." He replied softly, expectant eyes with their dilated pupils following her every move. Brimming with so much love and lust, it took all her effort to pace herself.

"Close your eyes. I trust you not to have to blindfold you." As if the thought caused excruciating pain, Devraj shut his eyes. His Adam's apple rose and fell as she lowered her moist self onto him. And the torture of exquisite, leisurely and thorough kissing and exploring began.

"Don't move or you lose." She whispered against his mouth, as he tried to kiss her, her fingertips fluttering over his taut torso. Her tongue taunted, her lips sucked and her teeth lightly nipped at his ear lobes, down to his jaw and corded throat muscles. She loved his bulging shoulders and chest narrowing towards his hips. From the display he'd put on for her minutes earlier, he knew it, too. Now she was ready to collect on the promised paradise.

"And if I win?" He growled grinned, breathless.

"You're going for a wild ride you'll never forget."

From his bliss-ridden smile and the single intake of ragged breath, both their fates were sealed.

The she-devil! The minx! Dev grinned. The insatiable woman sleeping in his arms made him feel invincible and sated as an emperor.

"I love you, my Lia." He whispered, his heart drummed the truth repeatedly, just like during his own release. He was willingly under her bewitching spell. His muscles complained deliciously   from   the   rigorous   workout.   What   an unforgettable—but definitely repeatable and addictive—night.

No matter how enmeshed they were, he knew she wasn't ready to admit her love for him. But surely, she was becoming as addicted to him, too.

Life without Lia was unimaginable. His bachelor existence had been like a long journey leading nowhere. But after last month's breakup Dev feared losing her. She was his oasis, his true soul mate. Staring down at her relaxed, angelic features, he knew he had to bring her to the simple realization; they were destined to be together.

Chapter Twenty Seven

DESPITE HAVING SO many things on her mind, like her flourishing art career and the exciting sexual roller-coaster ride with Devraj, Lia was filled with a new anticipation on the momentous day of Gabe's Bar Mitzvah. Today, according to Jewish law, her thirteen-year-old son was becoming a man.

But she was quaking at her adamant decision to invite Devraj and Sanjay.

They were future family, after all, and Danielle was determined to have Howard meet her future husband. Lia's insides coiled at the possible calamities that could ruin this special day for Gabe.

Having never enjoyed big crowds, especially with critical family eyes following her every move, she felt selfish and disrespectful to both sides, the memory of her grandparents and the as-good-as-divorced one. The Goldmans were, and always would be, her children's family.

But she had her second chance now.

Lia's breakup with Devraj had taught her a valuable truth: She couldn't live her new life in denial, without Devraj. They were deeply in love and they were so relaxed and right together.

With disobedient fingers, she dressed and fussed with her honey-brown hair and plum silk skirt suit with a deep neckline. Giving up, she rushed into Danielle's room.

"I need your help with my hair, sweetie."

"Wow, Mum, very sexy. Are you deliberately goading the relatives, or is this just for general rebellion?" Danielle eyes sparkled as she concentrated on manipulating her mother's hair.

Lia faltered. "I'll wear the jacket; it'll be respectable enough for *shul*."

"Sorry, Mum. You look wonderful. Devraj is bringing out the real you..." Danielle smiled, then asked, "What about me? How do I look?"

Lia wondered if Danielle was as calm as she appeared.

"You're perfect, darling."

"Don't you think Dad will like Sanjay once he meets him?"

Lia saw her concerned expression. "Let's hope so, darling." Silently she prayed that she was wrong about Howard's obstinacy.

On her way down the stairs, Gabe's grunt stopped her. "Do you need any help, Gabe?"

"No." A split moment later, she heard, "Yes."

Entering his room, Gabe's pink cheeks and the messed up black bow tie, told her enough.

"I—I wish I didn't have to r-read all the stuff out in f-front of everyone." Gabe's voice squeaked as he fought her ministrations. Then seeing her attire, his eyes widened. "W-why are you wearing such a—a—" He couldn't seem to find the right words.

Maybe her high heels made her silk skirt and top seem sexier than she'd anticipated.

"I'll be wearing a jacket with it." Frowning he stiffened his upper lip and wouldn't meet her eyes. He was so dashing and tall, her heart beat a proud drum for her son, now a young man.

"You've really changed since Dad left."

"How?" He still wouldn't glance at her as she finished straightening his tie.

"I—I don't know. Just different." Then he glared at her, "Mum..." His almost desperate expression made her worry if his nerves would cause him to break out in a high temperature again. Was all this worth it, these ancient centuries-old traditions and cultures? How had spirituality helped her in her life?

As he tried to form the words, knowing how hard he'd practiced his portion of the Hebrew text, she said gently, "You know your *parsha* inside and out—"

"It's not that." He moved away from her as if she was radioactive.

"I'm sorry, sweetheart." She could have shot herself for interrupting him. How often had she asked Howard and Danielle not to do that?

He hesitated. "It's about you and D-Devraj."

"Yes?" She couldn't breathe easily. Although he didn't

appear as derogatory as he had before the break up, was he going to mention the taboo subject?

"If he hadn't come into your life, w-would you still divorce Dad?" He scrutinized her.

"Yes, why?"

"Or did Dad leave because of me?"

Don't even think about crying. She put her arms around him. "Oh, darling, how could you think such a thing? I was the one who asked *Dad* to leave. I had to start a new life."

"I know it's because he didn't want me. And you didn't love each other. Dad told me you moved out to the guest room before I was born, and you never shared..." His lips trembling slightly he glanced down at his shoes.

"Oh, Gabe." She'd been so blind. "None of this is your fault. Why would you blame yourself for our marriage? Dad loves you, we all love you. You bring so much joy to us all." She was about to hug him, but he slithered out of her reach.

"I know, b-but..." The honking of a car interrupted him. With a resigned sigh that brought his shoulders down, Gabe turned towards the door.

"Wait, Gabe. They'll wait."

"N-no, I want to get this over and d-done with. I can't change a-anything, anyway." He mumbled, shuffling away from her.

"Gabe, stop. Please come here." She patted the space beside her on his bed. Hesitantly he plopped himself down next to her and she put her arms around him. "Is this what's really been troubling you? Or is there something more?"

"Why did you have to pick D-Devraj for your b-boy friend?" Gabe moved out of Lia's arms, tie crooked again. "I—I recognized him from all those pictures you had in the sewing room when I was little, that you've always had the hots for him—"

"What?" As someone rang the doorbell, Lia ignored it.

Turning to her son, who said, "It's too convenient for you to divorce Dad just as Devraj comes on the scene. Dad says you've been having an a-affair with Devraj all the while you were m-married." And suddenly Lia understood.

She envisioned all those interrogations, when Howard and Gabe were supposed to bond. Fury boiled within her that he'd obviously manipulated and confused their poor son about the facts of their stale marriage.

"Our marriage hadn't been right, Gabe, and I never met Devraj again until after I'd asked Dad for a divorce, but the most wonderful thing about our marriage is I have you and Danielle. Soon Dad will get someone new to love and he'll settle down and won't be so angry—"

"Dad says all women are selfish and no good."

Gabe's bitterness constricted the air within her already tight rib cage. "That's how *he* feels, but don't let his opinions cloud your judgment, honey." She tried to hug him, but again he shrugged her away.

"Why not? It's true, you didn't want him, and so he's out in the cold."

"Gaby," Lia unfurled her fists, reminding herself none of this was Gabe's fault. "Those are your father's bitter words, and he's wrong to involve you in adult stuff."

"I'm not a b-baby; I understand a lot m-more than you know." Gabe's cheeks turned crimson. He looked at his white-knuckled fists on his lap.

Lia's voice softened, "Gaby, I never did anything wrong while we were married and I'm definitely not doing anything wrong now. Life's complicated, but remember I'm here for you." Gabe refused to look at her. "All right, honey? None of this is your responsibility. And when you're with Dad, all you should be doing is having a great time together. Please don't worry about the rest, all that's between your dad and me, and no one else."

"That's what Sanjay and...Devraj said."

"I promise your dad won't get you entangled in this again." Her expression and determination must have got through to him, because his shoulders relaxed slightly.

"Now give me a hug, honey."

He shrugged, but let her put her arms around him.

"I love you, darling, and this is one of the most special days of your life. You're maturing into a young man, so dashing and grown up. I'm so proud of you. Enjoy today." She kissed his forehead, smelling his shampoo scent.

Her eyes followed him as he picked up his overnight case. Soon, Gabe would be moving on like Danielle, independent and grown up. The days and especially the nights had sometimes seemed long, but the years sped by.

She repressed her constant nagging guilt about the affair and not being the loving nurturer Gabe obviously needed.

Her jaw tightened thinking of Howard. She vowed to get it through to her ex-husband—how naturally that word came to her—even if it took a blazing branding iron.

But today she'd make sure it would be one of her son's best days of his life, so far.

The party was in full swing. The photos, the food, the cake, the speeches were all behind them. Gabe seemed less glum, but Lia suspected his confidence had more to do with having his friends around him. He was patently relieved he'd survived the ceremony and most of the party.

The DJ was in his element. As the dancing began, she caught him shoot furtive glances towards one of the girls' tables, near the dance floor.

Inwardly Lia quivered. Her son was growing up. She eyed Howard at the far end of the crowded banquet hall. Gabe *would* be allowed to flourish.

"Looks like that's the girl he told Sanjay about." Devraj inclined his head towards the small group Gabe kept sneaking a peek at every few moments.

"Which one?" She asked,

"That pretty, dainty, blonde girl in the turquoise. Annabelle, I believe."

"Wow, I'm impressed. Most men would call that blue."

"It pays to know an artist." He placed a casual hand around her hips, and it took all her strength not to wriggle away. Her parents-in-law radar was on full alert, feeling eyes boring into the back of her head through the large space.

"Very pretty. She's a daughter of one of Howard's clients, and I believe they go to the same school."

"Gabe certainly has good taste." Devraj grinned. The uncanny sensation of being scrutinised increased as their arms connected and stayed together. She caught sight of her soon-to-be ex-mother-in-law, Grace, and Howard's younger brother, Leonard, glaring at her and Devraj.

Looking away, she drew nearer to her lover.

"Let's dance." He said softly in her ear, as if attuned to her every mood.

Weaving their way through the crowd, Lia smiled at the guests. It felt alien and yet natural to be swayed and held in Devraj's arms. As the DJ played dance tracks that the Bar Mitzvah boy's friends and the relatives could enjoy, Devraj held her tight, leading her. It reminded her of their time at the villa mere weeks ago. She could never go there without him now. As she moved slowly in his arms, keeping their rhythm, even under the scrutiny, all she wanted was to feel those strong fingers on her back, lowering to hold her closer against himself. But she felt him tense, and then he let her go. She followed his gaze.

A few feet away, Danielle faced her father. Howard's back was ramrod straight and unyielding as he shook his head. Danielle's imploring expression left no doubt as to their subject: the silent young man standing with them. Danielle seemed close to tears. Lia quelled her urge to run to her daughter's side. As she nearly succumbed, she saw Danielle put her arm around Sanjay's waist.

Sighing, Lia started towards father and daughter, but a

burst of boyish laughter caught Lia's attention. She saw Gabe rushing out of the banquet hall, as if unable to decide where to hide.

Devraj brushed her arm, saying, "He may prefer to speak to his Dad, or even Sanjay, but as they're otherwise engaged, I'll see if I can help."

Lia smiled her gratitude, he squeezed her hand and followed Gabe's retreating form.

Looking back at Danielle, she prayed for a miracle, that Howard would suddenly grow into a *mensch*, and become a good, kind, decent and honourable human being. Why couldn't he prioritise his daughter's happiness, instead of his reputation and principles?

She had to talk to him, despite feeling impotent to change much, if anything.

Chapter Twenty Eight

WITH HER ATTENTION split between her son and daughter, Lia didn't notice Grace, who materialized before her, with her younger son in tow.

Her cool mother-in-law was elegant from the perfectly styled platinum-blonde, stiff hair down to her pumps. "I can't believe your brazen behaviour and at my own grandson's Bar Mitzvah, no less." Her nasal voice was a cross between the queen and the Wicked Witch of the West. "It's most unsuitable to be flaunting yourself with that, that..."

"If I've never been good enough for your son, then as long as I'm out with anyone else but him, you should be quite happy."

Grace gasped. "You've never talked to me like that."

"I knew you'd never hear me."

"I never said you weren't good enough for Howard." She had the decency to avert her eyes.

"But *I* did. I warned him." The frowning Leonard resembled his brother. His mother stopped his further words with a glance.

"You didn't have to say it, Grace. Excuse me, I have my son's Bar Mitzvah to enjoy, and a new life to get on with."

"You may gallivant with whomever you wish," Grace said with that tight-lipped resolve Lia recognized so well. "But don't encourage this ridiculous idea of my granddaughter considering marrying that most unworthy boy." Grace held up her nose.

How predictable and staid the Goldmans were. And where was her father-in-law, the quiet Jonathan? Probably sinking his reality in the bottom of a Scotch bottle at the bar, she thought uncharitably. "Have you or Howard met Sanjay?"

"Of course not. Unlike you, we won't encourage this—"

"Then you're judging this young man by the culture he was born into."

"Of course we are. But *you* wouldn't understand with *your* background." She talked as if Lia was a bastard mongrel of dubious origin, when the Abrahams could retrace their ancestry back five generations in South Russia, and even further back to Spanish Jews before that. It struck her that living three generations in England hadn't broadened the Goldmans' blinkered views of the world. Their engrained elitism would have been laughable if it wasn't so unfair.

"You're her grandmother, but as her mother I'll fight for what's best for Danielle."

"You can't mother a bag of flour." Leonard scoffed, his chin wobbling, his blue eyes even colder than his brother's. "Howard should have listened to me, instead he's going around saying you're temporarily separated." He sniffed righteously.

"Not everyone's as lucky as you in marriage. And how are all your children? See them much?" Lia was gratified to see his face grow the same shade of plum she recognized too well.

The three-time divorcé was on the prowl for the next victim to massage his inflated, chauvinistic ego.

"Anyway, we all know preserving his reputation and his business is Howard's number one priority." Lia realized that without her support Danielle might have been cornered, blackmailed, or bribed out of her chance with her Mr. Right. On the other hand, Danielle wasn't as naïve as *she'd* been.

"And although it's none of your business, I happen to be in love with Devraj and I'll see him whenever I please. Now, excuse me."

Gasping again, her mother-in-law's over-blinking increased in frequency. Lia turned away and felt Devraj's presence beside her. She returned his grin with a satisfied smile. Ceremoniously, she entwined her arm with Devraj's.

Being with him always soothed her soul.

"So that's the way I hear you say I love you? Or were you saying that just to goad them?"

She raised her face to him, "Do you really not know the answer to that question?" When he grinned, she planted a kiss on his lips.

"Let's revisit this conversation later." He smiled.

She nodded as her eyes scanned the place where Danielle had been a few minutes ago. But she couldn't see her daughter anywhere. Her frustration grew at seeing the smiling Howard, *schmoozing* with one of his clients.

"I have to find out what's going on, Devraj." Lia said apologetically reluctant to let his arm go again.

She reached Howard's side with a bright hostess smile, "Excuse us, for a moment." Gripping Howard's arm Lia smiled at the couple, to all the world, a smiling soon-to-be-ex-wife sharing an intimate secret about their children. She manoeuvred him towards a quieter alcove by the large French doors.

"What are you doing? She's—"

"They'll all wait, you can return to your *schmoozing* in a minute."

"That schmoozing put bread on the table, and paid for all this."

"I'm not arguing. But stop being so obstinate about Danielle and Sanjay. Do you think you'll stop them from getting married by cutting her out of your life like this?" Her tone was calm.

"I'm her father—"

"And your priority should be her happiness, not your principles. They love each other. At least they haven't run off and got married. Meet him, give him a chance, he's not a—"

"I don't care. She's broken the rules and she'll have to choose between what's right and—"

"You're making her choose between you and her Mr. Right?"

"He's not her Mr. Right, for God's sake. She's an immature, confused eighteen-year-old."

She didn't ask him why *he'd* married an immature, confused

eighteen-year-old. What was the use? "How do you know he's not? Would you rather miss out on your daughter's happiness or see her married to someone like you and be miserable?" She kept her voice low so only Howard could hear her in the music and the hustle of the festive occasion.

His features grew increasingly tense. "*You* filled her head with those fairy tales, and bloody Indian movies. *You* were miserable because you were an ungrateful b—"

"I don't think this is the time or place for this conversation." Devraj materialised by Lia's side like a lifeline, and Howard's jowls moved and clenched. She saw his fists by his sides. His face reddened as if he was about to blow a fuse. "How dare you bring them into our son's Bar Mitzvah?"

Before Lia could reply, Devraj stepped closer to him, drawing attention from some of the nearby guests.

Howard took a small step back.

"A more apt question would be, where your Bar Mitzvah son is, and why you're not with him when he needs you."

"Don't you give me fathering advice." His eyes flared with contempt.

"I was offering—" Devraj studied the now sweating Howard.

"I know what you're offering." Howard blinked rapidly, casting Lia the same accusatory look she'd received from the other Goldmans.

Devraj squared his shoulders and Howard took another step back, nearly colliding with a dancing couple behind him.

"Get him out of here or I leave." Howard glared up at Devraj, and then dismissed him.

"You selfish bas—" She said, but Devraj's hand on her upper arm stopped her words. Then she said, "Even on your son's biggest day, you still make it about you."

As she took Devraj's hand, Howard flinched but didn't break eye contact with her.

"I'll go, Lia." Devraj said.

"No, Devraj, I'd like you to stay, please." She continued staring at Howard. "You're my date for tonight or any other night I choose. I'm a free agent, unlike my soon-to-be ex-husband when *he* was gallivanting—" She moved closer to Howard. "And if you really want Danielle to make the right decisions then meet her, be there for her. She's missing you."

"Right. If she was, she'd—"

"Stop, you're the adult, the father. Think hard, she needs you." She sighed. "But right now our boy needs you; find him, talk to him." Her voice became lower, "and don't ever manipulate Gabe. If you ask or say anything about me to him again, and trust me, I'll know—you'll be childless, as far as the courts are concerned. And make sure you sign the papers as soon as—"

"Why?" His smug expression turned belligerent. "Can't you wait to finally marry your dark knight—"

"I'm not the Lia you knew."

"Like I really knew you." Howard hissed.

Ignoring his words she added, "Accept that Sanjay and Devraj are sticking around, and if you don't come to Danielle's engagement, with the rest of your family, it'll break her heart. Don't alienate our children, or you'll end up growing old and

alone. For once, put your pride aside and stop hiding behind
your hypocritical double standards of traditions."

With one last branding stare at the fuming Howard, Lia
turned and smiled at Devraj. At the bold admiration in his eyes,
her smile melted into a dazzling happy one.

Dev's respect for his adored woman climbed. That emerging
resolute determination and the tenacity she'd possessed years
ago was resurfacing at last.

But he didn't like the mutinous expression on Howard's face.
He wondered if the old boy would have a heart attack. No. He
wouldn't want the poor birthday boy to lose completely the
sorry excuse he had for a father.

At least he knew what Gabe's issue was.

When he'd followed him, finding him hiding behind a huge
plant in the corner seat, Dev suspected Gabe wouldn't want him
anywhere near him.

At first, he'd been tempted to turn back and let the hatred
in the boy's eyes massacre some braver soul. Then he thought
of Gabe's options. Neither his father or Sanjay were available.

He jumped into the emotional quicksand. "You probably
want some privacy after all the excitement..."

"B-bloody right." Gabe's dark eyes brooded, his jaw set, his
lips resolute as his mother's mouth.

"If you talk to someone outside the circle of your friends and
family—"

"You're definitely outside the—the circle."

"Fair enough." A sigh escaped him. "Congratulations on

becoming a man." He didn't offer to shake hands. There'd never be a truce. The strange tightness in his upper chest made him wish...

The silent Gabe ignored the passers-by. When Dev was about to turn away, the boy's lower lip quivered as he said, "What kind of a man am I going to be if I can't even a-ask for one l-lousy dance from a g-girl?" He hit his knee.

Dev paused, relieved that this had nothing to do with what the others were outraged about—the Shah men, the outsiders.

Without invitation, he sat down, giving Gabe plenty of personal space. "When I was fourteen I was dared by my so-called friends to ask a girl I liked to the school dance."

Slowly Gabe glanced sideways at him.

"I couldn't do it. I came out in a cold sweat." Dev continued, "She was gorgeous; no way, I thought she'd tell me to get lost. But I didn't want to look like a complete wuss."

"So what did you do?" Gabe sounded impatient.

"I bought myself more time, saying I'd ask her the next day. Only the next day I woke up with even more spots." Dev smiled at Gabe. "You're lucky you don't have them."

Gabe shrugged, staring at the carpet. "I've g-got other p-problems."

Dev nodded. "So, I reminded myself what my uncle used to say. What's the worst that could happen? I answered myself, I'll be rejected."

Gabe nodded. "Yeah."

When he offered no more, Dev continued, "And then what? I'd never be able to face my friends."

Gabe nodded, appearing even more miserable, "They don't realize that I'm ...shy."

"To your friends this is just fun, but what if this girl says 'yes'? You're the Bar Mitzvah boy. What if she feels special that you chose her out of all the others?"

"I don't even know if she l-likes me."

Dev could tell how much it took Gabe to admit this. "She came to your party, didn't she?"

"Yes, but..." he shrugged, clamping up again.

"She may like you and you'll never know, and what I've learned in my business—it's all about seeing the right opportunities and then taking them."

"It's what Sanjay told me." He flushed.

"Wow, Sanjay gave you advice? He must really like you, he usually keeps all our trade secrets in the family."

Gabe gave him another sideways look, frowning. "He's trying to get on my good side so I don't get in the way of him and Danielle."

Dev couldn't help grinning, "Do you really think you could?"

Gabe shrugged, "I don't think any of my opinions matter to anyone." Then he studied his short nails on his lap.

"I think you underestimate the power of your opinions, and before you say I'm only trying to *schmooze my* way into your good books—which wouldn't be a bad idea—I'm only sharing my personal experiences—man to man."

Gabe watched him, most of the hostility gone from his eyes. "You're on the level here? You really th-think I should ask A-Annabelle for a d-dance?" He swallowed as if his suit had turned into an arctic-proof boiler suit.

Dev nodded, "Seems the perfect opportunity."

"So what happened to your date when you were fourteen?" Was the youth stalling or was he genuinely curious?

"I'm embarrassed to tell you."

Gabe lips parted, as Dev asked, "Can I trust you with this? Promise not to use it against me?"

Gabe shrugged, a small nervous grin playing on his lips, "OK."

"I never asked her, but my best friend did, and they got married in college."

"I'm s-sorry." Gabe's disappointment moved Dev. Small steps in the right direction. Lia would be glad to see her son happy.

"Don't be, they divorced two years later. She didn't turn out to be a nice person. Anyway, I met someone very beautiful in college, and that was when I dared myself to ask her out. Eventually it worked like a charm." He could hear Michael Jackson's "Do You Remember" in the college cafeteria, recalling his intrigue when he'd first laid eyes on the young girl oblivious to her sweet beauty and talents. His chest constricted. He no longer felt sad, because he had her in his life, and he'd never let her go.

"You're talking about M-Mum, aren't you?" The slight thinning of the boy's mouth gave away his underlying resentment.

"Yes, and one day I may tell you about it. Man to man. But right now, I've got a hunch you need to see your father, or..."

Instead of a relieved yes, he saw Gabe's subtle change, seeming more alert, almost defensive. "Or do you want to go for it?"

"No, I-I think I'll see Dad." Shaking his hand, Dev's gut told him Gabe would have let him hug him. Then he remembered that to Gabe, they were adversaries.

After interrupting Lia and Howard's heated argument and watching him march away to find his son, Dev quelled his futile thoughts of 'he could have been my son'. Instead, he was glad to be getting to know Gabe with every outing with Sanjay.

Now he put a protective arm around Lia.

"Thank you for being here. I know it's selfish but what would I have done without you?"

"You'll never be alone again, my Lia."

She linked her fingers through his and her eyes followed her son. "Oh, look Devraj," Lia smiled, as Gabe danced with the radiant Annabelle. Her voice quivered with pride, "Thank you for getting Howard to help him."

He swallowed the lump in his throat.

Chapter Twenty Nine

LIA HAD ASKED Devraj to stay overnight for the first time. The house was quiet, with Gabe away at Howard's place and Danielle at Sanjay's flat. Her daughter was hardly home these days, but within a few months, the responsible young woman would be engaged and soon after that, married.

Instead of feeling guilty, all she thought about lately was when and how she could spend every spare, rejuvenating moment with Devraj. She wouldn't allow Gabe's tight-lipped attitude towards Devraj dampen these feelings too much.

Astride her lover, uncaring of the early morning light filtering through the blinds, Lia was about to let herself go completely when Danielle's voice called out.

Then again, more clearly—closer—and Devraj's fast reaction swathed them both with her quilt with one swift motion, before the door flew open.

"Oh, my God. I'm so sorry." Danielle disappeared as fast as she'd appeared.

Almost immediately, Lia heard Danielle's door closing, down the hall. "Hey, Casanova, thanks for that quick reflex action." Lia lay panting against his sweat-sheened rising and falling chest. "Never tell me where you learnt that. Let me believe you're agile and fast from those dancing lessons." She pushed away the image that may have greeted either of her children, her ass up in the air on top of a very naked male body.

"That'll teach you to lock the door." His voice was gruff as he continued to caress her, his heart thumping against her swollen breasts.

"And you can stop sounding like a satisfied Cheshire cat." She smiled, tickling the fine dark hairs on his pecs, enjoying how the mere caress of her fingertips aroused his nipples.

"Hmm, I feel like a *very* satisfied Cheshire cat." He pulled her mussed head down to kiss her inflamed lips.

"Darling, your stubble hurts." She pushed away from his divine body. "As much as I'd love to..."

"Say that again." Rolling her on her back, he pierced her with that adoring expression.

"Which part?"

"Darling..." He whispered.

"Darling." She smiled and welcomed another deep, possessive kiss.

"Why can I never have enough of you?" He grumbled against her shoulder.

"And I can't get over you." God, she adored him. And he was becoming so important and indispensible to her.

"Don't *ever* get over me."

Reluctantly, she pulled away from his arms and left the rumpled bed. She felt his eyes following her every move as he folded his arms behind his head, resting against the pillowed headboard. He made her feel perfect just the way she was.

"Promise?" He asked.

"Promise." She sealed it with a quick kiss, and escaped him before he could catch her and drag her into his arms again.

Chapter Thirty

"WHAT'S WRONG, DANIELLE?"

"You mean apart from Dad refusing to acknowledge Sanjay last night? If you weren't busy playing kissy-face with Devraj, I'd have appreciated a bit of backup, Mum."

Lia counted to ten, then to fifteen. She couldn't blame Danielle, but she wouldn't allow her to push the same guilt buttons and detract from another wonderful night. Even now, imagining Devraj in her shower sent tingling sensations throughout her body.

"Please don't talk to me like that."

"Sorry, Mum." Danielle sank into the kitchen chair. "And I know I shouldn't have barged in on you like that, but you've never had—"

"From now on, please knock."

"OK, I'm sorry." She got up from the table, and within a minute carried back two steaming mugs of coffee.

Lia welcomed the strong scent of the brew. "Thanks."

"Are you, like, making Devraj breakfast in bed or something?" Was it her Daddy's-girl loyalty, or did she want to talk? Was Danielle considering other people's plans and feelings?

Lia smiled. "We hadn't thought that far." Lia stifled a huge yawn. A couple of hours of sleep in Devraj's arms weren't enough, after such a busy weekend.

Lia studied her daughter's strained features. "You've been crying, what's happened?"

"I don't know if all this'll work out between Sanjay and me. And it's for real this time." Danielle's sheepish expression turned sad, her chin quivering.

"I know you're really hurt that Dad won't accept Sanjay, but we both have to accept that he can't change his life-long beliefs. He may well not come to your engagement. Be prepared for that."

"But why should I have to choose?"

"It's the unfairness of life, Danielle. Sacrifices have to be made."

"Sanjay wants to get married as soon as possible, and to travel to India, and I'm not even sure of anything anymore." She wiped away more swelling tears. "At least we have your—and Devraj's—support."

"Yes, I was alone in the same situation. Unlike you, I didn't have the courage, and it was so much more complicated with Baboola and Dedda, even though I couldn't imagine life without Devraj, but I still couldn't leave, feeling guilty and afraid if anything happened to either of them."

"I got all that last night too from Grandma. So why did you marry Dad? Did you think you'd forget Devraj?"

"No. But your father would probably have been a good husband to someone who loved him more. I didn't work as hard at the marriage as I could have. I wasn't mature enough. But it was hell without Devraj." She sighed, feeling some of her inner warmth dissipate. "Just make sure this is true love and then hold on to it. I can't imagine my life without Devraj now." Lia smiled.

"I'm glad to hear that." Devraj's voice made the two women turn to the kitchen entrance.

"Have you been eavesdropping?" Lia brightened at the sight of her lover in his dark suit and dress shirt without last night's tie. His sleeked back hair gave him an even more regal air.

"Next time remember I have fast showers." He lingered on their kiss. "If you don't want me to hear your secrets."

Bringing his mug of coffee Devraj sat next to Lia, and held her hand. "Are you going through with this, Danielle?"

Danielle sighed and nodded.

"So, don't expect to have everything perfect. How much do you love Sanjay?"

Danielle regarded Devraj. "How much do you love Mum?"

"More than my life." Silence filled the kitchen.

"I feel the same about Sanjay." Danielle bit her lower lip.

Moved by Devraj's emotional reply, Lia said, "Then you and Sanjay should stick to your plans, and if you only have a handful of relatives at the engagement or the wedding—"

"So what?" Devraj finished her sentence. "You've got each

other."

"I know..." Danielle was thoughtful. "So are you two going to marry soon?" Danielle smiled.

The wind was knocked out of Lia's lungs, a heaviness pressing on her chest.

"It's up to your mother." The hopeful tinge in his eyes threw her into a mini-panic.

"Let's not discuss that right now." Lia got up, letting her hand drop from his.

She saw her daughter's and her lover's expressions change.

"Me and my big mouth—sorry." Danielle got up, and looked at Devraj, as he dropped his gaze to his coffee mug.

"I have to see Sanjay..." She left them in the suddenly tense atmosphere.

"A clam should take lessons from you." Devraj stood behind Lia as she stared out at the overcast, cool September morning, from the kitchen window.

She sighed, summer was ending.

Enveloped in Devraj's arms she felt his caress lower from her shoulders to the length of her arms. He pressed against her, his torso warming her back.

But when he nuzzled her neck, fingers of claustrophobia engulfed her. "I'll have a shower and then after breakfast we could go for a walk." She turned in his arms to face his poker expression.

"So now you can admit you love me, but you can't imagine spending the rest of our lives together—despite your words to

Danielle a few minutes ago?"

"That's not fair. We're having such a wonderful time together, why complicate —"

He swore. "So it's still about fun to you." He moved away.

Bloody hell, she couldn't do anything right. "It's just so intense, Devraj."

"So? That's how I feel whenever we're together, every time we touch." She averted her eyes, her face burning, as he added, "You told Danielle to hold on to her true love. Am I not *your* man?"

He didn't play fair. All those nights and days at the villa, washed over her. She felt hot all over, until she reached inside the freezer and emptied some ice cubes into a clinking glass. Some spilled through her shaking hands over the counter.

"That's right, let's cool down." His voice was too near, too seductive. "Let me help my Lia." Even if he dumped the whole tray of ice down her wrap, she knew it wouldn't calm or cool her.

But apparently, he had other ideas. Devraj popped an ice cube between his white teeth, caressing it with his lips. Holding her gaze, he slowly pinioned her hands behind her.

With measured strokes, he ran his cool lips, trailing a delicious wet ribbon between her outer lips, her chin, down the side of her throat. She tried not to gasp aloud, but holding her breath was making her lightheaded.

Was Devraj supporting her?

Feeling his erection against her hip, she wished she didn't need him. Moaning, her resolve melting like the ice cube, she closed her eyes. Devraj's tongue teased the side of her throat, as he leisurely pulled away the too warm satin to reveal her breasts. With another ice cube, he punished first one hard nipple then the other.

She gasped. "You don't play fair, Devraj."

His low chuckle reverberated like a contented purr. Devraj freed her hands. "I appear to be doing the wrong thing..." He whispered in her ear. "I was trying to cool you down, instead— "

She kissed him hard and deep. "Shut up." She breathed against his lips, loving that heavy lust-crazed look in his eyes. "If you want to live another day, another moment, take me— now." She held him, like she was on fire and he was her firefighter.

"Yes, ma'am." He laughed softly again before picking her up, bound for heaven.

Chapter Thirty One

IT WAS NATURAL to feel this nervous, Lia reasoned. Today on this cold, rainy November evening was her daughter and future son-in-law's official engagement, at the Shah house.

As they entered the impressive mansion, Danielle's serenity made Lia doubly proud of her. Her daughter positively glowed in her sari-like cream holster-necked dress with gold beads at the yoke, tiny waist, and hem. Her flawless makeup and jewels enhanced her alabaster skin-tone and her large blue eyes held a new maturity within them.

The relaxed Devraj looked like the king of the castle, greeting them in the large foyer. As their coats were unobtrusively removed, Devraj held Danielle's hand up to his lips and smiled, "Sanjay certainly knows beauty inside and out. You're breathtaking."

Danielle blushed. *A first for her*, Lia thought smiling.

"But not as beautiful as my Rani," he whispered, placing a lingering kiss on Lia's cheek.

What a transformation Lia saw in them all. Devraj appeared much less intense and more fun loving, going with the flow.

Even Gabe wasn't as moody as he'd been a few months ago. With a growth spurt over the past few months, her nearly six-feet-tall son was filling out and becoming more confident.

She knew the sports trips he regularly went on with Sanjay and Devraj had much to do with that. The three had obviously gelled on the cricket grounds. Gabe had acquired this passion overnight with the incentive of building a stronger physique and stamina, under Sanjay's mentorship.

Gabe's stutter recurred only at times of high stress, such as exams or the upcoming school Christmas party. He'd even mentioned at their last week's family dinner that he wanted to ask Annabelle out to the cinema. He'd taken advice from the ever-obliging Sanjay.

Lia let herself enjoy the sumptuous surroundings of the Shah property, marvelling at the female guests in their gorgeous light and gem-coloured saris and their dashing partners. She felt vibrant in her chiffon, rich pink-coloured tailored dress, with the sensuous off-the-shoulder neckline. She'd bought it for a small fortune because of the way the decadent material hugged and accentuated her trim figure. And Maxine and Patricia had insisted it was 'her'. Where would she be without them?

She had yet to get the special dress for Danielle's wedding, planned for next June.

She tried not to fret over finances at this moment, still not feeling right about using any of her grandparents' money towards a wedding they would have never accepted. Although she appreciated Devraj's discreet generosity offering to foot many of the costs, she was determined to pay for the wedding on her own. She'd do it all, somehow. Although her job had become more like second nature, she was still adjusting to her new independence, juggling her family, her career, and her relationship with Devraj.

As gracious and intuitive as ever, Devraj had been supportive as the groom's father figure, but let Lia forge on with the wedding plans with no interference. Instead, he'd given a hefty lump sum as an advance, which the young couple had put down as a deposit on a large three-bedroom flat in Muswell Hill. Seeing it made her appreciate how mature and determined they were to stick to their set, practical marriage goals.

Lia had been further warmed but not surprised at her lover's generosity, when she'd found out that—along with a few other commercial and residential properties worldwide—Sanjay's current bachelor flat had also been gifted by Devraj a couple of years earlier. Now it would be one of the couple's first income properties.

Sanjay whisked Danielle away, and the atmosphere turned a little cool when Surita greeted Lia. Unlike the excited and beautiful Malika, Surita's haughty air left little doubt about her true feelings. Yet, she was the epitome of graciousness, limply shaking Lia's hand.

She hadn't dared count on Surita's stoical acceptance of the upcoming marriage. Apparently, family duty and obeying the head of the family continued to be upheld in the Shah household.

People changed, well, some did for the better, and tonight Lia prayed Howard would miraculously change his mind—if not his parents—and surprise her by attending the celebration, reinstating her faith in love and family bonds.

With dozens of friends, from both Danielle's and Sanjay's side, this happy occasion promised to be a great hit.

In the meantime, her nearly nineteen-year-old daughter braved on. Anyone could see how much they adored each other.

Lia remembered her sombre words to her last night. "You're marrying the man of your dreams, darling. Never take each other for granted."

An hour into the party, with still no sign of the Goldmans, Lia wondered why she was surprised.

Although Danielle and Sanjay were thoroughly enjoying themselves, mingling among the throng of their friends and Sanjay's group of relatives, she noticed her daughter frequently searching the entrance of the huge room.

"I'm going to kill Howard and while I'm at it, I'll poison his parents." She whispered to Devraj through gritted teeth, while smiling at the guests.

"They aren't worth making me suffer while you're serving time. Don't make me kiss you through that glass or the bars between us."

"Well, just for you," she smiled at him and saw Danielle's face light up, greeting the newcomers. Lia's heart leapt to see her Aunt Eliza hugging Danielle. Behind her, Maxine and

Patricia were perusing the brightly lit hall leading into the huge cathedral living area.

"I'm so happy you're here." Danielle hugged her great aunt again, "Come and meet Sanjay's mother and Aunt Surita..."

Lia sighed, trying not to let the disappointment mar her family's partial joy. Bless her aunt, the black sheep of the family.

"Don't play with his heart, Lia." Jim smiled in that charming way Lia remembered from college, but the seriousness in his gleaming gray eyes didn't escape her. "Devraj's crazy about you."

"I'm crazy about him, too."

"Then why don't you marry the guy?"

"I've tried that and it's not for me. And maybe it's not for Devraj either. He seems quite content."

"I've tried it twice, but I'd tie the knot again, if I had half the connection you two have. He's always been like that about you."

Flattered, but laden with guilt, she shook her head. "But we both know he's an independent spirit, too."

"If that's what you need to believe, fine."

"For such a die-hard romantic I can't believe you've not been ensnared by wife number three, already." She smiled at Jim

Devraj's voice interrupted them, "Hey, stop flirting with my woman. Friend or no friend you even look at her a certain way and you're dead, partner." Devraj put his hand on her waist, giving her a playful mocking glance. Then he whispered in her ear, "Aren't I enough for you, Queenie?"

She smiled back. He was perfect for her.

"That's what I get for playing cupid." Jim rolled his eyes, and then squeezed his best friend's shoulder. "I'm off to find myself my own woman." He winked. "I hear you have some very nice friends. Care to introduce me?" Jim gave her that Hollywood knock-em-dead smile.

Lia smiled. "Remember, I knew you at college, Jim, stay away from my friends. And you did very well on your own without my or anyone else's help."

Chapter Thirty Two

THE SMILING COUPLE in the band crooned their versions of classic songs that Dev had chosen. The excellent band had promised to include a mix of up-to-date pieces the young couple and the guests would also enjoy.

Dev smiled at Lia as the sound of Kenny Rogers' "Lady" surrounded them on the dance floor area. She hugged him closer as Chris De Burg's "Lady in Red" followed. Her eyes shone so brightly he knew she was moved by his choice of songs. When the lead singer sang Louis Armstrong's "What a wonderful World" Lia looked at him. "I thought this was Danielle and Sanjay's night, not for you to enjoy the music down memory lane."

"There's something for everyone to enjoy, and I plan to take every opportunity, any ammunition available to make myself indispensable in your life." Why didn't he feel like a romantic sap with her? In a lower voice, he added, "and I have especially fond memories of you in that sexy red dress." Her smile and sigh were evident proof of her happiness. After all, that night after the dinner with Malika and Surita, they'd made fresh new memories since their teens. He'd have gone crazy if he hadn't made love to her. The way she'd looked at him...

When the applause stopped and the leader of the band introduced the future bridegroom's uncle to deliver the speech, Dev strode to take the microphone with pride.

"Dear friends and relatives. We're so happy you could join us for this very special celebration of Danielle and Sanjay's engagement." More applause. "As poets and musicians have so eloquently expressed over the centuries, love is the only thing we need to sustain us, rejuvenate us. True love conquers all barriers, including prejudice, jealousy, and cultural divides. And here's my heart-felt toast to a young and awe-inspiring couple who show us just how strong and unbreakable a bond of love can be." He raised his champagne flute in the direction of the young couple and grinned. "May you always be blessed with happiness and carry each other's love in your hearts, and a broom in your hands to sweep away all the rest that may come between you. Don't let anything get in your way."

Drinking a toast to everlasting love and happiness, Dev was rewarded by Lia's face overcome with gratitude and love. He sauntered to her side and held her close.

Despite Surita's calm smile, Dev knew his sister-in-law too well to fall for her polite acquiescence. Excusing himself from his cousin's side, his heart hammered against his ribcage, as his eyes followed Surita wading through the crowd. She wasn't offering any samosas from her tray to anyone else, her eyes centered on Lia.

Striding urgently toward his beloved, he hoped he'd reach her in time as his suspicions multiplied.

Dev saw Lia turn from her conversation with one of Danielle's friends, as Surita held out the tray to her. Without hesitation, Lia smiled and picked up a samosa. She was about to put it to her lips when he stroked her hand.

Retrieving the triangular pastry from Lia, he glared at his sister-in-law. He bit into it and chewed. He tasted the familiar yet extra hot tang of cayenne and chili peppers.

He broke contact with Surita's challenging expression long enough to see the red flecks of chili.

He swallowed. "You know very well Lia's allergic to cayenne and chili pepper, Surita." He saw from the corner of his eye, Lia shrinking away from the platter, her hand going to her throat as if imagining how she'd have felt by now if she'd bitten into it.

"I made a mild batch specially. I must have picked up the wrong plate."

Dev gave her the *'I'll deal with you later'* gaze she understood too well, from the narrowing of her dark eyes.

Now there was no politeness in her face or demeanour.

Chapter Thirty Three

THANKFULLY, THE ENGAGEMENT celebration had ended well despite the absence of Howard and his family, and Surita's attempted sabotage. Thank goodness, Danielle had no inkling of it to detract from her happiness. Lia couldn't imagine anyone being so vindictive as to risk someone's life. But although Devraj had prevented a catastrophe, she *should* have been paying more attention.

But it added an ominous feeling to the shortening winter days. Ever since they'd made up in the summer, Lia had to quell the fear that something would happen to pull the rug of contentment from under her. That familiar gut instinct whispering that she'd lose all that she held dear.

Having spent the rest of the weekend with Devraj, after Gabe returned from Howard's flat, all three strolled in the woods in the brisk November afternoon.

Now that the engagement party was over Lia could catch up with more work-related projects. Devraj's faith in her abilities and appreciation made her love him even more.

Lia felt the stakes getting higher with her art and her career when, last week, one of her pieces had won first place in the national 'Europe's Sexiest Celebrities and Royalty' juried show at the London gallery. Maxine and Patricia had exhibited five of her earlier large works, which had been framed and prominently hung on the high walls of the bright gallery.

Her love and adoration for the model must have been evident.

Just like following her October's successful solo exhibition, it had taken Lia days to feel the ground under her feet. It was a fabulous boost to her ego when her family and friends came to share in her monetary and emotional triumph. Devraj had smiled at her with pride shining in his eyes.

It was alien, yet refreshing, having someone interested in her and her creativity to such an extent. Her intermittent travels to Paris only made their reunions sweeter and more poignant.

Over the following weeks, Devraj and Sanjay continued to become a closer part of the family.

There was more sense of fun and playfulness, even laughter in the house in the past few months than in the years she'd lived with the father of her children. Devraj and Sanjay were the two knights. To help Lia, Sanjay and Danielle did the weekly grocery shopping, while Devraj often came laden with their favorite take-out dinners accompanied with roses, "Just because." He'd say.

She especially enjoyed seeing him in her leopard print

apron, looking like a domesticated, sexy manservant.

Having Devraj as a houseguest on most weekends, apart from when he absolutely had to travel, these days Gabe seemed to take his presence in their home more stoically. He was either growing up, or keeping his resentments quiet not to upset his mother.

Either way, she enjoyed the conversations at the early breakfast or leisurely dinner table, when Devraj, and sometimes Sanjay joined them. Communicating mainly with Sanjay, Gabe didn't exclude Devraj as the three continued their trips to play or watch tennis, cricket or football.

If out of loyalty, or because Howard may have stopped using him as a mole, Gabe never mentioned their weekends together.

Hoping the father-son bond was growing stronger, Lia also kept praying for Howard to come round about Danielle's choice of life mate. With the wedding nearly seven months away, surely, there was time for a miracle to happen. But apart from the gift of having her first love back, miracles seemed very unlikely, especially where the Goldmans were concerned.

And that feeling of foreboding—nothing to do with her work or her children—kept growing within Lia.

Instead of feeling as if Lia was constantly teetering over some cliff, life was gaining some balance.

She allowed herself to relax a little and go with the flow. Everything was going smoothly, but a little too fast.

Although she loved it, her growing workload was increasingly demanding; promoting the second new gallery in

London, while creating fresh artwork in any spare time she could wheedle out of her days and nights. Maxine and Patricia requested more of her 'sensuous, unique art pieces'. Especially the large life drawings and acrylics that were becoming her trademark. Devraj was her muse.

Her growing closeness with Devraj sometimes continued shaking up her fears, making her question where this ever-revolving roller coaster of love and intimacy was leading them.

Unknown territories.

Devraj was becoming indispensable, like he'd jokingly threatened months earlier. She didn't want to be beholden to anyone in her life. The thought of any commitment brought out a hot flush, quaking at the thought of *again* losing her identity, of losing herself or her hard-earned independence.

The still cold-March evening added to Lia's sense of sudden disengagement. It would come over her unbidden, staying for a few minutes or sometimes hours. She couldn't wait for the rain to stop and spring and budding trees to flourish at last. She was a summer spirit. But somehow, this winter the cold didn't seep into her as it used to years ago.

"I've just got to pick something up at my flat for Jim." Devraj glanced at her before concentrating on the road. With one hand firmly on the steering wheel, his other one linking his fingers through her cold ones on her lap.

As she entered the dark hallway of his flat behind him, the lights came on and the sea of familiar smiling faces shouting "Surprise!" nearly made her knees buckle.

Her throat constricted with high emotion. Holding her

flushed cheeks while Devraj embraced and kissed her forehead, she laughed as flash bulbs went off simultaneously.

"Surprised?" Devraj grinned down at her. She should have suspected something was amiss earlier, but she was distracted. The ultra organized Devraj would never forget anything, and make them late for a double date.

"Yes, thank you Devraj. But you know my birthday isn't for another month."

"Therefore I had the complete element of surprise. Right?" Nodding, she smiled at his delight.

Lia's best friends and Danielle, whose smiles were beaming at her, had been privy to Devraj's plans. It seemed everyone was here. She saw Aunt Eliza talking with Malika, but noticed Surita's absence.

"Now I'd like you to meet a friend of mine." Devraj inclined his head and a familiar face came closer through the crowd.

"Omigod!" Lia's pulse went rampantly wild. "Kris Darshan." She thought she'd faint like a groupie.

"You recognize me." The tall Bollywood star from her most recent favorite movies shook her hand. "So, Devraj wasn't exaggerating your love of Bollywood movies." His generous smile overflowed with amusement.

She couldn't help staring. This Bollywood royal who gave the Bachanans and the Khans a run for their money was even more gorgeous in the flesh; all those well toned muscles from all that dancing, that divine smile and those green eyes were mesmerising.

Last year, weeks after separating from Howard, as a true

fan, Lia had bought all Kris Darshan's movies from the beginning of his career, viewing them late into the nights. Not only was Kris handsome, his tall frame moved like liquid when he danced. Despite the beautiful actresses like Aishwarya Rai or Alisha Rath or Kareena Kapoor, Lia had eyes only for Kris on the screen.

Taking in a deep breath, she exhaled. "I feel like a teenager seeing her dream hunk. I absolutely love your movies and your dancing." She giggled, shaking his hand.

"Hey, remember me?" Devraj made a show of leaning toward her, looking into her eyes.

"Seems like you have a loyal hunk of your own."

"And don't you forget it." Devraj's eyebrows arched, his arm around her hip bringing her closer to his side. Flicking his head slightly towards Jim a few steps away, he added, "I've already warned my best friend and partner to lay off my Lia."

"I thought *I* was your best friend, Dev." Kris gave his best hurt expression, grinning back.

"That was before you became so famous I hardly see you."

"Look who's talking? But now I see what's been keeping you in London months at a time."

"Less of the charm, Kris." Devraj hit him playfully on the considerable forearm.

"I saw a write-up on you in the India Gazette, Lia. Your art's amazing. I'd like to have you paint my portrait sometime. I know Dev's got his own contacts, but if you want any introductions to anyone in Bollywood, let me know. Dev, you have a very talented lady here. You both must come and visit me in Mumbai."

Aunt Eliza rushed over with her digital camera. "Can we have a photo of us altogether?" She looked like a groupie herself, her large brown eyes glowing in her animated face.

"Of course." Kris was as easy-going as she'd imagined he'd be in real life. After more photos, he faced Lia and Devraj with a regretful expression. "Now, I'm afraid duty calls. 5a.m. shoot on the London Eye tomorrow. It was an honour meeting you." Kris leaned over her hand and kissed it.

Was this a dream?

She nearly forgot to reply, "I'm the one who's honoured. I can't believe... Listen to me going on." She laughed.

Kris bestowed another one of his gorgeous, sparkling smiles and then was gone.

Turning to her real life hunk, she was lost for words. Then she threw her arms around his neck "How did you manage...omigod." She hugged Devraj so hard she was surprised he didn't complain.

"Danielle told me about your secret crush so I thought I'd do something about it. If I'd known you'd get this excited," he whispered, a low chuckle rumbling in her ear, "I'd have got him on the plane sooner."

"This is the most wonderful present I've ever had. No one's ever made such a fuss over me. I love you." She felt overwhelming tenderness for this considerate, romantic man.

"I love you too, and this is just a prelude."

An ominous shiver crawled up her spine. But she swept it away, kissing him on the lips.

When she glanced at Gabe, she was awed again at how her smiling son seemed to have blossomed even further in the past few months. Or maybe she was too busy with work and enraptured with Devraj that she was missing these developments. His voice had become thick and manly, his stutter a thing of the past.

Appearing quite at home, Gabe turned back to the computer game he was playing with his friends, Stevie and Jordan.

Her heart constricted at how easily the thoughtful Devraj could charm everyone. Although Gabe never divulged anything about his outings with Sanjay and Devraj, gauging from how he always joined them on their expeditions, she knew he valued their company.

Her heart leapt and lurched in a different way as soon as the jovial music quietened and Devraj's baritone voice demanded attention. He started by taking her hand, singing her praises for her extraordinary artistic skills, her sense of *joie de vivre*, and her values of family.

She blushed furiously when he talked about how beautiful she was, and was ready to run from him and everyone's attention.

Finally, he pulled her to himself, saying, "You complete my life by being in it. I can't imagine it without you."

Just as she thought she couldn't feel any more exposed, Devraj went down on one knee, let go of her hands to produce a blue velvet jewelry box.

Holding it open for her, he held her eyes and said, "Marry me, my Lia."

The room went quiet. Like the calm before the expectant bursting of applause. But none came.

From the corner of her eye she spied her girlfriends, and Danielle and Sanjay all smiling at her expectantly. But when she imagined her grandparents regarding her from Heaven, she became disoriented.

Then her eyes settled on Gabe. He stood like an inanimate statue.

Jim seemed to be holding his breath a couple of steps away to Devraj's right.

Her expression must have given her away. Devraj's face lost the hue of the healthy tan.

Through a haze of tears, she rushed away and locked herself in the bathroom.

Everyone had gone home and if Dev had allowed her to, he knew Lia would have left too.

Sitting on the rim of the tub he stared at her back as she stood holding on to the vanity table as if for support.

"You can continue doing all the stuff you're passionate about. Marry me. I want us to be together like we'd dreamed in college."

Finally, she looked at him, biting her lower lip. "*You* can't trust me without a piece of paper. I'm sorry I embarrassed you, but why couldn't we stay as we were? It's been so amazing. Now I can't think straight."

He stood up, his patience fraying. "What's there to think about? Either you want to spend the rest of your life with me, or you don't. I need you, Lia." He pulled her into his arms. She stood unyielding against him, lowering her head away from his waiting lips. "You're my only love. I'll want *you*, always."

Slowly she pulled away in the tomb-silent flat. "I can't do it. Not again." She turned away as if to leave.

"Lia, all I did was ask you to be my wife, and you're walking out on me, again?" Dev's heart pounded against his chest and not in the good way he'd enjoyed in the past months. Panic made him desert-thirsty. "Any excuse to push me away."

"You'll never understand my need for complete freedom. I've never really been on my own, going from my grandparents' house to another gilded cage, unable to love or move forward. I've been in that prison filled with guilt and compromise, the kind you'll never understand."

"You don't think I get that? You believe I've been free all these years? Just imagining anything happening to my family, or losing you again, makes me break out in a sweat. And contrary to your misconception, I know about guilt. I should have been on that private jet with my father, uncle, brother, and brother-in-law. And as if my punishment of losing you wasn't enough, and then losing my heartbroken mother... where was I when she'd needed me? Living in my own kind of prison, hell. Running from memories, in limbo waiting for some meaning after you left me. After losing you, being left alive was my punishment. You can't know the impotence of being unable to help my heartbroken sister, and watching my brother's widow turn more bitter, hating me for surviving."

His vision blurred and he blinked rapidly to clear it,

"Leaving my dream to become an architect was the least I could do to make it up to them and Sanjay. The family business is a legacy for Sanjay and his future. But not one day's passed when I'm not haunted that instead of his father, I shouldn't have been on that plane."

He averted his gaze from Lia's tear-filled eyes. "You're such a great father figure, Devraj, you're amazing."

He welcomed her hug.

"I know what it took for you to tell me—anyone—this. I can't stand seeing you hurt, Devraj, but..."

Her sigh snapped him out of his past. Ignoring his errant tears, he held her forearms. "I realize that I shouldn't have proposed to you in front of everyone, but we've come so far together. Let's leave behind the past, we have a great future in front of us." Gently Dev cradled her like a precious angel. But looking at her, her face held a fleeting glimmer of deep regret and sadness. He shook his head. "You don't know what you're sacrificing." His blood curdled in frustration.

"There's no middle ground here. You want too much from me." She almost whispered imploring eyes filled with held-back tears, and any intended desire to punish her dissipated. The lump in his throat grew, and he hated his lack of control and pride.

"I love you even more now than I did twenty years ago, if that's possible. You're all I need, Lia, and you're crazy about me. If you weren't so obstinate and dead-set on capturing this damned elusive sense of independence, you'd see we're perfect together."

She shook her head as he continued, "Don't you want to wake up with me every day? What will it take for you to see I'm your destined husband?" He inhaled deeply and exhaled. "If you push me away, this time I won't come back, no matter what happens."

Lia was torn, but stayed silent as Devraj said, "I'm done with doing all the running, like a romantic fool, waiting for you to wake up. It'll kill me not to have you in my life. We can get married and have children—"

"No. I can't." Panic jarred her.

"You mean you won't." He backed away, disappointment dimming his eyes.

"No. I won't consider such fantasies."

"You're young and healthy." As his fingertips made contact with her shoulder, she broke away as if scorched.

Was his love making him blinkered? She'd given away her best childbearing years to another man. If they married, eventually he'd resent her, realizing she *was* too old.

A choked groan escaped from deep within her. When he took her in his arms, she welcomed the need in his embrace.

"God, I love you so much, my Lia." Then kissing her, he held her face tenderly between his hands.

Tears streamed down her face. "It's killing me to hurt you but I can't give you what you need." She sighed. "I love you, but—"

"No buts. Stay with me, tell me you'll marry me."

All she heard was 'give me your soul.'

Tensing, she let him go, unsure if she was disappointed with him or herself.

Maybe she was incapable of truly loving unconditionally. Loving her children that way didn't count.

She loved Devraj but since he'd returned into her life she hadn't been prepared to sacrifice her art career or anything of herself. He loved her too much, whereas she knew she could never love him enough.

"I need to be alone, Devraj." Numb, she saw no other way out of the Shangri-La they had holidayed in for the past year.

He was no longer next to her. When she saw his stony expression she almost shivered.

"Once again, I give you your precious freedom, Lia." There was no emotion in his voice or his eyes. "You'll *never* appreciate me, what you've got right here, right now. You've got your freedom for good. I can't go through this torture again. You've ripped my heart out for the last time. Goodbye." He gazed at her as if he wished her ten thousand years of his own misery.

Then he stormed out of her life, leaving her cold and even more alone.

Chapter Thirty Four

IT WAS ONE long week after Lia's final breakup with Devraj when Gabe ran down the stairs and greeted Sanjay. "Where's Devraj?"

"I thought he said he'd call you." Glancing at Lia, Sanjay added, "Uncle Dev left for India this afternoon."

"When's he coming back?" Gabe studied Sanjay intently.

"Not sure." Sanjay gave another sideways glance at Lia. Was he blaming her for Devraj's travelling bug? "He said I should call him if we need anything. He may not be back until the wedding."

Realization marring his face, Gabe turned to his mother, "Why hasn't D-Devraj been over?"

"Oh, Mum." Danielle said registering Sanjay's expression. "Not again."

Bracing herself, Lia looked at her son.

"What did you do?" He demanded, his broad shoulders raised. "Why? Why do you p-push away all the men?" His glare accused her of the worst sin, before turning away from them all and loudly running back up the stairs.

Lia could do nothing right. But she'd vowed to concentrate on the positives. Her career, her freedom, and her children's happiness. She reminded herself again to spend more energy being a patient and caring mother to Gabe.

When he was calmer, she'd explain they didn't need Devraj in their lives. Her future looked bright, so why did England suddenly seem empty, and India was once again an exotic temptation?

You can't have your cake and eat it, too. She reminded herself.

A slow and agonizing week had passed after Lia's final breakup with Devraj. The welcome, warm April weather continued to grace London.

Lia tried not to show her surprise at the visitor at her door. Maybe Howard, now officially her ex-husband, was coming round to the idea of Danielle marrying out of their faith.

Hope blossomed for Danielle and Sanjay, who in eight weeks would make their union legal.

As they sat in the living room, Howard looked out of place in his own home of nearly twenty years. "I hear you've come to your senses and broken up with that guy again."

"If you asked Gabe—" Her hands balled into fists.

"No, relax."

She took in a deep breath and let it out slowly.

"Danielle and I had lunch together yesterday." He said.

A good start, she thought.

"I tried to talk to her about this... marriage, but I couldn't get through to her." He continued, obviously unaware of her tension.

"Like father, like daughter. You know how determined she can be."

"I don't know what else I can do." Then he looked wistful. "What went wrong with us, Lia?" He motioned to their wedding photo on a side table. She'd forgotten to pack it away with the past.

Rallying from the question she said, "let's not go into any of that again, Howard."

"Really, I want to know if there was something I could have done differently."

"I've been thinking about our marriage lately and I'm sorry about everything. It takes two to make a marriage. It was so unfair on you. I should have tried harder to love you more. But we have two beautiful, smart children. For their sakes—"

"Now, without the shadow of the guy, can we try again?"

Had she misheard? But Howard's face confirmed he was serious. "No, Howard. I'm sure you'll find the right person who'll love you properly." She got up.

He got up too, his flushing skin and frown betraying his disappointment. "I can see you're really set on this. So what's ahead for the Ice Queen? A life of escaping into canvases and journals?"

Her heart jolted inside her, "How did you know about the journals and those drawings?"

"How did you think I knew about Devraj? Your grandparents wouldn't have dared mention anything. But those diaries certainly opened my eyes about my wife. I could never compete with him."

Cringing from the descriptive diaries, as well as the extent of her unfairness to him, she looked at Howard and said, "I'm truly sorry, Howard. You deserved more. I shouldn't have married you or anyone." She realized it was the first time in years that she wanted to hug him. She didn't reach out, but saw in his eyes loneliness and grudging acceptance.

"I'm sorry, too." His voice was a little choked.

But even now, her thoughts jumped to Devraj, wondering where and with whom he was, at this moment.

The phone rang and she jumped away from Howard as if her ex-lover had materialised between them. Reluctantly she picked up the phone with a shaking hand and heard the loaded silence and then a dying click.

Don't be ridiculous, Devraj wouldn't call.

Their breakup had been final.

He'd promised never to love her again. But in the past few days, there had been one too many phone hang-ups. The one early this morning, finding her still awake at 2a.m., made her heart lurch, gripped with fear that something may have happened to Danielle, before remembering her daughter was sleeping at home for a change.

They all had to move on.

"Howard, please come to the wedding. It would make it perfect for Danielle to have you walk her to the *chuppa*. Please,

Howard, for your little Danielle?"

He shook his head, unshed tears in his eyes suddenly looking so much older than his years. "I can't." With a shaky jaw, he pressed his lips together, as if trying to compose himself.

Then he rushed out of the room and out of their house.

"Good bye, Howard." She whispered and closed the door, letting go of one more piece of her past.

Chapter Thirty Five

LIA COULDN'T BELIEVE how slowly and yet how fast Danielle and Sanjay's wedding day dawned. The eight weeks had moved on fast forward during the day and had stuttered into exhaustingly sleepless, endless nights. The June day was as beautiful as Lia had prayed it would be.

Proudly perusing the glittering surroundings, she savored the culmination of all the hard work.

What a year it had been, she marvelled. Everything had changed for her that fateful April day over fourteen months ago, when she'd grasped and held on to freedom, independence and passion to express herself through art and in Devraj arms.

She pushed thoughts of Devraj away, as butterflies quivered within her already unsettled nervous system. How she'd meet him after their heart-wrenching break-up, she didn't want to contemplate, knowing he'd never comprehend her rejection as anything but cowardice.

She concentrated on the magic of the special day.

Maybe Devraj would give her a wide berth like he had last night at the rehearsal dinner. He'd been engrossed with the many relatives who'd come from India, Australia and North America.

With over four hundred guests attending the wedding, surely they could avoid any connection, politely greeting and smiling at each other at the head table. She prayed fervently for strength.

One thing that felt perfect was the destined joining of the young lovers. In the past few weeks, she'd proudly witnessed them growing closer and coming up with their own solutions.

They were mature and becoming increasingly self-assured through each other's love. It wouldn't be easy, but they were meant to be together. Discreetly she'd remind them to keep working at their marriage—which, as a constantly evolving entity, needed to be fueled by love, communication, and compromise—despite inevitable storms of life.

She wished she'd had her own guidance before it had hurt so many souls. She could have been kinder to Howard in their marriage.

Something stirred within Lia as she scanned the smiling bride and groom sitting under the marriage canopy, which paid homage to both the traditional Jewish *Chuppa* and the Hindu *Mandap*. Her heart danced and somersaulted at seeing Aunt Eliza beaming a few steps away from them, all dressed to the nines. Her aunt was becoming a recognized and sought-after concert pianist, travelling all over the world. Unattached to anyone romantically, the fifty-six-year-old diva always said, "no more time or inclination for complications such as love or relationships."

How she wished Howard had come after all. But she accepted that some things never changed. Even if the ceremony would be an authentic mix of the two traditions, to her ex-husband all this was a farce, an insult to the sanctity of real bonds of marriage.

It was hypocritical, but Howard was... Howard.

Lia's eyes settled on the Reform clean-shaven Rabbi with a lively disposition, and the praying *Pandit*, who together, would uphold the traditional and modern aspects of the bride and groom's vision of their union.

The groom's mother, Malika who had that ageless beauty, looked stunning in a candy-pink sari with the delicate gold detail in the same hue of her blouse. The red *sindora*, vermilion powder had been applied above her forehead, and her dark chocolate eyes sparkled with pride.

On the other hand, Surita, on the grounds of being a suddenly pious widow had decided not to attend the wedding.

Lia had been explaining to Maxine and Patricia the turn of events two weeks ago, which had led to a major shake-up at the Shah home. "The other night Sanjay told me that Malika made a small comment about how happy she was about at small incident in the news, where widows had openly celebrated *Holi* in March at a widow's ashram in Vrindavan."

"Isn't it one of those festivities where people throw powdered paint at each other?" Patricia asked.

Lia nodded, "Yes, and Surita became indignant at the

widows' audacity at breaking traditions—because widows aren't allowed to mix with the others or have fun or joy—and celebrating the festival by throwing flowers and colored powder. That night Surita decided to dedicate the rest of her life to spiritual pursuits, like a *brahmacharini.*"

"What's that?" Maxine's eyes widened.

"I think it's some kind of devotional, spiritual calling."

"I think Malika is a much more spiritual and giving person than Surita." Maxine sniffed.

"These days, Sanjay was telling me, Surita wears saffron coloured saris, the same colour the monks wear. And she refused to discuss or be part of this wedding."

But looking around, Lia sighed. "Now I'm going to mingle and be the mother of the bride." She'd make sure her daughter and soon-to-be-son-in-law had the most memorable experience possible. Then the honeymoon couple would be Hawaii-bound.

"You look adorable and this is an exquisite do. As always you've surpassed yourself, Lia." Patricia smiled again.

While Gabe looked forward to staying at last year's French summer camp in Provence, because this time his friends Stevie and Jordan would be joining him, Lia would paint up a storm at the villa. She'd dig into her latest project of Bollywood and Hollywood celebrities for the upcoming show in the autumn.

Kris Darshan and a few of his friends, whom his manager had contacted on her behalf, were included in her new project.

The world was her proverbial oyster.

She must be tired, she sighed. The creative excitement

would return as soon as she was embroiled in her paintings, she prayed.

Suddenly the familiar prickles brought her to her full height as she caught sight of Devraj at the double doors of the banquet hall. Even with all the milling guests, his presence had the same effect as it always had.

He stopped at the mouth of the huge doors as if making an entrance. The regal king Midas perusing his land and its people.

Lia's throat constricted, as her heart thrummed an irregular rhythm. Would she always feel like this whenever she saw him? He was only a man, after all. She gritted her teeth.

Her eyes settled on the young woman with him. She was almost as tall as Devraj, in a tantalizing, red mini-dress scantily covering her long, sculpted body. The nubile beauty flicked her silky, long mane of ink-black hair—so similar to Devraj's color—smiling at him with a lover's familiarity.

His arm draped around her bare shoulders, he grinned broadly into her large over made-up eyes.

As Lia tried to keep her mouth from gaping, Devraj made contract with her and instantly dismissed her by focussing back on the Pussy Cat Doll look-alike. He seemed intent on her glossy plump lips as if he'd tasted their nectar only moments earlier, and couldn't wait for second and third helpings.

The music, the scent of the hot hors d'oeuvres being discreetly circulated to the guests, the ambiance and even the bride and groom, all vanished momentarily.

Lia forced herself to turn, to stop staring, but failed.

He leaned to hear what his obviously entertaining companion said, and inclining his head back, he laughed that sexy resonant laugh. He introduced his date to his relatives and friends as if Alisha belonged with him.

The saving grace was the dramatic music announcing the beginning of the ceremony.

The bride and groom along with the Rabbi and the Pandit, sat on the rich-colored silken orange, red, and pink pillows, surrounding the low sacred fire in the center in front of them.

It all painted a poignant picture for Lia.

The dashing, princely Sanjay was resplendently regal in the beautifully sculpted off-white silk brocade suit with subtle gold embroidery on the narrow, stylish collar. The *sherwani* style jacket brought out the golden-bronze tone of his tan skin, his shining dark hair and brown eyes. Utterly composed, he possessively glanced at his bride.

Black kohl eyeliner accentuated Danielle's twinkling eyes, bringing out their vibrant blue. Now, with her eyes downcast, she was bedecked in a red sari wedding dress, which mother and daughter had customised to add the modern twist in its cut, along with the subtle gold edging. The whisper thin shimmering gossamer veil covered her wild mess of honey-blonde curls. At the henna party two nights ago, intricate henna patterns were painted on her hands and feet, and on some of her female friends and relatives limbs.

The exquisite 22-carat gold jewelry, with its ornate designs, given by her soon-to-be-mother-in-law added an exotic princess feel to her perfectly made-up face.

She was exquisite, and breathtakingly calm.

She resembled the bride Lia had sketched and re-sketched in the college cafeteria two decades ago, next to the Bollywood bridegroom with a face so like the groom's.

Once again she was overwhelmed by the confirmation that unlike her daughter, she'd never been meant for any of this.

She wasn't as well rounded and self-assured as Danielle at that age.

She refused to contemplate how completely different and barren her next birthday celebration would be without Devraj in her life.

Recognizing too late, she admitted to herself that she had taken him too much for granted.

Chapter Thirty Six

EVERYONE SETTLED IN their seats for the ceremony of two melding traditions to begin.

Lia felt awed at the connectivity of the couple and the guests. Not allowing tears to surface, she reminded herself not to ruin her makeup. But despite being enraptured in the proceedings, proud at Danielle and Sanjay's tenacity and determination, she couldn't help but steal a glance at Devraj.

They were about to be related but not in the way he'd wanted.

He stood opposite her, at an angle behind the bridegroom. His expression was stony, as if he was alone even when surrounded by family and friends. He certainly couldn't be brooding about her rejecting him as he'd obviously already turned over *that* new leaf to find a nubile Bollywood girlfriend.

Concentrate on your daughter.

But her eyes kept stealthily homing in on his features. He was evading her glances like Superman avoided Kryptonite.

The die-hard bachelor obviously didn't want to stand anywhere near her, probably missing his girlfriend.

For an egocentric moment, she wondered if he'd hooked up with the woman to make her jealous. Of course not, why should he? He could bring anyone he wished, he was free, after all. Like *she* was.

Don't begrudge his happiness, if he's moving on.

Her pride was bruised, but she'd get over it. Who liked being replaced with someone so young and perfect, while she couldn't imagine going out with another man? She reminded herself of her need for independence and how despite all his supportiveness throughout their relationship, Devraj's 'all or nothing' archaic ultimatum, at the end, had left her no choice.

She'd been right after all, to bring them both to their senses.

She focused on the Pandit and the Rabbi taking their turns in chanting the evocative, spiritually awakening blessings and mantras. Her thoughts swirled around her like incense in an ancient temple high on a Himalayan mountain. The breeze of possibilities opened the doors within her starched world. What if she'd gone against everyone's orders and eloped with Devraj in her teens? What if she *had* married him and had his children?

No! No more 'what ifs'. If it had been fated, they'd have found a way like the wedding couple had.

After tomorrow, she'd be totally autonomous. And alone.

She must be tired, because suddenly she felt hollow inside. She hadn't been eating much and the chronic bug, which she couldn't seem to shake off for the past weeks, left her feeling constantly queasy and exhausted.

She'd take better care of herself in Provence in the few uninterrupted weeks to get proper sleep, paint, and pamper herself. Guilt free.

So why did the impending months, even years of freedom seem like an infinite prison sentence?

After the bride and groom exchanged the fragrant garlands of cream and white carnations and jasmine—just like the ones she'd sketched years ago—the Pandit tied their scarves together, symbolizing the eternal bond of soul mates, pledging to love and be true to one another.

Sanjay led as they slowly took their first steps as husband and wife around the sacred fire. These steps represented them walking together and carrying out the seven promises, encompassing the strength, prosperity, and happiness of the couple's hopefully prolific union forever. It was the most moving moment Lia could remember.

Beyond them, Devraj's glare pierced into Lia's.

She couldn't move or turn away.

She felt so connected to him, and suddenly he seemed unable to pry his gaze away from hers. But she refused to misread anything within them. They'd both move on.

Malika placed the *mangal sutra* necklace around Danielle's neck, the Hindu symbol of being a married woman.

As Sanjay stomped on the small glass goblet wrapped in a napkin in front of him, everyone applauded. This was a Jewish tradition to remind them of the sadness of the world even in periods of pure and unadulterated joy.

Tears blurring her vision as the now married couple smiled

into each other's eyes and kissed.

"*Badhae Ho!*" Someone congratulated.

"*Mazal Tov!*" Someone else joined in and the string trio became louder with the joyous music of celebration.

The newlyweds disappeared to spend the first moments alone as a married couple. The guests mingled with the soft sounds of the music almost swallowed up by the happy sounds of the huge crowd in the elegant, bright hall.

Lia escaped into the banquet dining area and marvelled at the dozens of vibrant colored flower centerpieces on the large white damask covered circular tables twinkled from the mirror coasters underneath, catching the crystal lighting. The cream and chocolate moiré contrasted with the large gold piped bow ties of the hundreds of chairs. The classic gold highlights winked welcomingly from the dozen, extravagant, brilliantly lit chandeliers throughout the tall ceilinged hall.

She scrutinized the variety of the main dishes being arranged on the serving tables, in the huge silver-lidded platters. The pungent yet comforting scents of the international foods, familiar, and beloved, intermingled together. Chicken soup, roast chicken and beef as well as mushroom blintzes smothered with more classic mushroom sauce, were to be served alongside deliciously fragrant vegetarian curries, saffron infused basmati rice, tandoori and butter chicken, *pakoras*, and *samosas*.

A choice of breads, such as *naan* alongside bagels and *challa* rolls were artfully arranged together.

The myriad of desserts was going to be a decadent oasis of

its own paradise, later in the evening.

With one last glance at the perfect picture of the dining hall, she smiled and nodded at the two head organizers.

As she walked back into the loud crowded hall, yet again she felt a magnetic pull to Devraj. He was talking and smiling with a guest she didn't know.

The voluptuous kitten was by his side, confident in her surroundings. Devraj draped his arm around his companion.

Before she grasped his intention, they strode toward her through the mill of happy faces.

Chapter Thirty Seven

ROOTED TO THE spot, Lia faced Devraj. Subtly raising an eyebrow, he said, "Baby I'd like you to meet the bride's mother, Ms. Goldman." Then with a smile, he said, "and this is Alisha Rath whom you probably recognize from her movies."

Lia nodded. The Bollywood star who'd risen from Miss India to become the Princess of Bollywood at such a young age, was even more beautiful in the flesh. What was Devraj doing with a twenty-something year-old? But she'd rather swallow shards of glass than say anything that could be misconstrued.

"Nice to meet you." Alisha said with her soft, familiar accent. Her famous haughty, low voice matched her sultry features and flawless form. Then she smiled. Those dimples were so like Devraj's that Lia looked away from her and suddenly wanted to scratch out those large almond eyes and rip her out of Devraj's arms.

But he was no longer Lia's.

Through choked airways, she tried to form some

hypocritical response as Devraj peered down at her. She couldn't even admit how much she enjoyed Alisha's movies. "Nice to meet you, too." She was about to turn and rush away.

"*Mazal Tov.*" It felt alien hearing Devraj congratulate her in the Hebrew words. "On pulling it all off. Now you have everything you ever wanted. Right?" he asked. "You know, Baby, Lia Goldman is an excellent artist."

Studying Devraj for a moment Alisha turned to Lia with a new expression of registration. "So *you're* Lia?" One beautifully arched eyebrow rose as the sexy eyes turned cool.

Lia got the head to toe inspection. She held her fists against her long russet and chocolate silk outfit, which earlier had made her feel glamorous, but now made her feel like a dowager. Feeling dismissed by the glamour-puss, Lia couldn't bear being compared to someone as ideal in every way for Devraj.

With a tight smile she said, "She seems a little younger than some of your other...friends."

The steady, non-committal expression on his face didn't change as Alisha answered, "But Devraj is in excellent shape. Aren't you, *Jaanu?*" Alisha's red talons played on his designer black jacket lapel, as she batted her false lashes at him with an expert eye of a sophisticate who knew him well.

She called him 'her life'. *Sickening!* Lia wished she hadn't picked up any Hindi words from viewing Bollywood movies.

"Yes, for someone his age." Lia conceded. "How old are you now? Mid-forties?" What was she doing?

Let it go, move on, be the mother of the bride.

But neither her brain nor body listened.

Instead of grinning or dismissing her words, Devraj replied softly, "You know how old I am. And aren't *you* 'painting' young French sculptors?"

She couldn't help repeating the word he'd emphasised. "*Painting*, yes. In a few days, actually." She refused to meet his eyes, but when she did, she saw his jaw muscles working.

He pulled Alisha closer, who said, "So you're the one Kris was talking about, nah?" That dimpled smile could have fooled millions with its plastic warmth. "I just finished a movie with him. So you rejected Devraj's proposal?" She shook her glossy head, stroking her long manicured fingers on Devraj's hand resting on her hip. "Your career must mean so much more than mine does to me, nah? If—or when—I get a proposal from such a special man, I wouldn't hesitate for a moment." Alisha exchanged a private glance with Devraj. "I know where my loyalties lie."

Rage nearly choked Lia at the mere split second of the image of him on top of Alisha, his aroused body worshipping...

Lia was surprised her hands weren't around the woman's neck, squeezing.

Devraj grinned, obviously enjoying Alisha's open invitation, and lapping up the lavish compliments. This was what he'd needed from Lia.

"Isn't it true that Indian men expect to be prioritized above all else?" She ignored Devraj's eyes narrowing subtly, his free hand balling into a fist by his side.

"You can't know Devraj that well, otherwise you'd recognize he's unique, nah?"

Lia dared look at Devraj. "It must be refreshing to have such an adoring and fervent fan."

"I'm the fervent fan. Aren't I, *Rani*?" He smiled at Alisha, leaving Lia feeling like a sixth wheel in a cramped sports car. So now Alisha was his queen!

She caught her breath, grateful for the hubbub around them and said, "I wish you luck. You make a beautiful couple. You'll have gorgeous children. Obviously you'd start a family straight away as Devraj seems impatient to sire a son or two."

The new fury igniting in Devraj's eyes would have warned a sumo wrestler to back off, to shut up, as his expression promised ninja-like lethal retaliation before he erased it.

You rejected him, why are you doing this? Her common sense demanded. But her mouth seemed to be motored by outside forces.

He threw her a steady glare before turning his attention to his new 'Baby'. Fluttering her eyelashes like hummingbird's wings, Alisha smiled coyly at Devraj, and if that were possible, she melded herself even closer into him.

"But you probably wouldn't want to spoil your young figure. If I was an actress or as beautiful—"

"Yes, Baby is perfect, but you were always so modest, Lia. Even in college."

"You never told me you knew her back then." Alisha said.

How much older could Lia feel?

"Anyway, we haven't discussed that yet, but I'm sure Devraj would wait for a couple of years if I wish. Wouldn't you, *Jaanu*?"

If the woman said that word again Lia would grab her

gorgeous main and not let go until 'Baby' was left with small clumps of hair on her scalp.

A pause made Lia wonder at Devraj's real thoughts. "I'd wait forever, *Rani.*" That gorgeous, dimpled smile was ever ready.

"You see?" Alisha laughed that perfect actor's laugh. "I just love it when you call me that." Then flicking that still intact hair, she glanced at Lia. "It means—"

"I know what it means." Lia couldn't help interrupting.

"Yes. Lia likes anything Indian... The movies, the music, the Taj Mahal...Don't you?" His lips curled as if enjoying her suffering.

"Visit us when you come to Mumbai on your painting expedition."

Right, that's what she'd do. As if she could set foot in India without it ripping at her heart.

Whose fault is that?

She had to get away from them now.

"So, see you around, Lia. And I hope you enjoy your freedom in Provence."

She shouldn't have been surprised at their darned telepathy. As if he hoped the ghosts of their days and nights spent at the villa, would haunt her.

As if loathe to share Devraj's undivided attention, or maybe her woman's intuition felt the tension, Alisha caressed his cheek with a long, red-tipped finger and gently turned his face to look at her. "Can we meet your lovely sister?"

"Absolutely, *jaan.*" He stared at those plump lips again, tempting Lia to kick his shin, as hard as she could, to wipe that tiger-that-caught-two-mates smirk.

His ego well-pampered once more he propelled his woman away.

But Lia became speechless seeing the raw emotion before he threw her another haughty glance over his shoulder. Then all that was left behind was the cloying scent of the woman he held protectively.

Even if this was his nephew's wedding and he could invite anyone he wanted, how dare he flaunt that woman like that? Lia spun round and slammed right into Jim.

"Whoa. I'm glad I saw you, otherwise I'd have been flattened on the floor." Jim laughed, steadying her by her arms. "You OK?"

From the corner of her eye, she spied Devraj's hesitant steps falter as he watched them. Lia gulped in some air, drained from not breathing properly for too long.

"Don't let it show." Jim whispered with a sympathetic smile. "You made your bed—"

"Please don't, Jim. I'm sorry. I've got to ... play hostess." She walked away, her head held high, her feet unsteady, her heart heavy and confused.

Move on. Devraj obviously has.

She hoped Devraj would avoid her for the rest of her life.

Chapter Thirty Eight

DEVRAJ DIDN'T SEEM keen to deliver his speech. When he eventually stood next to the married couple, the contrast between the enthusiastic delivery at the engagement and now, almost made Lia cry.

He said all the right things, but it didn't feel like it came from the heart. He finished with, "Some people know when they're meant for each other. They can't be apart for too long, and Danielle and Sanjay are the epitome of true love. Just make sure—" Was Lia imagining his eyes on her for a second? "Just make sure you always work at your relationship, and don't let anything or anyone come between you. And Sanjay, remember the most important phrase, 'yes, darling, you're right.'"

Applause followed laughter, before everyone drank the toast.

Then the MC instructed the bride and groom to make their way to the dance floor for their first dance as Mr. and Mrs. Dutt. Danielle had changed into a slinky, classic white evening gown and Sanjay wore a black tux. Everyone clapped and smiled.

Goose bumps awakened every pore of her skin at the couple's choice of "Unforgettable", which was sung as a duet by the band's lead singers. When they mixed it with "When I Fall In Love", Lia bit her lip to stop it from trembling. She concentrated on her daughter and son-in-law on the dance floor, who had eyes only for each other.

Her gaze darted back to Devraj, who picked up a short, stout glass obviously filled with straight scotch, or something equally potent. He appeared to be affected by the Nat King Cole duets, with which he'd romanced Lia at the villa, dancing, making love...

Forcing her attention on the newlyweds, her lower lip quivered at the intimate way they smiled into each other's eyes and kissed once more. As they finished their heart-wrenchingly sweet dance, Lia didn't stop her tears.

Then the band kicked up the music, starting with the Jewish *Hora,* and the classic, merry *Klezmer.* Everyone, it seemed, joined in the joyful circle dance. She was carried along in the inner circle with the bride, groom, and the beaming Malika.

As the music skillfully changed into a Bollywood hit from a *Dhoom* movie, and while vibrating with the energy of the celebration, Lia caught Devraj lean close to Alisha's ear. When she nodded and smiled, he led the actress onto the dance floor.

They reached it as "Jai Ho," from the "Slum Dog Millionaire" movie, ended.

As the tone of the music changed again, Lia retreated from the crowd. Slightly panting, every fiber of her being commanded her to look away, stay with her daughter and son-in-law, but she couldn't.

As she came to the edge of the dance floor, she instinctively knew what she was about to see.

The music turned into a pulsating beat of sexy Latin rhythm.

A dance for lovers.

Despite other people on the floor, she saw only Devraj and his supple partner. Perfectly matched in their coloring and regal confidence, even if Alisha was much younger, Lia knew Devraj's stamina could easily keep up.

Again, her thoughts stirred up venom in her veins.

As Devraj and Alisha danced, their palpable energy and passion were evident in their synchronized steps and glances. Drawing her arched back into his chest, his hands travelled down her arms. He swung her by her hips to face him.

The sexual charge between them may as well have been lit in neon green.

Even the bride and groom stopped and joined the other spectators on and off the floor, leaving a reverent space around the dancing couple.

Lia didn't know where Alisha ended and Devraj began as the golden-tan Barbie entwined one long leg around his tall form. Dipping back, she closed her eyes as if in ecstasy.

He carried her easily, with one toe-tip of her high-heeled shoe dragging behind her.

What complete trust she had in her partner.

He'd never danced with me like this.

Lia reminded herself to breathe deeper.

The musical momentum picked up, matching the couple's urgency. Even from here Lia saw their possessive need to fulfill each other's sensual hunger.

Devraj dipped, manoeuvred and teased Alisha's proffered throat with his mouth. They meshed, as if they'd practiced the amalgamated dance steps of tango, salsa, and mambo, forever. Moving with the arrogance of Patrick Swayze and Antonio Banderas, Devraj would have given her idol, Kris Darshan, major competition on the dance floor.

Now Lia couldn't breathe.

When she'd seen him dance in the college competition, she hadn't been aware of the power of sexual magnetism. That first dance had made her turn away from reality and risks of being friends with him. Now, her lover's dance blew away any residual illusions or doubts she may have had about her breakup.

Lia could never belong in Devraj's world.

Devraj's brooding profile demanded complete surrender as he leaned over Alisha, cradling her lithe body, which slanted so low that her shining, long hair catching the lights, touched the floor. She gazed up at him with the passion of a gypsy, a princess, a devoted village girl for his taking.

Alisha brought his face closer and her lips were a whisper away from his.

Lia was afraid she'd vomit.

Dev heard the applause but even while staring down into Alisha's face his concentration centered on Lia.

He manoeuvred his nubile, smiling partner to stand and bow to the crowd around them, and saw Lia a few feet away.

Shame gnawed at his ulterior motives to make her jealous, to make her taste some of his pain. With one glance at her pale face, he saw he'd pushed his love to the edge. He wanted to run and beg her to forgive his idiocy.

"Go to her, Dev." Alisha said, regret tingeing her beautiful face. Gratitude replaced his guilt for her true friendship and for being such a good sport.

Staring into her surprisingly mature eyes, he saw her pride intermingled with subtle hurt. They told her the role she'd performed since being introduced to Lia wasn't all for show. He suspected she'd have liked more. And Alisha deserved more.

But they both realized he still loved the woman who was now rushing out of the hall with a stiff back, head held high.

How Lia must hurt.

Fresh waves of shame overtook him. He brushed Alisha's cheek with his lips. He had to get to Lia, to eradicate the agony he'd inflicted on her. Even if she still loved him this scenario may have pushed her away forever.

Why hadn't he used his common sense, or listened to his gut? Because when facing Lia all he'd seen was that warring pride bordering on arrogance that she'd survive without him, while he couldn't stand another moment without her.

But now he may have killed his chances of winning her.

Chapter Thirty Nine

THE APPLAUSE HAD erupted from the dance floor, shaking Lia out of her nightmare. The image of Devraj, making that woman his sexual slave had forced her to rush away. The dance had felt like a protracted life sentence, relived in excruciating slow motion.

Hiding in the cool tiled powder room, the luxurious surroundings were lost on her, as beads of perspiration cooled on her pasty face. She felt old, seeing herself in the unflattering lights around the mirrors. She turned away from her reflection and jumped when—after hearing a gust of joyous music and voices erupt and die almost immediately—she saw Devraj leaning against the closed door.

She heard him bolt it shut.

"What are you doing?" she demanded. "Someone may—"

"They'll have to wait." His deep voice lowered further. "How does it feel?" He came nearer. "Seeing me with Alisha."

She sighed, turning away from him. It was over. "I don't care a—"

"Then why were you so jealous and so uncharacteristically bitchy?"

Peering at him in the mirror, she silently dabbed a tissue to her forehead and pale cheeks. Instead of answering she said, "Some dance—most entertaining. I'm sure the guests and bride and groom appreciated the professional performance."

His jaw tensed and he broke eye contact, but only for a moment. Then he was right behind her. The movie "Unfaithful" sprang to mind and waves of heat rippled through her, interspersed with freezing cold sensations.

Even if Lia loved him...

Whoa! Stop thinking like that. It was *too late.*

They were never supposed to be alone again.

"Now that you've gloated, go back to your new woman. You're perfectly matched."

Grabbing her arm, he swung her to face him.

His features were so close, she saw tiny new lines at the outer edges of his eyes. "You don't believe that and we both know it. I've been a fool, Lia." The remorse and need within those amber depths told her what she'd been afraid to believe.

No, her ego was playing tricks on her.

She looked away from him.

"Did I make it too easy for you to take me for granted, by always being there for you?"

She glared at him. "Let me go—"

"Admit it, Lia. You still love me." His lips were too close to hers. She gaped at the door behind him and shrugged his hand off.

But he wouldn't let her go.

She felt dizzy. Would it always be like this between them?

She closed her eyes, shaking her head.

Right on cue with their telepathy he said, "So you're going to be content with us seeing each other at family gatherings, me with another woman, even married to her?"

She glared at him. Even if he was goading her, she tried to control her nausea. Her legs felt like watered-down jelly. Surely, he was bluffing that he'd also marry for the wrong reasons. "Avoiding each other, knowing we could have been together. Hmm?" He asked impatiently. "Even Gabe—the one person you were so positive would never accept me—even he sees what you refuse to admit."

As he was about to stroke her shoulder, the image of him holding another woman crowded in on her she flinched away from him.

Devraj shook his head. "Life doesn't have to be this hard."

Inhaling, she recoiled against the cold marble vanity unit.

As he neared her and he touched her she cried, "Don't touch me. I can smell her perfume on you."

He backed away.

"It's over. And *she* can give you children."

Devraj's fury was palpable. He shook his head, his stiff jaw tightening further. He turned away, his fists by his sides. With a few long strides, he stormed away, unlocked the door, and it thrashed against its frame behind him.

Rushing into the nearest cubicle Lia made it just in time to vomit the bitter bile and the little food she'd managed to eat.

Finally, it was truly over.

Tears of remorse and deepest loneliness overtook her as she leaned against the claustrophobic partition.

What was she doing hiding on her daughter's wedding?

She didn't care.

She didn't know what she wanted anymore.

Devraj had probably tasted many fruits between their years apart, but now the image of him and the gorgeous Alisha was forever branded on her brain. She felt weak and dirty and admitted she'd always love him despite trying to convince herself otherwise. It had never been only about their physical attraction for each other. It was always true love.

What had she done? She'd pushed the love of her life into another woman's arms.

And now she'd lost him forever.

Chapter Forty

LIKE THE ANGEL of mercy she was, Aunt Eliza entered the ladies room within moments of Devraj's exit. Helping her cool her forehead with a cold, wet flannel, her aunt shook her stiffly coiffeured head. "He's a wonderful guy, but—"

"Yes, I'm sure his girlfriend will readily agree with you."

"As I was going to say—but he's as stubborn as you are."

"I don't feel like talking, Aunty."

"You know very well he's only brought her here to get you riled up, and it worked beautifully."

"I'm such a fool for showing how I felt, what's it matter anyway?"

"You're both fools. Stop playing these childish games, you're dying to be together, I can practically see the lightning between you two across the crowd."

"You're such a romantic."

"Romantic-Shromantic, you both need a good head-butting." She sighed and shook her head again. "Dancing with her like that...And you—you burying your head in that villa, painting. Those canvases and all the fame won't keep you warm at night, you know. You think I wouldn't give up my piano in a heartbeat for a love like yours? I've just accepted it doesn't happen in everyone's lifetime. If you're afraid to repeat my mistakes then remember this; I became besotted and obsessed with those men, who weren't right for me, but you're running away from the right man who loves you. Huge difference. Just go after him. He adores you. It's not too late." Aunt Eliza smiled sadly. "Stop hankering after Bollywood movies and go after the real thing right under your nose." She placed a delicate finger on her niece's nose, her wise eyes full of concern and sympathy.

"You're so clichéd." Lia smiled despite her lousy insides making her want to curl up and die.

"Don't knock clichés, my dear girl, they've become common because they're true." Her aunt embraced her to her ample bosom embroidered with peacock colored sequins. "We all see that he's good for you, always was."

Dev sat in the garden feeling like a rotten bastard. Making such a spectacle of himself in front of his relatives and friends. What an actress Alisha was, jumping into the role with no preparation. But his tactics had backfired, badly.

He'd gone after the stubborn woman he loved, and apologized, only to be shunned again. Had she really stopped loving him? Was she that set to leave every part of her past behind?

She held on to that hard-earned independence like a medal,

a lifeline. He shut his eyes at his self-disgust and remorse, at how she'd recoiled from Alisha's fragrance on him.

He'd given Lia her freedom while all these weeks planning revenge with tonight's foolish stunt, at his own nephew's special day. Even last night had been torture watching Lia's joy at the rehearsal dinner. Orchestrating the evening for everyone, and ignoring him as if he was a stranger.

Now it was time to grow up and to move on.

A rustle brought him up short. Against all hope, he prayed it was Lia coming to find him and maybe whack him upside the head. He'd welcome any contact with her after the way she'd treated him with censure and denial. Even while her eyes had followed him all evening, like he could never resist gravitating towards *her.*

Gabe nearly passed him in the dark, and then seeing him hesitated. "Er...I just needed some air..." Gabe explained, sounding so grown up with the burden of the world on his maturing shoulders.

"Me too. Do you want to sit here for a minute?"

Gabe shrugged and sat on the bench much more readily than at the Bar Mitzvah last September. They were related now, not the way Dev would have liked, but still...

The silence broke when they spoke simultaneously. Finally, Gabe asked, "How's your car nowadays?"

"Good." Then Dev asked him about school and listened, then said, "I'm sorry I've been too busy to get in touch. I've..." How could he tell him that it was heart-wrenching? That he was afraid to call again and hear Lia's voice. When he'd tried to text

Gabe, the words seemed meaningless and he'd given up.

"I understand. Have you played cricket lately?" Gabe said.

"Not since we last played together. We should start that up after you return from summer camp..."

Gabe slumped in the seat, kicking at the pebbles at their feet, "I'm not sure...Mum's talking about moving to Provence permanently. I t-told her I hate French, but I have no choice...I'm sorry to dump on you like this."

"I don't mind, Gabe. Have you told her how you feel?"

"Sort of. She's been so busy. Although she does try and include me in the plans..."

"I'm sorry. I wish there was something I could do."

"You can. Ask her to marry you."

"It's my asking that broke everything up, remember?" Dev sighed.

"But that was ages ago. She misses you. I know she does. Maybe this time she'll..."

"She doesn't want to have anything to do with me."

"Oh, after seeing... your new girlfriend?" Gabe's disappointment was palpable in the semi darkness.

Dev sighed again, "Yeah. But she's not my girlfriend. I shouldn't have invited her."

"You hardly know her?"

Gabe sounded so hopeful, Dev grinned. "I'd hoped if your Mum saw me with someone else..."

"You tried to make her jealous?"

Shame built within him at his childishness. He shrugged.

"But why did you give up on Mum?"

"Sometimes you just have to admit defeat."

"But you've always told Sanjay never to give up. You told me never to give up about Annabelle, and you were right."

The thudding pain in his chest quadrupled. How could he explain to this young man that his mother preferred freedom and independence to all those highs and lows of their past and their new, shared emotions...those nights, the laughter and closeness?

Obviously, he'd never understood Lia's complexities or her needs. Not in her teens, and not the fully grown woman he loved even more.

He had to stop torturing himself like this.

"Some people are destined to be together, and some aren't. Maybe Annabelle is the one for you, and maybe she's not. But she'll make you realize how special you are and you can have a great time until either of you change or grow into different people."

"Is that what's happened with you and Mum?"

Dev shrugged, sighing.

Gabe watched Devraj clam up as he himself did when Dad used to ask about Mum. These days, after having taken Sanjay's advice and telling Dad he didn't want to talk about Mum, they were becoming closer, spending more time than they ever had when Mum and Dad had been together.

"No one will ever make me feel like your Mum, and that'll just have to be enough for me. I'm sorry to be dumping on *you* now, but I know you understand what I'm feeling. I hope she'll be happy with—whatever she'll do." Devraj's voice was heavy.

"You really love her, huh?"

"Like a complete fool. Always have." He grinned sadly.

Without hesitation, Gabe reached for Devraj's shoulder. Even in the dimness, he felt Devraj's sadness.

"I have to talk to her, as I'm the one to blame for your first break up."

Devraj's smile turned sad. "No, Gabe, you're very kind. But at least I'm happy about one thing. Look at *us* right now, I knew you'd grow up and understand what it's all about. But no, this is between your Mum and me, and you aren't responsible."

"Just like Sanjay said that my parents' breakup wasn't my fault, either. I mean, I know that, but..." Even though he was supposed to be a man now, he wanted to cry.

As if aware of his inner turmoil, or maybe his breaking voice had given him away, Devraj turned to him and squeezed his shoulder. "None of it's your problem, you understand? Adults make mistakes, fall out of love. That's life." The sincerity in Devraj's eyes was too much to bear. He could have had this man as a sort of father, and he'd blown it.

Unable to stop the choking cry from escaping, he almost catapulted his head against Devraj's big shoulder and let his tears fall.

He didn't care if Devraj thought him a wuss, or sissy. He only cared about this moment, right now. Really being heard and understood.

Sanjay was really lucky to have this man for his uncle.

Now he knew Devraj was right.

Gabe wasn't to blame. Adults made stupid mistakes, too, just like kids who thought being born was their fault. Like Devraj had admitted he'd made a mistake tonight about bringing that woman.

He'd make it right between Mum and Devraj. If there was a way he'd find it. This gave him the resilience he'd been searching for. A few moments passed and he moved out of Devraj's arms, wondering if he looked like Mum after she'd been crying, with her puffy face. He wiped his eyes gingerly with Devraj's offered tissue.

Inhaling a bolstering breath and letting it out again, he said, "I'm going to find a way to bring you two back together."

Devraj nodded with that regretful expression on his face, "I appreciate it pal. You can try but I don't think it'll do any good. But I'm so glad we had a chance to really talk."

"Yeah, so you can keep it over me about what a sniveling baby I am." Gabe grinned despite himself. He knew Devraj would never break their unspoken pact. This was man to man. "I'm sorry I've been such a, you know..."

"No need for any of that, remember I'm used to having Sanjay around." Devraj grinned back at him. "Even if he's married now, I'm sure he'll still have his moments."

As they got up, they shook hands. Was this really good-bye? It gave him a strange heavy feeling in his stomach and rib cage. Although Stevie and Jordan would be at camp with him, Gabe knew he'd miss Devraj, knowing he wasn't around.

Sanjay was cool, but Gabe had a different connection with Devraj. "Can I reach you, if I need to...you know...talk to someone?"

He also knew he had to work fast, to sort this out. In two days, his mother would drop him and his friends off at camp for most of the summer.

"Sure, call my mobile. I'll be away this week but if you can't get hold of me, call my secretary and leave her a message." He reached into his jacket's inner breast pocket and gave Gabe his business card. "And Sanjay always knows which part of the world I'm at, whenever you need to talk. Man to man."

Chapter Forty One

"DEVRAJ'S A COOL guy, you know." At Gabe's words, Lia tried not to swerve on the slick road to Heathrow. Stevie and Jordan were in the back engrossed in a game on the iPad. "Devraj gave me his private mobile number and told me that I can call him anytime."

"That's great, Gabe."

Before she could change the subject, he asked, "So was he just a fling?"

Staying calm, not showing her surprise, she was relieved his friends hadn't registered the challenging question. "I didn't even think you'd think such a thing, never mind say it."

"We had a man to man talk after the wedding, and although it's private, I'll tell you, Mum, he's the best guy I can imagine you with."

"Oh, you can?" Lia smiled tightly, the ever-ready pain in her chest rising. She gripped the wheel with white knuckles. "That's nice, but Devraj and I have already discussed it all and everything's finished."

"But it's not, Mum."

"Of course we'll all see each other at different family gatherings," Lia breathed in deep relaxing breaths. "And hopefully at birthdays and when Danielle and Sanjay have babies..." She wanted to cry again.

"I'm old enough to know the difference between friendships, marriage and when people are really in love."

"I know you're old enough, but it's too late—"

"It's not," Gabe's voice broke as he sat up, his body turned towards her, staring at her.

In her mirror, she noticed Stevie and Jordan gaping at them. "Devraj really loves you, Mum. People make mistakes and he said he made one when he brought the—"

"I'm sorry, Gabe. We're starting our new life—"

Gabe huffed. "That's another thing. You said we'd be honest with each other and make decisions together. Well, number one, I don't want us to move to Provence or anywhere." Then quickly added, "and number two, Devraj loves you, and always will. So there." Then, mouth tight, he slumped back, arms against his growing chest.

Stunned into silence, Lia wanted to summon up her anger at Devraj manipulating her son, but knew he'd never do that. She'd seen them together, and knowing how fatherly he was to Sanjay. Concentrating on the rain soaked road ahead, she tried to keep to the speed limit and not dawdle or hesitate.

As his friends returned back to their game, at the red traffic light Lia sneaked a quick sideways glimpse.

Gabe was shaking his head as if fed up of the stupid, stubborn people around him. When had her son grown up to be even more mature than she was?

She stared ahead. *Look forward, Lia, not back. You've got exactly what you wanted.*

Chapter Forty Two

HAVING LOOKED FORWARD to complete isolation, Lia felt deflated when she finally arrived at the suddenly too quiet, quaint villa. It had nothing to do with the decadent joy spent in Devraj's arms, she admonished herself.

She'd been certain she'd revel in her freedom. Both her children were happy and settled for now, with Danielle on her three week honeymoon, and Gabe... Lia had some serious thinking to do about her son.

She had the whole summer, right now, she'd unleash her artistic creativity. But entering the sunlit room where her materials and canvases waited, the prospect of starting to paint didn't appeal yet.

After months of anticipation, planning and getting life in order she suddenly seemed drained and out of focus.

This was the first time she was truly alone without any obligations, since her marriage—even *before* that, she realized.

She'd catch up on her sleep, first, truly rest, and then take it from there.

But hours turned into days and nights when Lia found herself gazing over the beautiful landscape of Provence, willing it to work its magic. She may as well have been a robot. The long, haunting nights spent staring at the old moon-shadowed ceiling found Lia praying for peace or at least some rest.

If it weren't for her mobile, she'd have lost track of time.

Hoping to get into the swing of things, relaxing her mind, she started preparing a fresh canvas with gesso. But she gave up half way, slowly washing the brush out in the large water jar.

After the sixth night's restless sleep, she awoke with a jolt. She'd dreamt of being in Devraj's arms yet again. Would she ever get over him?

She grabbed her towel, donned her bikini, and went for a swim in the too silent, sunny paradise.

As she dried herself, and let her wet hair dry in the heat, she threw on her sundress and her legs started her towards Jean-Pierre's place. She wasn't sure if he was around but she reasoned the ten-minute walk in the perfect mid-morning through grapevine lanes would do her soul good.

Jean-Pierre answered the door with shorts and an open shirt. His blond hair spiked up sexily, his blue eyes wide in surprise.

At the warm welcoming grin, Lia smiled back and entered his cosy lair.

Settling at the tiny bistro table beside the small cottage, they drank coffee and caught up.

When Jean-Pierre leaned closer, studying her frankly with those warm eyes, little warning bells jingled in Lia's brain.

"So life's good for you, *oui*?" His sexy accent sounded low and filled with meaning she didn't want to hear.

Her heart beating uncomfortably, she nodded.

"Is it true what Maxine told me? That you broke up with your lover?"

Again, she nodded slowly and looked away, ostensibly finding the views behind him interesting.

When Jean-Pierre stroked her hand Lia sat up, her back rigid against the iron chair.

Studying her face, he said slowly, "So, *now* will you take me seriously, Lia? You know how I've felt about you since that first time I sat for you."

Shooting up from her seat, she shook her head, breathing erratically. "I didn't realize and..."

Had she misunderstood their friendly banter over the past, giving Jean-Pierre mixed messages?

Or had she come here to eradicate her need for Devraj with someone else? Tears came unbidden as she stared down at the handsome young man. "I'm so sorry. I shouldn't have come."

Shaking her head again, she rushed down the small path towards the villa.

Her senses overloaded with bird song and delicious summer flowers and nature smells, she wiped her tears away.

She shoved Michael Jackson's taunting lyrics of 'One Day In Your Life' out of her mind. Snippets of conversations tripped over each other. Until now, she'd swept away Gabe's defense of

Devraj's integrity, and Aunt Eliza's words of canvases and fame not keeping Lia warm at nights.

What had she expected: That while transforming into an autonomous woman and painting exotic men's portraits, her love for Devraj would lose its burning obsession? How had it worked for her twenty years ago, or—despite her hectic work schedule and the wedding planning—had she got him out of her system in the past weeks?

She stood motionless feeling the heat of the midday sun and knew with blinding clarity what she wanted. What she'd been afraid to admit in her married years, and escaping for the past year since Devraj had returned into her life.

She admitted to herself that Devraj *was* her soul mate, that her adult love for him had fanned and re-ignited the meaning of her existence. She'd fallen even deeper in love with the genuine, amazing *mensch* she'd grown to understand and appreciate. With his spiritual and emotional intelligence, he'd always put others' wants and needs before his own. Especially hers.

While Devraj had fully given of himself, compromised and patiently waited for her to wake up, she'd convinced herself that he'd been asking for too much and had, once again, hurt and rejected him.

Now she was through with being terrified, or running scared, in the guise of keeping her freedom.

Here she was facing her one-woman show within a couple of months, and she didn't care about anything but wanting, needing Devraj. She relived the past year and the times they'd spent laughing, sharing, and rediscovering each other, when Devraj had always been there for her and her family. She admired anew how easily the die-hard bachelor had turned into a selfless, caring monogamous man, just for her.

Love meant risking the deepest part of you.

Even if she could live without the man she'd always loved, why would she?

Instead of seeing this revelation as a vice or weakness, she concentrated solely on how to contact him. She had to go to him, now.

Could he still love her? Or had she pushed him into Alisha's arms? She'd fight for their love, and tear him out of the clutches of any woman around him.

She prayed she wasn't too late.

She'd beg his forgiveness and settle for whatever morsel of love or sexual arrangement he came up with. If he did that at first to punish her, she wouldn't blame him.

Rushing inside the cool living room on unsteady legs, she picked up the phone. As her shaking fingers dialed the number of Devraj's flat, she shoved the images assailing her from 'Gone With the Wind'; Rhett turning away and flinging his famous parting line at Scarlett, of not giving a damn.

She'd swallow her pride and the bitter taste in her mouth that Devraj had been intimate with Alisha. Hadn't she been married to the wrong man for years?

Even if it took Lia another twenty years, she'd prove to Devraj they were destined to be together.

Chapter Forty Three

HOLDING THE RECEIVER like her lifeline, she listened as Devraj's phone rang and then clicked into voicemail. Panicking, she killed the connection. Her agitation grew; what if he'd intercepted her name and refused to answer her? After so many days of inaction, suddenly what she had to tell him couldn't wait.

She called his mobile and redialed the number twice in case her hasty shaking fingers had misdialed. But getting voicemail, she felt slightly faint and heavyhearted. Her left temple began to throb then the right, until she thought a vein would explode within her head.

Was he in Alisha's bed refusing to be interrupted by the world, like he used to turn off the mobile whenever he was with Lia?

Summoning all her new courage fortified by Devraj's love over the past year, she abandoned any remaining pride. She dialled Malika's number.

"The Shah residence," Surita's patient reply made Lia wish Malika had answered—anyone but Surita.

"Surita, it's Lia." She swallowed through her constricted airways. The silence made her visualize Surita's cynical expression, not unlike Devraj's own.

"Surita, I need your help, urgently—"

"What's happened? Is Sanjay all right?"

"Everyone's fine, but I need to get hold of Devraj, please." After another pause, she heard a slow chuckle filled with more venom than mirth. Closing her eyes Lia waited.

"It's funny that you too came to your senses about Devraj at the same time he has about *you*! I was just praying about this very thing." Further grating laughter reverberated in Lia's ear. "This is indeed revenge at its sweetest, nah?"

"Surita, if you care anything about Devraj's happiness, please tell me how and where I can reach him."

"Precisely because of that, I'll tell you only this: you're no good for him. And now he knows it." Surita emphasised. "Now you're out of his system. For that, I am grateful to God. You may be my nephew's mother-in-law, but Devraj will never to see you again. He's in India getting married, you cannot change destiny, and God's will. And *this* marriage will be a happy union with children. You met the young woman at the wedding, nah? So stop interfering in his life."

Lia grasped the phone so tightly to her ear it hurt, but her fist against her lips kept her from making any sound.

You've lost him. You're too late.

Blinking away the haze and the tears, she couldn't find the

receiver's home. It fell out of her hand swinging in a pendulum motion, its jarring dead tone confirming the end of her last hope. How could she feel more desolate than when she'd said goodbye to Devraj in her teens?

She let herself slowly slide down to the floor, hiding her face in her hands. She lost the sense of time and where she was, vaguely aware of the cooling breeze through the open window.

It may have been minutes or hours later, Lia didn't care. Who could help her, now? Could her friends somehow get his whereabouts?

When she opened her eyes, something caught her attention in between the cushions on the sofa where she'd become emotionally bonded with Devraj. Reaching for the silky red softness, she produced one of the scarves they'd both enjoyed using. How it had ended down here from their bed upstairs, she didn't remember. As if in punishment, it held traces of Devraj's subtle scent. The lump in her throat magnified as self-deprecating groans nearly blocked her breathing.

She closed her eyes, but she still saw him, like in those snapshots of them on the Avignon bridge, laughing, hugging. She remembered those summer days when he'd taken her on a Jewish Heritage Tour in Avignon. When they'd also visited other ancient neighbouring regions and explored the synagogues and sampled kosher wines and foods together.

How she'd taken it all for granted. He'd do anything for her.

Now, no magic or prayer could bring him back.

She needed air.

Making her way through her own fog onto the patio, did

someone call out her name from a distance? Or was she hallucinating?

Was it Jean-Pierre? She hoped not. She didn't want anyone near her.

She tried to focus but gave up. Putting her face in her hands she let the agony she'd bottled up for months, years wash over her.

She had to find a way to stop Devraj from making the same mistakes she'd made. He'd given her so many chances. Wasn't there any chance left?

She heard the rusty creaking of the iron gates. Then the familiar voice became louder.

She squinted against the sunlight. Was that man striding towards her the spitting image of Devraj?

Not again, with the fantasies.

Was this all she had in store for her for the rest of her lonely, creatively blocked life?

"Lia, for God's sake..." It *was* Devraj.

At the warming feel of his strong hands on her shoulders, she awoke out of her catatonic misery.

She gawked at the man she'd dreaded was lost to her forever.

"I've tried to reach you all day." His intensity made him more real. He was here in the flesh, manoeuvring her into the iron chair by the garden table.

Through her tears, she gawked at him and started shaking.

"I just got off the plane from Delhi when Gabe called to say you needed to see me. I got on the first plane over. It took me three hours to get on the next plane to Nimes. But even if he was playing Cupid and you didn't know anything about it..." His gentle fingers brushed away her tears. "Are you all right?"

"Gabe?" Her son had played matchmaking Cupid after all.

"I kept calling this number but it was constantly engaged."

"I thought you were in India getting m...I felt so devastated." But when he frowned and glanced away, her lips trembled.

He must have registered her panic, because swivelling the other chair he sat close to her. His arms tightened around her, as if willing his strength to transfer into her spirit.

Slowly she stopped shaking as he cradled her head against his shoulder. The sound of the birds filled the lavender-perfumed afternoon air.

"I'm not going anywhere. I'm not letting you go, Lia. Even if I have to handcuff you to myself. Ah, I see you've been reminiscing." Amusement crept into his voice as he eyed the red scarf she was clutching.

The breath left her lungs and then refilled with rejuvenating oxygen and his welcome scent. She tried to calm her palpitating heart and felt her cheeks tighten in an optimistic smile. She caressed his warm skin on his shoulders, throat and face.

Her smile turned into a deep sigh. A gurgle of laughter escaped her. Just in case he thought she was getting hysterical, she explained rapidly, "I tried to get you at the flat and on the mobile and then Surita said—"

Devraj's arms tensed around her. "What did she say?"

"That you're marrying Alisha."

Devraj shook his head and sighed. "One of these days she'll

have to stop... But right now, I only want to discuss us. Do you need anything? Water, something to eat? Let's get you inside."

She shook her head and held his hands. "I don't want anything. I just want to explain about...I've changed my mind about us—"

His face lit up, "Good. But let me say what I came to say."

She nodded holding her breath. Her heart, which had been about to shatter or at least stop beating a few minutes ago, was now playing havoc against her ribcage as if mischievous cherubs were playing tickles within her.

"All those hours on the planes and at the airports, I've had a lot of time to think, and here's my best offer—" he put a gentle finger against her open lips.

She hadn't planned to say anything. She didn't dare.

"We buy a place together, or you and Gabe move into my flat or whatever you decide—I don't care right now—and we live together. Because you must listen to Gabe's needs too. And I'd rather live in sin with you, share you...as long as we're together. Let's spend the rest of our lives building a love story worthy of the Taj Mahal."

"That's so beautiful, Devraj." Her vision blurred again as she blinked tears away to enjoy his every feature, every loving expression.

"And...nothing happened between Alisha and me. I swear on my mother's—"

This time Lia shook her head and put a finger across his lips. "I've got a better proposition for you. How about we get married as soon as possible?"

At this, his frown left and joy lit his face, those lips quirking in that sexy grin.

"You were right from the beginning, we're soul-mates, and I'm so sorry for what I've made you go through. No more running away. I love you, and I was about to fly to India and rip you out of that woman's arms, and demand or beg you to spend the rest of our lives together. I promise to make it up to you for being such an obstinate fool and coward."

A huge "Whoopee!" reverberated from Devraj as he laughed and picked her up clear off the ground. When he finally let her feet touch terra firma, he kissed her long and hard.

And everything fell into place.

She was home, in their second destiny, at last.

Epilogue

Agra, India, two months later

SMILING WIDELY, LIA took small purposeful steps towards Devraj who stood under the exotic, billowing wedding canopy. His four best men; his cousin Vikram, Sanjay, Jim and Gabe held up its poles.

Devraj's 'cat-that-swallowed-the-canary-and-the-cream' grin brought out the whiteness of his teeth against his deeper golden tan.

Lia wasn't complaining. She'd been captured in the same ridiculously happy bubble since she'd proposed to him two months ago. They were like two teenagers crazy in love, spending every moment together as if making up for the months, years they'd been apart, without reservation.

Now she'd buried her fears and denial in the sea of faith.

Nearing him, she saw that same hunger in his topaz eyes that flourished within her, and yearned to have him all to herself.

Even now, overlooking the incredible, regal Taj Mahal, under the balmy, early evening sun, she wanted to be out of her flowing cream-and-gold satin dress. She also wanted Devraj out of his dress shirt and dark suit. And it had nothing to do with the humidity the Monsoon rains had left behind. He looked so delicious and dashing and he was about to be legally and officially all hers.

Reaching him, she smiled as he put his arms around her, avoiding her protruding tummy. She revelled at the stirring in her belly. She'd never felt heavier, healthier or happier. In over three months they'd be proud parents. She'd become pregnant weeks before they'd broken up for the very last time.

Two weeks after their final and true reunion, having taken a pregnancy test on a strange impulse, the bemused Lia had shared the shocking news with Devraj. Devraj had been ecstatic, but his stunned and elated reaction had been marred for a moment when he'd asked, "Are you marrying me just because of the baby?"

She'd arched her eyebrow, hands on hips and glared at him. "I hadn't thought of even taking the pregnancy test till just now. What do *you* think?"

His lopsided grin had burst and he'd swooped her into his arms. "Just checking. But really, you found the perfect way to get me to change my bachelor ways, including trading in my convertible for a more practical—family—car." His pride had been contagious, as if they were the unique Adam and Eve having created a first and only miracle. "Thank you, Lia. God, I love you..." He'd sealed his words with a deep kiss.

What she'd thought were symptoms of perimenopause and the constant bloating and craving for watermelon and cream cheese, were the classic hints of a life growing inside her.

She should have known better.

They'd eloped, with the whole family in tow.

Now, about to officially tie the knot, as Devraj sent her a smouldering look, Lia forced herself to stay strong and not snatch his head down to kiss him.

When last night Danielle and Sanjay had discreetly told her and Devraj of their own baby news, Lia had been beside herself with joy. To hear this at the pre-wedding dinner at the sumptuous Oberoi Amarvilas with all their friends, Aunt Eliza and Malika, was a gift Lia could never have imagined. And the Oberoi was the dream hotel she'd drooled over when researching places in Agra years ago. How often she had dreamed of seeing the Taj Mahal at least once in her life. And here they were, getting married and expecting their own baby—with a first grandchild to come soon after that.

When Lia had asked if Danielle minded having her mother with a young baby, Danielle's eyes had widened with shock.

"Are you kidding? It's the perfect arrangement. Whatever you go through I'll be learning along, and we can spend more mother and daughter—and baby—time together."

Her daughter was growing into a loving young woman.

Now as Gabe stood holding up his corner of the canopy, he smiled at his new stepfather with a secret grin, as if he'd orchestrated the entire thing.

Lia's Aunt Eliza stood next to Malika, who before the

ceremony had excitedly explained about the generosity of London's community for her new expanding project, The Shah Orphanages. Shah Industries was a big sponsor, of course.

Ever since Surita had returned to her own family in Punjab, continually becoming more devout, Malika was flourishing into her own gregarious personality. She was even dating one of Gabe's teachers: A dedicated, passionate pioneer in protecting children's rights and quality of life across the globe.

Lia still couldn't believe Devraj's wonderful surprise, the perfect wedding gift: he'd shown her the blueprints of a classic holiday home to be built on land he'd purchased close to Patricia's villa.

She couldn't wait to start designing, helping build and make new memories with her growing family. Seeing Gabe and Danielle and their new lives unfolding before them, Lia thought she'd burst with pride.

The ceremony binding Lia and Devraj together culminated in a sincere burst of applause. Uncaring of the crowds of their party and the passers-by whistling and congratulating, the beaming bride and groom embraced as if they'd won every jackpot and had all their dreams come true. With the prospect of sharing the rest of their lives together, surely Lia could exercise some patience until they were alone.

Couldn't she?

What Came Before and What's Coming Up Next?

If you enjoyed **Second Destiny** and haven't read the story of how they first met and fell in love in college, then you may like to read **First and Only Destiny**.

Also check out **Breaking the Chains**, coming out in the winter 2014.

Visit Gloria Silk at www.GloriaSilk.com or email her at contact@GloriaSilk.com. Tell her what you thought about **Second Destiny** or anything else you'd like to share with her about reading or writing.

She would be delighted to hear from you.

About the Author

Ever since she was little, Gloria Silk knew that creating and sharing her romantic stories with others, was her passion. She always loved reading contemporary and historical novels that grasped her imagination. After many years of running art and design related businesses and being a published non-fiction author under a different name, Gloria now writes intense, sensuous love stories full-time.

Her special interests are in intercultural romances and family bonds. What can be more important in life than love and family?

Born in Russia, Gloria Silk has visited and lived in amazing, exotic places, including some in Europe and the Mediterranean. Her favorite in the world, by far is Hawaii.

Being a writer gives her the privilege to explore, travel, and meet wonderful, new and exciting—and sometimes eccentric—people. Her background in English literature, writing, and psychology helps her create unique characters for her stories. Especially the charismatic heroes and feisty heroines who find themselves in sticky situations with each other, their families, and their cultures. There is nothing more satisfying than knowing readers love her warm heroines and the gorgeous enigmatic heroes, like *she* falls in love with them.

When she is not painting in various media or watching romantic movies, or cooking up a storm for her family and friends, she hangs out with her writing friends and other creatives.

Although she was brought up in England, she now lives—and writes—in the Toronto suburbs in Ontario, Canada, with her husband and teenage daughter.

If you enjoyed this book please consider reviewing it and telling your friends about it. Gloria Silk would also love to hear from you. Contact her through her website, www.GloriaSilk.com and she will notify you about her next book releases. Partial proceeds of all Gloria Silk's book sales go to Canadian Cancer Society.

www.ingramcontent.com/pod-product-compliance
Lightning Source LLC
Chambersburg PA
CBHW060946120726
47910CB00002B/505